Death by
Chocolate
Snickerdoodle

Books by Sarah Graves

Death by Chocolate Cherry Cheesecake

Death by Chocolate Malted Milkshake

Death by Chocolate Frosted Doughnut

Death by Chocolate Snickerdoodle

Death by Chocolate Snickerdoodle

Sarah
Graves

KENSINGTON
PUBLISHING CORP.

www.kensingtonbooks.com

KENSINGTON BOOKS are published by

Kensington Publishing Corp.
119 West 40th Street
New York, NY 10018

Library of Congress Card Catalogue Number: 2020945443

The K logo is a trademark of Kensington Publishing Corp.

ISBN-13: 978-1-4967-2919-4
ISBN-10: 1-4967-2919-6
First Kensington Hardcover Edition: March 2021

ISBN-13: 978-1-4967-2921-7 (ebook)
ISBN-10: 1-4967-2921-8 (ebook)

10 9 8 7 6 5 4 3 2 1

Printed in the United States of America

One

It was a warm golden morning in late September in the remote island village of Eastport, Maine, and the air smelled like sea salt, pine needles, and smoke from the grass fires burning in fields all around the edges of town.

"If only it had snowed more last winter," said my friend Ellie White as we hurried down Water Street together.

Tourist season had nearly ended, and the shop windows in the two-story brick or wood-framed downtown storefronts held postcards, T-shirts, coffee mugs, and ball caps with lobsters, lighthouses, and eye-patched pirates embroidered on them, all on sale at a big, winter-anticipating *50 percent off*!

"Or if summer hadn't been so dry," I added.

To our right, past the fish pier, the boat basin, and the massive concrete-and-steel breakwater, which stuck out over the waves, Passamaquoddy Bay spread wide and blue.

On it, small fishing boats motored slowly, their crews hauling up rectangular wire lobster traps and stacking them on deck, later to be brought to shore.

Because it was nearing the end of lobster season, too.

"Or if," said Ellie, "we could just get a little rain right now."

But that seemed unlikely; the sky was the same relentless clear blue as it had been for weeks, and we were all beginning to feel a little anxious about it.

"One spark down here is all it would take," said Ellie, and she was right. The nineteenth-century structures weren't built to modern fire codes, and while our local volunteer firefighters were well trained and dedicated, they weren't miracle workers.

Ahead, our store's sign—a wooden cutout of a moose head, his big, googly eyes and goofy grin suggesting he'd just eaten something tasty—hung out over the sidewalk.

"Well, at least that hasn't burned down yet," said Ellie with a wan smile. The night before, several acres of dry grass had been charred black before the fire trucks could get there.

THE CHOCOLATE MOOSE said the ornate stenciled lettering on our front door. Ellie turned the key, and the little silver bell over the door jingled prettily as we went in.

Sunshine slanted in through the shop's front bay windows, lighting up the half dozen cast-iron café tables and chairs placed against the room's exposed-brick interior walls.

The air in here smelled like warm chocolate, butter, and sugar. Owned and run by Ellie and me, the Chocolate Moose made and sold cakes, cookies, brownies, éclairs, scones—just about anything you could bake with chocolate.

I glanced back out the window and noticed wisps of smoke drifting across the water; something was burning, again, somewhere nearby, and a trickle of unease about it went through me. The fires hadn't approached the town yet, but . . .

Fortunately, I had plenty to distract me.

"Once all those fishing boats get in with those traps, their crews are going to be hungry," said Ellie, straightening the chairs and spiffing up the napkin holders on the tables.

I flipped a bunch of wall switches, then lugged trays of cookies from the cooler as overhead the big old paddle-bladed ceiling fans began turning and the radio began playing WSHD, the local high school's student-run station.

The Bee Gees burst bouncily from the speakers my son, Sam, had set up for us here, as I began filling our glass-fronted display case with the variety of treats we'd made for today: chocolate pinwheels, ginger-chocolate biscotti, and the ever popular chocolate-chip lace cookies, which are like regular ones, but so delicate, they might float right away from you.

"Good thing we've still got the lobster fleet coming in," I said.

Did the cooler sound a little different this morning? I wondered. Inside its motor, had its sound changed from a gentle mutter to something more resembling a high, unhappy . . . ? I thought it had, but then it settled itself and ran normally again.

"Although not for much longer," I added, meaning the lobster fleet.

Summer business had been good. Ellie's treasured old family baking recipes, plus the top-quality ingredients we used, drew tourists in droves. Only her genius-level organizational skills and my dismal but slowly improving ability to just shut up and do whatever she said had kept us sane, even when we were baking practically twenty-four-seven.

Once the summer people had gone home, though, sales had dropped off sharply. We were, after all, a community of only twelve hundred year-round residents, and money was tight around here at the best of times.

Ellie started the coffeemaker, then booted up the cash register and the credit-card reader on the counter. Finally, she opened our laptop computer.

"You've got that right," she said. "From now until next summer," she went on, scanning the incoming email, "I'll be glad for any customers we can get. I don't care *who* they are. Speaking of which . . ." She read the screen. "Huh. We just got a special order."

"And?"

The kitchen timer buzzed; somehow when I wasn't looking, she'd gotten a tray of snickerdoodles—the batter made the night before and left in the cooler—into the oven.

"You won't like it," she said as she hurried back to the kitchen to slide snickerdoodles from the tray onto a wire rack.

"*Why* won't I?" I asked, following her and watching the just-baked treats. Each one wrinkled delectably as it cooled, a kind of magic I never got tired of. "I mean, it's for cookies, right?"

Wielding the spatula, she didn't look up, which right there was a bad sign. "Yes," she said slowly.

"So?"

Strawberry-blond and blue eyed, with small, finely carved features and a lot of gold-dust freckles sprinkled across her nose, Ellie was ordinarily a wide-open book expression-wise. But she still didn't answer. So this was going to be a thing, and possibly not a good thing, though I didn't see how a cookie order could be bad. After taking a warm snickerdoodle, I poured coffee from the fresh pot and sat at one of the café tables.

"Lay it on me," I invited.

"Twelve dozen," said Ellie, and I didn't quite choke on my bite of cookie. "The triple chocolate ones," she added, moving the final snickerdoodle to the rack. "There is one problem, though . . ."

"Ellie!" I swallowed coffee to wash down the swear words I wanted to say. Triple chocolate cookies were delicious, but they were also complicated and labor intensive. "Ellie, have you forgotten that the annual Eastport Cookie-Baking Contest is this weekend? How can we possibly also make twelve dozen—"

"By Saturday," Ellie called out from the kitchen, where she was already scrubbing the baking tray. The smell of hot soapsuds mingled pleasantly with the aroma of snickerdoodles.

"For the Elks," she added as I got up and carried my cup into the kitchen. "Or is it Elk?" She shook her head impatiently, a blond curl bouncing out of the hairnet she wore in the shop. "They're having a regional meeting."

"Fine," I said. "Good for them. But how many cookies can an elk eat, anyway? Besides, don't they usually just browse in forests? Chomp on leaves and berries and so on?" I held my cup out to her. "I mean, when you stop to think about it, are chocolate cookies even *good* for . . ."

She gave me a look of long-suffering amusement. "Very funny. But I don't think whether it's good for them is exactly the point here." She took the cup and dunked it into the soapy water. Then her tone changed. "I mean, we talked about this, remember?"

I did. We had. "But—"

"We said if we wanted to get through next winter without all the financial problems we had *last* winter . . ."

Right. Just one big expense—such as, for instance, if an entire brick wall should happen to collapse without warning off the rear of our building and land in the alley out back, the way it had the previous January . . .

Well, let's just say that a nice, soft cushion made of cash would've softened the blow considerably.

"I know," I replied unhappily. "Building up the bank account before winter really sets in would be great. But still, the contest . . ."

Eastport's annual cookie-baking contest was a local tradition. Anyone could enter, and there were no rules; if you turned your boxed mix into something better tasting than my from-scratch creation, you won.

But that didn't often happen. Eastport people had their own treasured old family recipes and wouldn't dream of foisting any packaged concoction on the judges. It was what made the contest so exciting—and competitive.

"What if we made the same cookies for both?" she asked as she wiped the cup dry. "For the contest *and* the special order?"

She slipped out of the bibbed apron she'd tied around her slender middle. Beneath it she had on a white cotton tunic with rolled sleeves, blue denim clamdiggers, and Keds, and despite the perspiration glistening on her brow, as usual, she looked like a million bucks.

"Brilliant," I said. "Chocolate batter, chocolate chips, chocolate frosting . . . How could they possibly lose?"

"Plus," she agreed, smiling wisely, "a secret ingredient."

I nodded. It was a dagger of white chocolate stuck into each cookie's top that made them so good that they could imperil your very soul. We'd even nicknamed them mortal-sin cookies.

"There is still one problem, though—" she began, but just then the little silver bell over the shop door rang again and I went to see why.

"Hi, Jake!" a pair of lively young voices rang out.

That's me. It's short for Jacobia—accent on the second syllable—and I'm Jake to my friends.

"Hi to you, too," I greeted the ruddy-cheeked young women who'd just entered the Chocolate Moose.

After dropping their backpacks full of schoolbooks by a table, they hurried to the display case and peered in.

"Oh, there's dream bars!" said Anna. She was the tall, blue-eyed one, her flaxen hair braided into a thick plait that ended halfway down her back.

"And éclairs," Helen sighed happily. She was a dark-eyed, curly-haired brunette with red lips and a dimpled chin.

"One of each, please," said Anna, opening her purse.

They both wore overalls, red ribbed-cotton river driver's shirts with men's plaid work shirts over them, and faded ball caps: red for Helen, blue for Anna. I took the money, gave back change, and poured two coffees over ice, light and sweet.

"On the house," I said of the drinks, and after a bit of polite struggle, during which I pointed out that they were already poured and would be wasted if the girls didn't drink them, the two stubbornly self-sufficient young ladies gave in gratefully at last.

"Studying for a test?" Ellie emerged from the kitchen with a towel in her hands as the girls pulled textbooks from their bags.

"Yes!" groaned Helen, rolling her eyes. "Algebra."

"Not me," said Anna, shaking her head indulgently at her sister. "I'm just her study coach."

"Good for you both," Ellie said approvingly. After they'd lost both their parents suddenly in a domestic incident two years earlier, Ellie had become a sort of adopted aunt to them.

Domestic incident . . . That was putting it mildly. But I had no time to think about it, as now more customers began coming in. One after the other, they got and paid for their coffee and breakfast pastries—today's was chocolate prune, and don't knock it till you've tried it—and went out again, keeping me busy for nearly an hour.

But when the mini-rush was over, I looked at the girls again. Surrogate aunthood had not been extended to me as it had been to Ellie—for one thing, Ellie had a daughter nearly the girls' age—but they liked me well enough.

"You two aren't dressed for school," I observed. "And aren't you hot in those outfits you've got on?"

Canvas pants, those red long-sleeved undershirts poking out from flannel cuffs . . . I spied sweaters stuffed into their packs, too, and yellow windbreakers tied around their waists.

"Teachers conferences," Anna explained. At fifteen, she was a sophomore; Helen was sixteen and a junior.

"We don't have school today. So we thought we'd go out on the boat and get our traps, and that's what we dressed for," Helen added.

Which made sense; a seventy-five-degree morning might make the day feel like midsummer, but on the water it was more like fifty, and if you didn't get drenched by icy spray at least once out there, you weren't doing it right.

"But now it turns out Helen's got this big make-up test," Anna said, sounding put upon. "We thought she'd gotten out of it, but then the teacher set it up for the school secretary to supervise."

"Which was a dirty trick," Helen added indignantly. "But I've still got to be ready for it, unfortunately."

Both girls worked part-time on the lobster boat they were talking about going out on, and they had been allowed to drop a few traps of their own, besides, for extra money.

A plan formed in my head. "When's the test?" I asked.

"Two o'clock," said Anna. "But if you don't want us to be studying in here," she added hastily, "we can go—"

"Oh, no. You two are always welcome," I told her. These cheerful, energetic young women were a pleasure to have around. "But if you leave here now," I said, "can you still make it to the boat on time and get your traps hauled?"

"Yes," said Helen, looking puzzled. "They'll be going out soon, and the boat's due back in right after lunch. But . . ."

"Then why don't you go down to the dock, come back right afterward, and I'll help Helen with her algebra," I said.

Back in the old days, when I lived in the big city, I'd made a good living on my math skills, plus some other, less socially acceptable talents, which we'll talk about later.

"Great! Thank you!" the girls enthused, and after stowing their books behind our counter, they scrambled out the door.

But . . . "Do you think that was a good idea?" Ellie asked when they had gone.

Getting involved, she meant. The sisters were adorable, but their home life was complicated. A hands-off policy had always seemed best, meddling-in-their-affairs–wise.

"Probably not," I admitted. "But math is one of the few things I'm good at."

And being motherless was a subject I knew plenty about, too.

"At least we'll get a chance to feed them again," I said. "Why don't I run home and get some of those good baked beans you made and the garlic mashed potatoes we have left over?"

Because I happened to know that when you've been out fishing, hot baked beans over buttered mashed potatoes, with a salad and a rosemary biscuit on the side, is just what the doctor ordered.

"Good idea." Ellie got a coffee for herself and sat down to do our shopping list for the special order of cookies.

Which reminded me. "What did you mean, there's a problem about the contest?" I asked.

She began to reply, then stopped herself. "Never mind. If you don't notice it when you get home, then maybe I'm wrong and there isn't one."

"Okay," I said slowly and decided to take her at her word. We'd been friends for a long time.

The little bell jingled as I went out.

On Water Street, autumn chrysanthemums had replaced the geraniums in the planters outside the shops. Flags snapped briskly outside the Coast Guard station overlooking the harbor, and the breeze had shifted, so the air was damp from the spray blowing in off the whitecaps on the bay.

I stepped along quickly, not having brought my own sweater with me. Now the wind out of the north had an edge on it, under a sky whose summer azure had suddenly turned dark blue.

Uphill, past the library, the Happy Crab restaurant, and the flower shop, with its bright bouquets beaming in the window, I shivered a little; the fiery reds and oranges beginning to show in the maple branches overhead gave only the illusion of warmth.

Up Key Street, I walked between small, close-set cottages with picket-fenced dooryards, neatly swept front walks, and early Halloween decorations festooning their porches. A few had snow shovels already standing sentinel by their doors. I'd thought this was an affectation until one Thanksgiving, when I'd had to dig my own shovel out from under a foot of the icy white stuff before I could start roasting the turkey.

But now at the top of the hill, my own house appeared: a big old white clapboard dwelling with three redbrick chimneys, forty-eight old double-hung windows with green wooden shutters, two porches, and a granite foundation peeping up beneath it.

I climbed the porch steps and pushed open the back door. "Hello?" I called out.

No answer. I hadn't expected any. My husband, Wade, was a harbor pilot, which meant he guided ships through the powerful tides, treacherous currents, and underwater granite ledges that our bay had in marvelous abundance. At this time of day, he was at the port authority building, assembling his paperwork and getting ready to take a tugboat out to meet whatever freighter was on its way in, headed for our cargo port.

Probably everyone else was out, too, I thought, the house was so quiet. But then, hanging my bag in the hall, I heard a strange sound, a sort of sniff mixed with a faint whimper.

"Hey, what's going on?" I said, following the sound to the kitchen.

It was a bright, high-ceilinged room with tall, bare windows, beadboard cabinets and wainscoting, and a big kitchen table with a red-checked cloth spread neatly over it.

In one corner stood an antique potbellied stove; in the other, a soapstone sink. At the Formica-topped counter under the old beadboard cabinets stood my daughter-in-law, Mika, wearing black slacks, flat cloth slippers, a white shirt, and a three-month-old baby cradled in a fabric sling hung around her neck.

My little grandson, Ephraim. clung to her pant leg. He wasn't fussing exactly, but the look on his small, round face said it wouldn't take much to get him going.

"Hi," Mika managed, hastily brushing her blunt-cut black hair back from her face. She'd been crying, and I'd surprised her.

In front of her on the counter were a large mixing bowl, some eggshells, a bottle of cooking oil, and a bag of flour.

"Mika, what's wrong?" I scooped Ephraim up and away from her. She'd been crying hard, and from his red-cheeked, woebegone little face, I could see that soon he would be, too.

"Oh," she sighed with a hopeless wave at the mixing bowl. A fat tear slid down her cheek and fell into it. "It's all just so . . . I can't seem to . . . Oh, Jake, what am I going to do?"

"Now, now," I said, hoisting little Ephraim onto my hip while guiding his mother over to the kitchen table.

"Sit," I commanded, and she did. Mika ordinarily had a stiff upper lip that wouldn't quit. Since she and Sam and the kids had begun living here, I'd grown to love her a lot.

But now she felt wretched, I could see. Ephraim wriggled to get down; unwisely, I let him, and he reached up to his mom just as the baby began crying.

"Here, let me," I said, hoisting the infant from the sling to my shoulder, but little Doreen wasn't having any of me, either. Kicking and waving her tiny pink fists, she jerked her baby head back hard, as if trying to fling herself from my arms.

"Wow. She really owns her feelings, doesn't she?" I said, which at least got a quavery laugh out of Mika.

Ephraim held the baby's pacifier up to me in an offering gesture; then, just as I reached for it, he popped it into his own mouth and ran off.

"Oh," said Mika, "I should go get him before he . . ."

"Never mind," I told her. My new granddaughter had stopped crying and was asleep. I handed her to her mother. "He won't hurt anything," I added. "This house is so baby proofed, there's no way he could possibly—"

A crash sounded from the dining room. After putting my palm up in a "Stay where you are" gesture, I followed the sound to the dining-room table.

He was under it, with the tablecloth pulled down over him. What had been a stack of library books waiting to be returned lay around him on the floor.

"Oopsie," he whispered, peeking out, watching me carefully to see what I would do about all this.

But there'd been enough crying around here already. "Ssh!" I whispered, putting a conspiratorial finger to my lips.

"Sssh!" he agreed, and we tiptoed back to the kitchen, where Mika was still at the table and the baby still slept.

"Now," I said when I'd gotten out a new box of crayons and a coloring book and Ephraim was settled with them. "What's this all about?" I said as I sat across from Mika.

"Oh, Jake," Mika sighed heavily. "I feel so foolish about this. Even my doctor says I'm fine, physically, but . . ."

Tears threatened once more as I sat across from her; she gestured at the mixing bowl and ingredients on the countertop.

"This is going to sound crazy, I know, but I've made those popovers a million times at least. But now . . . I can't remember how!" she wailed.

"Oh, dear," I said, sympathizing automatically with her, not yet quite seeing the problem. "That does sound distressing. But can you not just look them up in the cookbook?"

Her answering gaze was hopeless. "Oh, sure. I can do that. But even then . . . Jake, it's not only that I've lost my memory of it, but it's also like I've never even seen the recipe before."

Then I got it. "Oh, honey, you've got mom brain," I said, recalling my own life right after Sam was born.

One week I'd been juggling millions of dollars for people, and the next, I could barely add and subtract.

"How long has it been now since you were working?" I asked my daughter-in-law.

A professional pastry chef in Boston before she married my son, Sam, Mika had moved here to Eastport and had had Ephraim, then had developed a freelance gig catering for business events. She'd done that until practically the moment before Doreen was born, and from the mess on the countertop now, I gathered that she was ready to go back to it.

Or she'd thought she was.

"Four months," she said as the baby stirred warningly and then slept again, to our relief. "But how could that possibly be enough to . . . ?"

"And in all those four months," I asked, already knowing the answer, "have you done anything at all other than take care of these kids?"

On the floor, Ephraim stopped scrubbing his crayons over the coloring-book pages and began tearing the pages out.

Mika got up to stop him. "Sweetie, let's not—"

I shook my head at her, indicating that it really didn't matter how many pieces he tore those pages into, and she sat again.

"Nothing," she admitted, biting her lip hard. "I've done nothing else."

Oh, man. Hearing this, not only was I not surprised Mika was having trouble with a recipe, but I thought, too, that it was a wonder her brains weren't actively leaking out her ears.

"Okay," I said decisively. "We're changing that. I don't know exactly how yet, but . . ." I got up. "As for that popover recipe, let's finish them together, shall we?"

Ellie would know that I had a good reason for delaying my promised return to the Moose. In fact, I got the feeling this was what she'd meant by "problem," and since she'd mentioned it in connection with the baking contest this coming weekend, I had to wonder whether . . .

But before I could finish my thought, just then my elderly father, Jacob, and Bella Diamond, my beloved housekeeper-slash-stepmother—and yes, I do know our family's relationships are complicated—came in.

"Oh," said Bella, sweeping little Ephraim up into her arms and cuddling him fiercely. "Who is this handsome boy here?"

Skinny and ropy-armed, with big grape-green eyes and a jutting jaw full of mismatched teeth, Bella had frizzy red hair and a voice like gravel being shaken in a metal bucket.

"My boy!" she declared, nuzzling Ephraim's neck while he wiggled and giggled. "And I'm going to eat him up!"

She was wearing a purple sweatshirt, red pants, and black high-tops that Ellie's tween-aged daughter, Lee, had decorated with silver glitter. Behind her, my dad scrunched his withered-apple old face into terrifying expressions, all of which made Ephraim laugh, then took him from Bella's embrace.

"Who da man?" he inquired of the little boy, poking with his lumpy, arthritic finger at the child.

"I am!" Ephraim answered stoutly, and then all three of them went into the living room to watch cartoons, a treat that Ephraim was ordinarily not allowed during the daytime.

But when Mika made as if to go in there and stop him, I shook my head at her again.

"The baby's out for the count," I noted. In my arms, she slept like an angel. "And your son will be safe, happy, and well occupied until lunchtime, no attention needed from you."

She tented her fingers and rested her neat, round chin atop them. "Leave well enough alone, you mean? Hmm."

"Uh-huh," I replied. "You remember how, right? So what do you say we make those popovers? I know you still know how to do that, too. You just need a minute to think. And I'll help."

"A minute to think," she repeated wonderingly. "I've heard of that."

After a few minutes of peace and quiet, Mika's autopilot kicked in, as I'd hoped it would, which was how my adorable daughter-in-law and I ended up not only mixing that popover batter but baking the popovers, too, and afterward eating them warm with butter and the strawberry jam Bella had made earlier in the season and put up in half-pint jars.

"Listen, Mika," I said as we sat together. In the living room,

Ephraim crowed with laughter as his favorite cartoon charac-
ters bashed and crashed into one another. "I know you probably feel like you might never get your brain back now that
you've got the kids," I said.

Not that she wasn't happy to have them. The thing about her
and the four months of child care was that she'd adored it.
She'd gone in whole hog, as Bella would put it, loving every
minute of it. But now I understood that she wanted to do other
things, that is, if she could remember them.

"And the truth is, there's a part you might not ever get
back," I went on. Might as well get the bad news over with.
"The part that's carefree. Unworried. The part that never,
ever—"

A shout from the living room made Mika's eyes widen for an
instant, until she recognized it as laughter. Apparently, the
channel had been changed, and my dad saw *SpongeBob Square-
Pants* as high comedy.

"But the good news is that you'll get your brain back," I said.
"Your skills and your drive, your concentration . . . all of it."

Mika didn't look convinced.

"Yes, it'll feel like swimming through molasses at first," I
said.

Right from the start, Sam had been fussy and fretful, and my
life had been all worry and fatigue nonstop. I'd felt that I was
pawing my way through thick fog, worried I might never think
clearly again.

I had, though. I had gone back to being a money manager
and had done pretty well at it. Also, being Sam's mom had
opened my eyes to the fact that his dad was a complete slime
toad and had given me the nerve to start a new life for me and
the kid.

But Mika didn't need to hear that part. "Just stick with it," I
said. "You can do it. I know you can. I wouldn't lie to you."

She sighed, but as my words sank in, her shoulders straightened and her lips tightened determinedly. "So it's not just me. You mean this whole new-mom brain freeze is, like, an actual thing that happens sometimes?"

Because it hadn't with Ephraim, or not nearly so much, her tone implied.

"Yeah, and sometimes not, but I don't know why," I admitted. Ellie hadn't felt any such thing when she had her kid, either. But I knew women who had—some to the point of taking medication for it, and feeling much better as a result, by the way—so I was about to add even more reassurances when—

"Mom!" Sam slammed in through the back door and rushed into the kitchen. Nowadays he was a tall, good-looking young fellow with curly dark hair and a lantern jaw. This morning he wore clean but raggedy jeans and a green sweatshirt and looked as if he'd just seen a ghost.

He sank into a chair. "Mom, Mika, we found a body. Billy did, I mean."

Billy Breyer, he meant, who worked with Sam in the yard-work and landscaping business Sam had started. Billy was also Helen and Anna Breyer's older brother/legal guardian, even though he was older by only a few years.

Hearing Sam's voice, Ephraim ran in. "Da!" he shrieked joyfully, clasping his arms around Sam's legs.

Mika got up, grabbed a teething biscuit from the jar on the counter, and lured the little boy back into the living room with it. Ephraim had never liked teething biscuits, but now that the baby got them, he would do pretty much anything for one, so he went willingly.

"Whose body? Where?" I demanded once the little pitcher's big ears were safely out of hearing range. The baby was still asleep.

"Alvin Carter's," Sam replied. "In his yard. Billy's still over there now, with the police."

"Oh, dear," I said, imagining all this.

Alvin Carter was a grumpy old curmudgeon who'd inherited his extensive land holdings, including a seaside estate here in Eastport, from his grandfather, a famous landscape designer.

Now Sam's yard-care outfit cared for the estate, and its current resident, Carter himself, was Sam's biggest client.

"Billy found him," Sam repeated. "He got there early to get everything ready to cut down a big old apple tree down in that gone-to-hell old orchard of Alvin's." He took a deep breath and let it out. "Not much I can do out there now, though, and I'd told Mika I'd come back at lunchtime to take Ephraim off her hands for a little while." He got up. "So here I am."

An odd suspicion struck me. "Sam, could you tell how Alvin died? I mean, did it look to you like a natural death?"

Because Alvin Carter was known all over town as the kind of guy who might've just dropped dead of pure meanness.

"Or did it seem more like . . ."

But he was also the kind of guy whom any number of people might've wanted to . . .

Murder.

"Oh, this wasn't natural. No way." Sam winced, recalling the scene. "Not unless Alvin's pruning hatchet buried itself in his skull all by itself," Sam added with a shudder.

Suspicions confirmed.

"Twice," Sam said, and at this I grabbed my bag and sweater from the hook in the hall.

"Come on," I told him, grabbing the leftover baked beans and mashed potatoes in their containers from the refrigerator and heading for the door.

Sam followed, I started the car, and we drove together in silence down Key Street, under the maples, whose high, yellow-leaved branches made a golden tunnel over the pavement.

On the bay, frothy whitecaps danced; a storm brewed out there somewhere, mounded thunderheads peeping over the horizon. But soon, if recent history was a guide, those clouds would vanish below it; rain wasn't in the cards, or at least not anytime soon.

On Water Street I pulled into a parking spot outside the Chocolate Moose and then ran in with the food containers. Ellie took them and popped them into the cooler while listening attentively.

"So you don't know who or how?" she asked when I finished telling her what Sam had reported.

Did it, she meant. Killed Alvin Carter. I shook my head, not wanting to spoil her pleasant day with the unpleasant *how*.

Heck, I didn't even want to know about it myself. The warm, sweet-smelling shop, with the big paddle-bladed fan turning slowly overhead and the radio playing Mozart, felt safe and pleasant to me, and I wished heartily that I could stay.

But if Sam and Billy Breyer were going to be talking to any police officers about any dead bodies, I needed to be there.

Because for one thing, it's not exactly any secret that in a cop's mind, the person who found a body was very often the person who'd turned the victim from a live one into a dead one in the first place.

Add to that the fact that Alvin had disliked Billy Breyer on sight. . . . My first question would be whether Billy had seen Alvin Carter alive this morning or only dead. If the former was true, the situation might get unpleasant, not that the latter would be a barrel of laughs, either.

"Uh-oh," Ellie uttered, looking past me out the Moose's front window.

After turning to follow her gaze, I spotted Helen and Anna Breyer coming up Water Street, past the big old granite-block post office building on the corner, both looking disappointed.

"Helen doesn't need to hear about this right before her algebra exam, does she?" Ellie said.

"Correct," I replied firmly as the girls trudged nearer.

In fact, I wished she'd never have to hear about it at all. But

Anna and Helen would both learn soon about their brother finding a body, wouldn't they?

He was their only remaining family, after all. And that was what worried me most: the family, I mean, and its deeply unsavory history.

Because this wasn't the first time Billy Breyer had gotten involved with murder.

Bloody murder.

Two years earlier, Billy had been accused and nearly convicted of killing his own father.

With a hatchet.

Two

My name is Jacobia Tiptree, and when I first came to Maine, I had an angry ex-husband, a young teenaged son named Sam, and a dozen heavy-duty manila envelopes stuffed with hundred-dollar bills, the envelopes packed neatly into the trunk of my car.

The cash was from my employment as a money manager for some guys who could be lovely to your face, but if they ever got a whiff of your trying to cross them, you'd be inside a steel drum at the bottom of the East River before you knew what hit you.

But what can I say? Growing up mostly on my own on the mean streets of Manhattan had been an education in survival methods; my two main ones turned out to be adding up numbers and keeping my mouth shut. Both of which I was good at. Moral judgments, though, not so much. I figured that someone would get paid by the fellows whose limos featured bulletproof glass and doors reinforced to the specifications of battle tanks, and it might as well be me.

Not until I woke up one morning when Sam was ten did I realize that (a) my husband, a noted brain surgeon, was also a monster, and that (b) Sam was turning into one, too. So I packed up all those hundreds, got Sam into the car by a combination of threats and bribery, got the car through city traffic onto the Cross Bronx Expressway and north toward New England, even though I was crying so hard, I could barely see; and once we were out of the city, I stomped the gas pedal so vehemently that the seat belt automatically yanked itself tight across my torso.

Then, after a series of deep, shaky breaths, during which I debated and rejected the idea of crashing the car into one of the highway's concrete overpass abutments, I began to explain to Sam about the mobsters, my earlier life, his dad's constant, deliberately cruel infidelities.

Among the last straws was finding out that a friend, one I'd comforted when her own husband went AWOL and with whom I'd shared confidences, had been regaling my husband with secrets I'd told her. As pillow talk. Laughing with him about me.

Well, I didn't tell Sam that part. But I told him enough. At the start of my rant, he was slumped in the backseat, his eyes full of the smoldering resentment and mistrust that I'd come to think of as normal for him. But when I finished, he was crying, and I was, too; I couldn't help it. For one thing, I felt so guilty about taking him away from his life, never mind that at the time it consisted mostly of first-person-shooter games, illegal drugs not found in any pharmaceutical catalogs, and late-night forays with his hideous little pals to scary neighborhoods where I wouldn't go without a chain saw and a rocket launcher.

"I'm sorry all that stuff happened to you," he sobbed. But then, "Am I ever going to see Dad again, though?"

I was ready for it, having already made the resolution. "If you want to see him, I will never stop you. Or when—"

If, I amended silently. Victor had never been Father of the Year, to put it mildly.

"Or when he wants to see you," I finished.

That's when Sam swallowed hard—he already knew what his father could be like—and changed the subject.

"Where are we?" he asked as we drove up onto a huge metal bridge over the Piscataqua River. Below, sunshine glinted off waves the color of molten silver.

"We just crossed into Maine," I told him, feeling a weight lift from my heart—I didn't know why—and a few minutes later I pulled into a rest area and parked.

When we'd visited the restrooms, bought snacks and sodas, and picked up a map, we sat on a bench outside. Sam unwrapped a candy bar and bit into it.

"Listen, Sam." Might as well lay the rest of it on him and get it over with. "I'm making a fresh start here."

Truth-telling time, and never mind that my heart was in my throat, as I wondered how he'd react.

"You can start fresh, too, if you want to," I said, and he looked skeptical, rolling his eyes at me while he chewed. I pointed at the map. "So tomorrow we're going here."

It was a small town called Eastport, on an island called Moose Island that was linked to the mainland by a causeway.

We got back in the car as the late-afternoon air softened with fog and a damp breeze sprang up, cool on my hot skin.

"What's in Eastport?" he wanted to know.

I glanced in the rearview mirror. His eyes, dark hazel behind long, curly lashes, were alert and curious as he peered out at the scenery around us: trees, mostly, and hilly farmland, right now in the process of being transformed into suburbia.

"No idea," I said, pleased that he'd asked. It was as if the farther we got from the island of Manhattan, the less power some evil spell had over him and the more the real boy emerged.

I pulled the car back out onto the interstate. "I want to see it, that's all."

But now he looked rebellious. "Well, I don't."

An exit sign read FREEPORT. I took it, then followed more signs to a decent-looking motel and pulled in.

"Fine," I said. "But just ride along with me, and after we see the place, I'll take you back to the city if you want."

I had no intention of doing so. But I'd fight that battle later, I figured. For now, he nodded grudgingly.

"I assume you do want to get some dinner tonight, though?" I added.

He did, and while we ate Whoppers and fries, I explained that we wouldn't even be staying in Maine for long—luckily, he didn't ask where we'd go afterward, since I had no idea—and we certainly wouldn't be lingering in Eastport, Maine.

Just from the size of the dot on the map, I knew the place was too small, too remote. For all I knew, we wouldn't even be spending a night there, and while Sam finished the rest of my fries and slurped up his milkshake, I told him that, too.

Which in retrospect was pretty funny, since the very next day I bought a big old house in Eastport and we moved into it, with Sam's enthusiastic approval, and the next thing I knew, he was a grown man and we were driving together again.

Only this time, it was to the scene of a murder.

Alvin Carter's long, curving driveway wound between tall oak trees with golden shafts of sunshine slanting through them.

"Listen, Sam, I don't mean to poke my nose in," I said as Carter's house came into view up ahead. The sweet smell of burning leaves hung in the air. "You do know Mika's having some problems, though, right?"

Sam sighed heavily. "Boy, do I ever. But, Mom, I'm doing the best I . . ."

Two Eastport squad cars were parked in the graveled circle in front of the house, a once lovely old Victorian mansion now showing its age in sagging porch trim and crumbling foundation stones.

Billy Breyer, round faced and ruddy cheeked, with a shock of dark reddish hair, peered out from the backseat of one of the police cars, which I doubted was a good sign.

"Okay," I told Sam, "let's check this out." Then the most urgent concern occurred to me again. "I hope you told Billy . . ."

We got out of the car. "Yeah, I told him to keep quiet," Sam said. "Just to say he found Alvin and that's all. But you know Billy. He's a good kid."

I did know. Still, owing to his history, Billy was going to be under at least some degree of suspicion until the actual culprit was found. At the same time, though, he was also the kind of innocent-hearted fellow who could talk himself deeper and deeper into serious trouble just by trying to help.

And this, in a nutshell, was what I wanted to prevent as I walked across the graveled drive in the sunshine, my sneakered feet crunching on the white stones.

"Bob," I said to the cop standing by the squad car, talking through the rolled-down window to Billy. The cop looked over at me with a frown, but when he recognized me, his face cleared.

Sort of.

"I should've known you'd show up," he said.

Bob Arnold was Eastport's police chief. And Ellie and I, I'm sorry to have to report, were the town snoops, or at least we were when murder happened to be involved.

"Of course you should've," I retorted to Bob, "but this is different. Billy's a family friend. What's going on?"

Bob grimaced briefly. With his plump pink face, pale blue eyes, and rosebud lips, generally pursed in an expression of mild skepticism, except for the dark blue uniform he wore, he didn't look much like a cop.

But Bob could move rowdy guys into his squad car so fast, their feet hardly touched the ground; and once he got them behind the perp screen in there, he could usually convince them that, considering the alternative, it was a good idea for them to be there. The alternative being a swat upside the head that would make their ears ring and their eyes roll around like marbles. Anyway . . .

"Somebody dropped the sharp end of a hatchet on Alvin's noggin," Bob said, brushing wisps of thinning blond hair back from his own wide forehead. "Billy found him, so I'm getting the details while they're fresh in his mind," he added.

That made sense. "So he's not in any trouble."

Bob shook his head. Billy looked back and forth at us as we spoke, like he was following a tennis match.

"Alvin's still down there?" I asked, already moving away from Bob toward the half acre of old apple orchard that spread to one side of the house.

I could see that he was, though. A blue chenille bedspread, which I imagined came from the house, covered a long, human body–shaped lump lying on the ground halfway down the path.

I looked back up at the house, which had so many gables, turrets, towers, porches, and elaborately carved wooden moldings that it looked as if bats ought to be spiraling up out of its chimneys, squeaking and flapping.

Haunted looking, in other words, its tall, dark windows peering down like so many eyes. Also, it was badly in need of maintenance, from the loose or missing shingles on its sharply angled rooftop to the sagging foundations that held it up from below but, from the look of it, might not do so for long.

All at once I wanted badly to get away from the place; it would've been creepy even without a corpse in the orchard. But I wanted to see the murder scene, so I started down toward it.

"Oh, no, you don't," Bob put in, stopping me. "Bad enough this kid here had to tromp all over the place."

Billy looked away, embarrassed.

Bob went on, "Anyone else messes things up more than that, I'll get the heat for it."

From the Maine State homicide cops, he meant; Bangor and Portland had their own murder squad, but the rest of Maine didn't. No doubt those state cops would arrive soon. Meanwhile, one of Bob's deputies stretched yellow tape in the orchard.

Drat. I changed the subject, walking back up towards Bob. "How come you've got Billy in the car, though? All he did was find the—"

If he'd just wanted Billy to stay put, Alvin's porch was furnished with elderly but still serviceable white wicker furniture he could've sat Billy down in.

"Yeah, he found it, all right," Bob interrupted, meaning Alvin's body, "and if that's all he did, I wouldn't have a problem with it."

A bad feeling came over me. "What else?" I asked quietly, and when the answer came, it was a beauty.

"Handled the weapon," Bob said, gazing out over the field that ran downhill away from the house, on the opposite side from the orchard. In the field, patches of purple asters and pale green milkweed rippled in a brisk onshore breeze. "Hands on the axe handle," Bob said in disgust. "Prints're all over it. He's all spattered with Alvin's . . . well . . ."

"But why?" I asked Bob. I mean, Billy was no Einstein, but surely even he knew better than that.

"He said he was trying to pull the blade out, that maybe he could revive Alvin," Bob replied in disgust.

My heart sank. So Billy hadn't just turned around, walked back up the hill, and called the police. Instead, being Billy, he'd tried to help.

"Revive him," Bob repeated, shaking his head. "Like that was even going to be possible." He sighed heavily. "Jake, I know a dozen people who, if they found Alvin like that, they'd slam the blade in farther. Hit it with a rock, make sure they finished him. But instead, Billy Breyer had to come along and . . ."

He was right. Alvin Carter's popularity ranked somewhere

between a toothache and bubonic plague; for one thing, the unpleasant old skinflint had terrorized every housekeeper in town
until the only one left who would work for him wore steel-
toed boots and bib overalls and carried a gun.

Mary Sipp was her name, and she was a fearsome character
in her own right. Her souped-up Dodge pickup, with the four-
barrel carburetors and the jacked-up suspension, was parked
by the house right now, and if I were closer, I wouldn't be surprised to see a shotgun in the window rack.

Meanwhile, around Eastport Billy Breyer was a well-known
good guy, despite his history. But well-known-good-guyness
was a fairly common trait among small-town murderers, I
happened to know, and I guessed the state cops probably knew
it, too.

"So now what?" I asked.

A resigned look spread across Bob's round pink face. His
voice could cut glass when he wanted it to, but now it sounded
regretful.

"Now I run Billy down to the station and keep him there,
feed him doughnuts and coffee while we wait for the state guys
to come and talk to him."

"How long will that take?" I was thinking of Billy's two
wonderful younger sisters, Anna and Helen.

But also of Billy, who had stopped gazing dumbly around—
really, he looked as if he was in shock—and now peered hopefully uphill at me from the open car window.

He hadn't killed Alvin Carter any more than I had, and Bob
knew it. But there wasn't much that Bob could do about it.

"I don't know how long, okay?" he said defensively. "What
I do know is, a lot of stuff that was on the inside of Alvin
Carter is now on the outside of Billy Breyer, and until I find
out why and how, I won't be a happy camper about it. Got it?"

I got it. Sam came over and joined us.

"And while I've got you here . . ." Bob went on.

"Billy wants to know, can we watch out for the girls?" Sam said quietly to me.

I nodded, and Sam went back to the car to relay this message. Bob didn't notice; his own message was meant for me. "Do not," he said firmly, "go near that dead body. Understand?"

He waved at the orchard side of the property, where the rows of overgrown trees, with tall grass growing between them, awaited serious lopping. I could see even from here that the ripening apples were wormy and misshapen, like twisted fists.

The rest of the place was the same, weedy and unkempt. Alvin hadn't had anyone doing outdoor work since an incident when he chased a lawn-service guy on a riding mower down the driveway while brandishing an antique dueling pistol at him. Then Billy and Sam had answered an ad placed by Alvin's steel-toed housekeeper, Mary Sipp. By that time she'd started bringing a machete to work with her so she could slash her way through a burdock patch to Alvin's kitchen door.

For Sam and Billy, the job meant plenty of work right through autumn and on into the winter, when they'd be plowing, shoveling, and firewood hauling.

All of which Bob knew. "This is bad for Sam, isn't it?"

"Yup. Decent paycheck, regular as a clock," I said.

"And *that* poor kid," Bob went on, angling his head back toward Billy Breyer. "Dad kills Mom, kid walks in on the scene, and he goes after the old man, kills him?"

This, horribly, was Billy Breyer's story, how he and the girls became orphans, and why the cops would find his personal history so intriguing, although I hoped not for long.

But for now . . . "Where's Mary Sipp?" I asked.

Bob shook his head. "The housekeeper? Sitting up there in the kitchen, crying her eyes out. Too upset to drive, she says, so her son came to get her."

So that accounted for the other car parked up there, a nondescript tan sedan.

"That woman's heart must be as big as the outdoors," Bob said, "to be crying over that old tyrant."

He moved away, toward his car, as Sam returned to me, hands stuffed in his pockets and his boots kicking morosely at a few fallen leaves.

"Billy's going to hang out with Bob until the state cops get here," Sam said.

He knew what that meant. Billy wasn't in custody, but if he wanted to leave, Bob would suggest otherwise. Gently, but still.

"Yeah," I said.

We got back into my car, with Sam behind the wheel this time, and followed Bob's vehicle out between the tall, silent oaks lining Alvin Carter's driveway.

"But it might not be a bad thing," I said. "Billy won't be able to accidentally get himself in even more trouble. Nobody will be able to say Billy tampered with anything at the murder scene, for instance."

Sam made a "Give me a break" face. "Billy? He'd never—"

"Right, but the state cops don't know that."

Sam looked glum as we drove back to town, past the airport, the Bay City gas station, and the IGA.

"This whole thing sure puts a wrench in my monkeyworks," he said as he pulled over in front of the Chocolate Moose and parked.

We got out of the car, and Sam tossed me the keys. Up and down Water Street, shopkeepers swept sidewalks, washed windows, and watered wooden tubs of red chrysanthemums, taking advantage of the fine afternoon.

"Maybe it would be good to get Alvin's attorney on board soon, anyway," I said distractedly.

Whoever that was. There was an estate to handle, probably, and the lawyer would know how, I assumed. But even as I said it, I already was thinking of Alvin's housekeeper, Mary Sipp, crying in Alvin's kitchen.

Mary was not the crying type, as far as I'd ever heard. And one other thing . . .

"Sam, did Billy say anything to you about why he was all spattered with Alvin's . . . ?"

Because what I'd seen was beyond the "I was trying to help and got some on me" level of spatter.

Way beyond.

"No," Sam replied, not wanting to think about it, either. He turned and gazed unhappily out over the water. "I asked him to tell me," he added, turning back to open the shop door for me. "But he just wouldn't."

Inside the Chocolate Moose, Ellie was taking a second batch of her simple six-ingredient brownies out of the oven.

Well, simple except for the chocolate buttercream frosting she puts on them. Also, she never overbakes them.

"So what's up?" she asked. "I saw Bob Arnold go by here earlier. He was really flying."

Now she was arranging the brownies from the first batch, all cooled and frosted, on a cut-glass platter with a bell-jar glass top.

I filched the last one before she could put it onto the white paper doily lining the platter, and bit in. Instantly, vast choirs of angels sang in my head; once the dopamine rush had faded, however, I was able to summarize recent events.

"And now Billy Breyer's going to be in the middle of it all," I finished with a sigh. "I can feel it coming."

A young guy with violence in his past would get looked at hard, especially when his clothes strongly suggested close proximity to the current victim. Like maybe *during* the event . . .

Ellie brought me a cup of hot coffee with milk in it. She could see I was upset, and have I mentioned yet that she is a good friend?

"I can see it all interests you," she said in what must've been the understatement of the year.

Because seriously, an old Victorian mansion; a body in the orchard, with an axe lodged where it shouldn't be; and a weeping housekeeper who had no reason to weep . . . Well, it was all right up my alley.

Back in the city, I'd minded my own business, a habit I'd picked up while learning to avoid that dreaded barrel ride down the East River. But once I'd got to Eastport, I'd discovered my inner snoop, and not much later I'd begun taking it out for a spin now and then just to give it a little air.

I drank some coffee, savoring the way its faint bitterness mingled with the chocolate in the brownie.

"This is going to hurt Sam," I said. "When Mika's not working, their budget's already cut to the bone."

"And if Billy's not available, Sam will have to put off jobs they've agreed to do?"

Ellie sat across from me at the table. "So what's your plan?"

"Well, first of all, I want another look at the scene before the state cops get here."

Once they arrived, they would take away as evidence any items they could find that might suggest what had happened to Alvin.

And *who* had happened it to him.

Just then Anna and Helen Breyer rushed in, their eyes wide with shock. "Jake! Ellie! Billy's been—"

"I know. I was there. Calm down," I said.

If I knew Bob Arnold, Billy was in no distress. Was just hanging around the cop shop, eating doughnuts and playing *Grand Theft Auto* on the department's computer.

"How can they *possibly* think . . . ," Anna began.

"Billy would *never* do such a . . . ," Helen put in.

Well, but he'd already done it once, hadn't he? That was what a prosecutor would say.

"Alvin was horrible," added Helen. "He yelled at Billy."

"All the time. Billy even said he'd quit," Anna chimed in. "Told Alvin that he could clean up his own damned orchard."

That got my attention. "Billy and Alvin had been together in the orchard before?" I asked the girls. "I mean, recently?"

Before they could answer, the bell over the door jingled hard, and a short, slender lady in a blue flowered housedress and a white cotton sweater came in. With fluffy white hair like a dandelion puff, bright blue eyes, and skin like parchment, she looked the way I hoped to when I reached her age.

But I did not aspire to her temperament. Prunia Devereaux was tart tongued and critical; her business in this world, she seemed to believe, was to make sure everything was exactly the way she wanted it, and damn the torpedoes.

Now she glanced alertly around the shop just to be sure we were keeping it to her standards, then approached the counter, where she narrowed her eyes at the fresh brownies.

"There's a wrinkle in that doily," she told Ellie. "You should replace that. It's such an untidy look." Then:

"You're in the baking contest, I assume?" she asked, changing the subject.

Helen and Anna had seen Prunia coming and had slipped out to the kitchen before the bell over the door rang.

"Probably," I replied.

When Prunia asked a question, she expected a reply. And it had better be the one she wanted, too.

"But we're not sure," I added.

Wrong answer. Prunia's pink-lipsticked lips tightened even more than usual. "I wish you would figure it out, then, so I can finalize the entry list. It sets a bad example for the others, you know, this lollygagging around, not bothering to make a decision."

I was gagging, all right, but it was because I was trying to bite back naughty words.

"Well, we're still thinking about it," Ellie said sweetly, but this did not mollify Prunia one bit.

"Younger women today have no discipline," she complained. "In *my* day, ladies would have the *courtesy* to—"

"Yes, I'm sure it's all very annoying," Ellie responded smoothly, coming from behind the counter to rest her hand on Prunia's forearm.

If I'd tried this, Prunia would've bitten my fingers off. But somehow Ellie guided Prunia toward the door without quite seeming to and opened it for her.

"Humph," Prunia sniffed, turning to rake the shop's interior with her ice-blue gaze. I wondered what Prunia must've looked like as an infant. Or had somebody been psychic?

Now, at the last moment, she spied something on the floor, and her eyes narrowed. *Suspicions confirmed.*

"I see my nieces have been in," she said disapprovingly.

It was Anna's book bag, bright pink and plastered with stickers about Girl Power!

"And if they've been this near the harbor, then I suppose they've been racketing around on boats again, too, instead of at home, learning to do something useful," she went on.

Distantly, the sirens atop the firehouse began blaring, summoning the fire volunteers yet again.

"Boats with *men* on them," Prunia added, her thin nostrils flaring. "And now look. They leave their things lying around on the dirty floor."

She made as if to retrace her steps and retrieve the bag, but Ellie blocked her, ignoring Prunia's jab about the floor—it was *not* dirty—while producing a brilliant answer. "No, please, let me take it to them. I've been meaning to give those two girls a good talking-to about their tomboyish ways, and this will be my chance," Ellie lied smoothly.

"All right," Prunia agreed reluctantly. "But don't hold back on the lecture," she added, shaking her finger at Ellie, who, as you may imagine, just loved having fingers shaken at her. "Maybe if they hear from you about what troubles a young woman can get into," Prunia went on, "they'll . . ."

She continued with more in this vein, much more, while a faint whiff of another grass fire somewhere drifted in. Ellie waited patiently for Prunia to reach the door and step through it, then at last closed it firmly and leaned her back against it.

"She hasn't heard. About the murder or that Billy found the body," said Ellie.

"I guess not," I agreed. "If she had, she'd be running in circles, squawking about it."

"Is she gone?" The girls' anxious faces appeared in the kitchen doorway. "Aunt Prunia, has she . . . ?"

"Yes. I heard her say she was your aunt." I hadn't known that.

Helen nodded glumly, emerging from the kitchen. "Great-aunt," she corrected. "On our mother's side. Unfortunately."

"It's how she tried to get custody of us," Anna piped up, "after our parents—" She stopped, her face changing. "Died," she finished quietly, looking down.

"You mean after our dad killed our mom and would've done the same to us, only Billy walked in on it and stopped him," Helen said crisply. "No sense sugarcoating it."

Anna nodded, biting her lip. The girls did so well in their daily lives, it was easy to forget the horror that they'd been through, and that Billy had endured, as well.

"Anyway," Anna said after a moment, "Aunt Prunia was bound and determined to get us and turn us into *proper young ladies*." Her lips twisted on the words. "But luckily Billy was eighteen by then, so she couldn't."

She meant that he had been a legal adult and had been able to have custody of his sisters. They had stayed with friends until their brother's court case ended, then had returned home with him.

"But now he might really go to jail?" Helen asked.

I had to admit that it was possible. "But listen, don't get too upset. We'll find him an attorney and make sure he—"

But this didn't seem to help how the girls felt. "You don't understand," Helen cried. "If Billy's not at home, even for just a little while . . ."

"Aunt Prunia will get us, just the way she's always meant to do," Anna finished. "She's been waiting for any excuse to go back to the family court, and—"

Outside, a breeze snapped the flags flying at the Coast Guard station and sent dry leaves whirling along the sidewalks. I turned from ushering the girls to a table by the window to find Ellie bringing out the lunch we'd planned for them.

"You just eat your lunches now," she said, putting the filled plates in front of them, along with some slices of fresh bread and glasses of milk. "You need your nutrition, and Jake and I need to talk."

Helen glowered mutinously. Anna seemed about to speak. But the delicious aroma of homemade baked beans and hot, buttery potatoes proved irresistible, and their forks moved toward their plates as I followed Ellie into the kitchen.

"They're right, you know," she said when I got there. "If what the girls are saying is right, and I have no reason to doubt that it is, then when Prunia finds out that Billy might be under suspicion, she'll be hell-bent to get those girls back under her control."

I took a breath. "And a judge might just go along with her," I said. It was my understanding that the courts took a dim view of murder suspects, giving-them-custody–wise. "But why does Prunia want them so badly?" I wondered aloud.

"Who knows? But you know her. She's never met anything she couldn't improve with a little well-placed . . ."

"Bullying," I said. "Nitpicking and faultfinding and criticizing and . . ."

And the girls confirmed this when Ellie and I emerged again

from the kitchen. "She'll make us wear dresses and pantyhose," Helen moaned as she scraped up the last of her potatoes and baked beans.

"And we'll never get to go fishing again," Anna groused. "She *hates* it if we get dirty or do anything unrefined. Which means we won't make any money."

What little they could afford to put aside from their tight household budget went into a small but steadily growing boat fund, because someday these two capable young women meant to have a fishing vessel of their own.

And they were right; Prunia would despise the idea.

"If she ever did let us get jobs, it'd be clerking in the fabric store or something," Helen observed in disgust. "And once she's had us for a while," the girl went on, "she'll go *back* to family court and say how well we're doing, and there we'll be in our little outfits and hairdos."

"Outfits," Anna repeated sourly. "I'll just die."

Anna's idea of an outfit was a yellow rain slicker and a black oiled canvas sou'wester, plus gloves, coveralls, and the kind of big black rubber boots that didn't slip on a wet deck.

"So," Anna summed up urgently, "if Billy goes to jail even for a little while, not only will we be stuck with Aunt Prunia, but we'll also never be able get our own boat."

"We have," Helen revealed tentatively, "some money, now. Not a lot, but we could get a few things together and—"

"And what? Run away?" I interrupted from behind the counter, and a pair of guilty faces said I'd guessed right.

"To where, though? Do you even know?" I asked, pressing them. "And, anyway, you two don't have idea number one of how to get along on your own," I told them.

But with that last part, I'd miscalculated. "Oh, yes we do," Helen said stoutly. "Billy may have custody of us, but we do all our family banking and bill paying. He taught us how."

Anna nodded. "And we put money in, too. It's not just

Billy's income that we live on. And all the taxes, we do those. And . . ."

As far as money went, in other words, they really did know how. But . . .

Oh, yeah? And what about long nights in a crummy apartment where there's never enough heat? I inquired silently, recalling my own early days as a runaway.

"There's a lot more to independence besides bill paying and taxes," I said, hoping I sounded persuasive.

"There are predators out there with smiles on their faces and cruelty in their hearts," I wanted to add. My ex-husband, for instance, had been devastatingly charming, and he'd had a bright future, and marrying him had been like pairing up with a pit viper.

"Look, at least let us drive you home," I said finally.

"I'll call the school and say there's a family emergency, so you'll need to postpone the algebra test," Ellie offered.

So she did that, and the girls agreed to come with us. Outside, the smoke smell had faded for now, leaving the day gold-washed with early afternoon sunshine.

Just past the old power station on Route 190, we took a right onto Norwood Road and followed it to a driveway peeping from between old pines. The little house tucked in under the trees had vertical wood-plank siding stained dark red, a long pressure-treated deck with some lawn furniture and a few big tubs of geraniums and potted petunias on it, and a mailbox on the deck rail.

"Let's us just see you inside," Ellie said. "And can we leave you our phone numbers? In case you need anything."

In the house—sparkling windows, clean-swept floor, a hint of bleach mixed with soapsuds in the air, and everything in order—I wrote on the notepad lined up tidily by the phone. Clearly, the three siblings had their act together in the domestic cleanliness department.

"Listen, ladies," I said on my way out, "if you ever want to take up housekeeping for hire . . ."

It was a joke, but back in the car . . . "Did you mean it about the housekeeping?" Ellie asked.

"No," I scoffed. "They're busy enough already. Why? Should I have?"

Ellie shrugged. "Bella's no spring chicken, is all."

I'd have liked to deny this, but I couldn't. Well into her seventies, Bella remained a marvel of energy and ambition, but her stamina wasn't quite hanging in there the way it used to.

"She does take naps," I admitted. "She and my dad both."

Ellie nodded, as if to say that of course they did.

"But Bella would never put up with my hiring more help for the house," I said.

Ellie nodded again, as if to say of course she wouldn't, but then . . . "Did you believe Helen and Anna about helping to pay the household bills?"

"With their fishing money? Sure," I replied, and paused. "But come to think of it, even if they quit putting some money aside to buy a boat with, I doubt they could support themselves completely on just . . ."

"Exactly. Without Billy's income, maybe they can't afford *not* to go and stay with Prunia."

We passed the Bay City gas station on our left. There was a dark blue state police car parked at the pump.

"In fact, I've got a feeling dear old Aunt Prunia might have all three of them over a barrel money-wise," said Ellie.

She was right. I knew what Billy earned, and I knew what things cost. And when I added it up in my head, even with the girls contributing, it was clear that these young people weren't making their whole nut, as my mobbed-up friends back in the big city used to put it.

And certainly there hadn't been anything left for them to inherit after both their parents died. So I had to assume that Prunia must be helping them. While waiting, I mean, for her chance to swoop in and seize control entirely.

"But never mind that now," Ellie went on, "because what I really want to know is . . ."

On Key Street I pulled into my driveway, past a crab apple tree that had begun dropping crimson fruit. As I drove over the mashed apple pulp, a tangy fermenting-cider smell floated up.

"How Billy got all spattered," Ellie finished.

At her words, an image of Billy sitting in Bob's squad car popped into my head. He'd been more than spattered.

Way more.

"Me, too, but at this point, I doubt he should be talking to anyone about that," I said, "other than a lawyer."

Which reminded me that he needed one, and I doubted also that anyone else had called one. But first, I should find out. . . .

Drat. I backed out of the driveway and aimed the car downhill toward Water Street again. "How about I drop you off at the Moose, and then I'll take Billy's things to him?"

Back at their house, the girls had pressed clean clothes and shaving gear into my hands. Maybe while delivering them, I'd find out that there'd been further developments and that Billy didn't need a lawyer at all.

But when I left Ellie under the googly-eyed Chocolate Moose sign and went around the corner to the police station, I learned that Billy Breyer's immediate future—not to mention Billy himself—was already under the control of Maine State homicide cops.

Three

Yeah, he needed a lawyer, all right. Big-time.

"What do you mean, they were already transporting him?" my son, Sam, demanded indignantly at the dinner table that night.

I'd spent the afternoon getting Billy the kind of attorney that you need when you are suspected of bloody murder. In *Cain v. Abel,* my old friend Mick Flaherty would've secured a not guilty verdict without ever breaking a sweat.

"Yeah, but if I do this, you owe me," Mick had said when I called to ask for his help.

"I know," I'd replied resignedly.

Mick took debt repayment seriously, and there was just one thing he wanted from me. But I would deal with that later, I'd decided, and when I'd told Mick I understood what I owed him for this, he'd agreed to get right on Billy's case.

"Billy volunteered to go," I told Sam at the table now.

Not that I liked the idea, either, and Mick had been livid when he heard about it.

"Jeez, Jake," he'd erupted, "you leave the kid all day with a local cop, then hand him over to the state boys? When were you planning to have him see an attorney? After they convict him?"

But Billy had been adamant, Bob Arnold had said, insisting he had nothing to hide and just wanted the questioning over with.

"So let me get this straight." My husband, Wade, looked up from his plate of stew, richly aromatic with beef, garden potatoes, and carrots, ladled over rosemary biscuits.

He took a swallow of his beer and passed a calloused hand back over his brush-cut blond hair. Then: "Alvin got his head bashed, Billy found the body, and then somehow Billy got, uh, incriminatingly splashed with, uh—"

He was searching for a way to say something non-gruesome about the condition in which Alvin had been found, and about how Billy had gotten way too much of that condition all over himself. But . . .

"Never mind," Bella Diamond interrupted admonishingly. She angled her frizzy, henna-dyed head at our resident toddler, who was listening attentively from his high chair.

A smile creased Wade's tanned, rugged face. "Yeah, huh?" he agreed, eyeing Ephraim affectionately. But then: "Anyway, now the cops think maybe Billy Breyer didn't *find* Alvin that way?" Wade said. "They think he might've *made* Alvin that way. "Billy says he tried to help Alvin," I explained, but not very forcefully.

Because the truth was, I didn't believe it, either. Or at least not quite the way Billy was telling it.

Upstairs, baby Doreen began crying. Mika, who hadn't eaten much, got up. Sam rose, too, and took Ephraim from his high chair.

"Mom, can you do something for Billy?" he aked in appeal

"The guy's no big genius, but he wouldn't swat a fly, you know that."

It was true. Sam's young business partner was just smart enough to live life in a kind, decent way: to raise two young sisters after a tragedy, for instance, and have them turn out great. So . . . plenty smart.

"I'll try," I said. "But let's see what Mick Flaherty says," I added. "Maybe Billy won't need anything more than a lawyer like Mick."

Sam sighed, looking unconvinced, and bore little Ephraim away to be bathed and read to. Bella got up to take plates out to the kitchen, and Wade rose to help her.

Which left just me and my father, Jacob, at the table in the dining room, with the old gold-medallion wallpaper gleaming dully and a small fire flickering companionably on the hearth.

"So." He lit his pipe, waggling his bushy eyebrows at me over the wooden bowl. "Interesting."

He was in his mid-eighties, with a face like a carved walnut and long gray hair in a stringy ponytail tied with a leather thong. A ruby stud glimmered in one of his earlobes.

I wore the other. They'd belonged to my mother.

"Kid's in a peck of trouble," he said, puffing.

He wore a black plaid flannel shirt over a black silk long underwear top and faded blue jeans that fit him as trimly now as they had when he was twenty. Sandals on his knobbly old feet, and a little gold ring around the third toe of the left one.

A clean old man, in other words, safe at home with his family now. But he knew what it was like to be in trouble.

He pushed himself back from the table, his bumpy knuckles whitening as he gripped the chair arms. "Well, Jacobia, I'm sure you'll do the right thing," he said, peering wisely at me from under those bushy eyebrows of his.

"I thought you'd have advice," I complained, looking up

from where I sat, with my stew cooling before me. The pictures my memory kept showing me had spoiled my appetite.

"And would you take it?" my dad inquired just as Wade came back in with a fresh beer and set it in front of me.

"Advice?" Wade repeated wryly. "Not unless it was what she meant to do, anyway," he said.

Then, "Finish your dinner," he suggested in kindly tones, so I tried again, and once I wasn't trying to talk while I ate it, that stew turned out to be delicious.

The beer was good, too, and while I made quick work of it, I listened to the pleasant clattering of dishes in the dishpan out in the kitchen.

Until, from the darkness outside the dining-room window . . . "Psst!"

Well, not that sound exactly, but you get the idea.

"Oh, come on in through the porch door," I said. "They're all probably expecting you, anyway."

Because the thing is, you can't go around making a habit of nosing into other people's bad deeds without *other* people thinking that you are *always* going to be going around nosing into . . .

Ellie came into the dining room from the kitchen with her own dripping cold beer bottle in her hand.

"So listen," she began after sipping from it.

A deep sigh escaped me. For a couple of hours now, I'd been hoping for a nice hot bath, and now that I didn't feel simultaneously starving and queasy, that big claw-footed tub in the upstairs bathroom was looking better to me by the minute.

I'd probably have to clear a whole flock of rubber duckies out of it, but maybe after that, I could sink down until my ears were underwater and I wouldn't be able to hear anybody.

"So," Ellie began again after another sip. "I've found out some stuff."

I still had no desire to abandon my current, extremely pleasant situation: fed, warm, and headed upstairs for a bath and bed. I may have even yawned hugely to demonstrate this.

But when Ellie got done telling me what she'd come here to tell me, without a bit of argument, I grabbed my jacket from the hook in the back hall and followed her outside.

"She was there?" I asked. "In their house?"

Ellie sped us out Route 190 in her little old Honda sedan. Under the lights of the empty IGA parking lot, a kid bounced a basketball. At the airport, the runway lights glowed for a small plane just now coming in for a landing.

Behind us, at the island's north end, a reddish glow showed where a new fire had sprung up; the white smoke visible against the dark sky said somebody had a garden hose on it already.

She took the next right turn onto an unmarked gravel road, swinging the steering wheel one way and then the other to avoid the deep, dried-out muddy ruts showing in the head-lights.

"Prunia," she confirmed, "was at the Breyers' house just now, bullying those poor girls."

She negotiated an uphill curve made even sharper by the overgrown wild roses spreading out into it from both sides.

"Telling them," she went on, "they've got no choice but to go and live with her."

I squinted out at the darkness going by, not a house light or anything else in sight. "But, Ellie, what's that got to do with us being out here right now?"

The air coming in through the passenger-side window smelled like doused campfires.

"You'll see." An orange sawhorse loomed dead ahead of us in the headlights, blocking the road. "Jake, we've got to help those girls."

CAUTION, the sign on the sawhorse read.

Yeah, no kidding, I thought. *I'm convinced. But why here?*

"Ellie," I began again as she stopped. "Ellie?" I got out of the car.

No answer. I was about to slam the car door, then decided to close it quietly instead. Maybe it was the silence there in the chilly darkness at the terminus of a dead-end road.

Maybe it was something else, like somebody lurking in the thickly treed area ahead, waiting to do who knew what. But that was silly. I shook the thought off as Ellie's voice came again.

"Anyway, from what I overheard, you were right. Prunia contributes a lot toward their upkeep, and Billy's, too."

"And she's threatening to take it away," I guessed aloud.

"Correct," Ellie replied. "All of it, unless they start doing what she says pronto. And she also said she's not paying for Billy's lawyer under any circumstances. She says a public defender's good enough for him."

Oh, terrific. I mean, nothing against public defenders, for sure. But this was murder we were talking about.

"Here's the kicker, though. Anna and Helen have their eye on buying their own boat, remember?" Ellie said.

I did, and it remained a fine idea. They'd be eating a lot of their own catch at first; you don't just start working on the water one day and make a living the next. But it was a start.

"Prunia says no more fishing," Ellie reported, hurrying ahead of me toward the thick stand of trees. "Which means no income for the girls, like they feared, so they'll never get the boat."

"Good-bye, bounding waves. Hello, frilly prom dresses," I said, and Ellie turned back to me, nodding in the gloom.

"I mean, not that there's anything wrong with a frilly dress," she said, her face pale in the moonlight.

"Right, but Helen and Anna aren't the frilly type," I said. "So far, anyway. But I still don't see—"

Ellie's flashlight snapped on, lighting up a sapling thicket. A narrow path of tromped-down grass and weeds led into it.

"Ellie?" I hurried to catch up, but she'd already vanished along the path, and now it hit me where we must be. The gravel road we'd been on that dead-ended at the sawhorse led around toward the back of Alvin Carter's property.

Suddenly she was right beside me again. "Just stay with me," she murmured. "We can get to the house by approaching it from behind, then cutting across the back lawn."

"Which we are doing why again?" She still hadn't told me, and I was beginning to think that this—whatever *this* was— might be a bad idea.

But she had the flashlight, so I had little choice but to follow her on the narrow path, swerving to avoid exposed tree roots and ducking under low branches. At last we came to an old cedar-post fence with rusted barbed wire tangled along it, and I tore myself up only a little bit getting through it.

"The state cops have been here already, right?" said Ellie quietly. "Gone through the house and whatnot?"

"Uh-huh." I'd gathered as much from Bob Arnold at the cop shop that afternoon. "And they've sent Alvin's body to Augusta," I added, recalling more of what Bob had told me. "Had the crime-scene people here for samples and photographs, too."

We were out of the trees now, looking downhill into a long swath of grass that ended at Alvin's tumbledown Victorian mansion.

"And took custody of the hatchet," I said. "Bob said they're going to start interviewing people tomorrow, talk to anyone who might know anything."

Not that Alvin Carter had a lot of social contacts. The list of interview subjects would be short, I was guessing.

"But, Ellie, right now I'm not going a step farther until I know why I'm doing this. Specifically why," I said, emphasizing the word *specifically*.

She'd been about to step out onto Alvin's back lawn, but now she turned to me instead. "All right." She took a deep breath and began. "I went to the girls' house just to tell them we'd support them any way we could. To make them feel better. *Not* to eavesdrop."

Out in front of the house, an Eastport deputy sat in his squad car on the graveled driveway. The gravel shone whitely under the moon; a few clouds streamed over it, but not any that looked as if they might produce rain, unfortunately.

The deputy's phone screen glowed blue, propped up on his steering wheel in front of him. He was there to guard against vandals, I supposed.

Nodding her understanding as I pointed cautioningly in the deputy's direction, Ellie went on. "But afterward . . . Well, I just couldn't help it."

"You went inside," I guessed aloud. "To talk with the girls after Prunia had gone?"

"Uh-huh." The few thin clouds slipped away, and the long, grassy lawn seemed to shimmer with light the pale bluish white of skim milk when what we needed was pitch darkness.

"So then what happened?" I asked, and she let out a sigh.

"Well, of course they were both crying, partly on account of Billy's trouble, but also . . ." She turned to me. "Jake, she's going to send them away to boarding school. Some kind of fancy place where you learn how to dance and which fork to use, but not how to do higher math or read poetry or—"

At a sound from behind me, I glanced back. "What was that?"

Again, a rustling sound.

"Anything *useful*," Ellie went on, stepping out onto the grass.

A *stealthy* rustling sound . . .

"Um, Ellie?" I quavered as clouds overhead thickened again and whatever it was approached from behind me. *Rustle, rustle.*

But Ellie kept going, flitting away down the dark lawn and into the deeper shadows at the corner of the house. The rustling sound stopped, but in a sneaky way, which made me think it was only waiting for me to let my guard down.

But that was silly, too . . . wasn't it? I took a deep breath and peeked slowly over my shoulder, to make *sure* nothing was—

Glowing green eyes regarded me, unblinking. My heart came up into my throat, and my knees went watery. Then the owner of those eyes took a step toward me, and another. . . .

A raccoon waddled onto the moonlit lawn. *Shuffle, shuffle.* I let my breath out just as someone grabbed my arm, and the sensation that went through me then was electric.

No," I uttered harshly, only to find a flashlight being shoved into my hands.

"Come on!" Ellie whispered urgently. "What've you been doing out here, anyway? You were supposed to be right behind me."

She took my hand. Flailing and stumbling, I followed her down the long grassy hill.

"Stick close to me, now," she muttered, hurrying along the orchard's fenced edge, between discarded farm tools and some old apple crates left to molder into the earth.

The fence was chicken wire, thickly intertwined with years of overgrown weeds. Sam and Billy would have had their work cut out for them here, and afterwards, they'd have needed tetanus boosters.

"Duck!" Ellie whispered harshly, and moments after I'd dropped down, the door on the squad car out front slammed and footsteps crunched across the gravel, toward us.

And if that deputy caught us, there'd be hell to pay.

"Did he see us?" I whispered, wondering which way to run.

"I don't know." Ellie tugged my sleeve. "This way, though, just in case."

After ripping away some of the weeds thickly matted against

the fence, she fashioned a small nest-like space in what remained. Then she yanked me in there alongside her and we huddled together, our backs pressed against the chicken wire and the weeds pulled back down over us.

"Don't you move a damned inch," she murmured.

And have I mentioned yet to you that dry weeds are itchy? And *sneezy* . . . ?

The deputy was moving along the fence toward us now, his flashlight beam strobing along the orchard's rows and into the grassy patches between the trees. Soon he'd be standing right in front of us, and if he happened to look down . . .

Well, we were hidden. But not *that* hidden. Ellie spied a few fallen apples, snaked her arm out for them, and then jumped up to hurl them out onto the driveway. The deputy's flashlight whirled away toward the sound of the fruit bombs landing on the gravel.

I stared at Ellie. "I can't believe you just *did* that."

She smiled back modestly, but then her look changed, and she gazed fixedly at me.

"What is it?" I managed to ask just as something bristly-legged skittered across my cheek on its horrid way to my left nostril and from there, I supposed, up into my brain.

"*Ellie.*"

Now it was on my lip, still moving along purposefully, and I had no choice but to remain perfectly motionless, since if I moved at all, I might start slapping at the thing while running around in circles, and then that deputy would find us for sure.

"Just a minute," said Ellie calmly as her hand approached my face. Her thumb and fingertips moved pincerlike, then pulled back with something kicking and wiggling between them, and oh, I did not like this one single bit.

But the scratchy, skittery feeling had vanished, so that was good. "What was it?"

"Never mind. Come on."

The cop's footsteps sounded once more on the gravel driveway. But once he found the apples she'd thrown, he'd be back. After all, where else would they have come from but the orchard?

"Ellie, I still want to know what the heck we're doing here and why at the *very next possible instant*," I gasped as I wiggled out from the weeds.

Crouched low, scuttling along, we reached the end of the fence nearest the house. Ellie stopped, looked up. I followed her gaze as a light went on in the topmost window. Then it went off.

A chill rippled through the hairs on my neck. "Uh, that just happened, right?"

Ellie nodded, seeming unconcerned. But then I realized that the deputy had returned to his car, put his headlights on, and turned the car so that the headlights lit up part of the orchard, turning the trees' gnarled branches to clawing wraith arms. And as the car had turned, the lights had lit the house's windows. That was why Ellie wasn't worried.

"Oh," I exhaled, relieved.

Now the deputy was on his way back down to the orchard, brandishing a flashlight in one hand and bouncing an apple up and down in the other. In the headlights' bluish-white glow, I could see also the small marker flags the state cops' evidence technicians had left to show where they'd found Alvin.

"This way," said Ellie hastily before hustling me over the side lawn toward the murdered man's back porch.

We scampered up onto it. She headed straight for the door; I hung back. The white wicker chairs on the porch looked as if they had been standing there for decades. At their feet lay an indoor-outdoor rug; it had looked good, too, once upon a time.

But never mind the condition. I wanted to flop into one of

the wicker chairs and rest. I wanted even more for that deputy not to find us. But most of all . . .

Most of all, I still didn't see what we were doing here. "Ellie, let's . . ." "Go home and make a plan," I'd have finished, but she wasn't listening.

Instead, she was pressing her face to each porch window. Finally . . . "There are night lights on in there," she announced.

Oh, wonderful. So if anyone *did* happen to be slinking around inside, they'd have no trouble seeing us.

She tried the door. Locked, of course. Bob Arnold would have made sure of it. But when she rattled the knob, the latch let go, and the door drifted open with a creak of old hinges.

Inside, silvery patches of moonlight spread on the floor. Dim shapes loomed in shadowy corners. A clock ticked hollowly somewhere, and a faucet dripped. *Plink, plink.*

"Ellie," I heard myself croak. "Ellie, *why* are we—"

But she'd already gone in.

Alvin Carter's old-fashioned kitchen held a farmhouse-style porcelain sink, beadboard cabinets with tarnished brass hardware, a massive old gas stove featuring a firebox on one side and a water boiler on the other, and a clothesline with a couple of dishcloths draped on it stretched over the firebox.

I still didn't understand why Ellie felt so determined about this. But then it hit me.

"Oh, Ellie. You didn't . . . did you?"

But of course she had. "Jake," she entreated, "those poor girls were so miserable. And so *scared.*"

And being Ellie, naturally she'd wanted to make them feel better, just as she'd told me.

"You promised," I said. "You told them we'd fix all this. Clear Billy of suspicion by finding out who really . . ."

Her face gave me my answer. "I did," she admitted simply. "I had to. Jake, you'd have done the same." Her eyes searched my face.

Finally, I said, "Yeah. You're right. I probably would."

And in any case, it was done now, wasn't it? And here we were in Alvin's house.

"So come on," I said. "Let's get this snooping session over and done with."

The old dwelling's high-ceilinged central hall ran all the way to the front entry. To our right lay the parlor, which Ellie had seen from outside, full of lumpy-looking furniture, fringed lamps, and rugs with swirly patterns that seemed to move when I looked at them too long.

The smell of wood ashes wafted from a rough granite hearth whose gaping mouth was blackened with soot. But despite the charmlessness of the place, I'd just about managed to relax and decide that in fact nobody else was in here with us, that Ellie was right and the light upstairs had been cop-car headlights.

Then something twined itself sinuously around my ankle. Leaping back, I let out a startled yelp as Ellie's flashlight beam probed the floor around me.

"Prutt," said the cat who'd just startled me out of my few remaining wits. A black cat with almond-shaped yellow eyes and a long, twitching tail shaped like a question mark.

"Oh, *prutt*, yourself," I said crossly. But the cat seemed to regard this as a welcome. After gathering itself, it sprang at me with a cry, then settled itself purringly in my arms.

"Oh, for Pete's sake." The cat wiggled happily. I tried dropping it to the floor, but it wouldn't go. "Ellie . . ."

Mindful of that deputy outside, my friend snapped the flashlight off, then went about rescuing me. Realizing from her firm, "Don't mess with me" attitude that the jig was most definitely up, the feline let itself be lowered to the floor, then streaked from the room.

Ellie headed after it, toward the hall stairs, and there wasn't anything for it but to follow unless I wanted to stay here.

"Wait for me!" I called, hurrying after them both. Because maybe it was just my nerves, but now the patterns in those rugs weren't the only things that seemed to be moving.

Alcoves with statues' shapes shifting unpleasantly in them, pressed-tin ceilings whose braided-vine motifs slithered like snakes . . .

Oh, stop it, I scolded myself impatiently, climbing the stairs and hurrying along after Ellie down the upstairs hall. But even without my admittedly overactive imagination working on it, the place felt oppressive, with too many ornately framed mirrors, murky oil portraits, and tables with alabaster heads perched on them, all making the house look like a junk shop.

But an *expensive* junk shop. We were on the second floor of it now.

"If there's a third floor . . . ," Ellie began quietly from the far end of the hall.

Right. Then there must be a stairway leading upward somewhere around here.

She aimed her flashlight at murky wood-paneled corners and swaths of faded wallpaper. The smell here was like that of an unaired cedar chest, mothballs and old wood.

Finally . . . "Oh, *here* it is . . ." Not waiting for me, she hurried up the steps to the third floor.

I hesitated. For one thing, we were getting too far from the exits on the first floor—for my purposes, that's where they'd have to be, wouldn't they?—and for another, what if Ellie was wrong? What if someone *was* in here, waiting for . . . ?

Well, I didn't know what they might be waiting for, and while I stood there worrying about it, Ellie cried out from somewhere above. Not a scream, really, more of a little "Eek!" But it was enough to rocket me up that damned third flight of stairs, and if somebody up there was trying to hurt Ellie, I would . . .

"What's wrong?" I demanded when I found her at last in one of the third floor's slant-ceilinged, primitively finished chambers. Unpainted plaster, stained and mottled by roof leaks; old windows so dilapidated, they looked as if a light breeze might blow them in.

"Nothing," Ellie replied with a weak laugh, still getting over her fright. "The cat jumped on me. Surprised me."

The solid black feline now sat atop a stack of wooden filing cabinets, washing its face and basking in the moonlight, which filled the old room with a gauzy glow.

That was when I noticed that all the file drawers had been opened and left that way, as if someone had rifled them in a hurry. Pale manila folders and sheets of paper lay scattered across the floor.

I crouched on an old carpet underneath a wooden desk to peer at the labeled columns of numbers printed on the fallen papers. These were Alvin Carter's yearly financial summaries, I knew at a glance, snapshots of income, expenses, taxes, and so on.

I'd created a lot of them back in my past life as a money manager. Now I scanned quickly and found nothing obviously amiss . . . but these records were from years ago. *Not anything of present-day interest*, I thought.

"Looks as if somebody didn't find what they were looking for," Ellie observed.

The mess really was epic. "Mmm. Or they found it at the end of a long search, instead of early on."

I stood up. A bare bulb with a chain switch dangling from it hung from the ceiling; a little while ago, someone had—or had not, if Ellie's theory was correct—turned it on and off.

"You're right, though," I said, looking around again. The

desk drawers held only pens, pencils, and an old metal tie clip emblazoned with the words CARTER'S DEPARTMENT STORE. "Looks like they went through everything. Then something spooked them—that deputy arriving, maybe?—and they got out of here," I said.

Or so I hoped. The "got out of here" part, I mean. We peeked into the other third-floor room, its doorway straight across from the first, but nothing was in it except one small window overlooking the driveway.

"If there was something here, it's gone now," said Ellie. She went in and walked to the window.

I wasn't so sure. All these records were pretty ancient. Why would something somebody wanted now be among them? Then . . .

"Darn," Ellie breathed, and I hurriedly joined her at the rickety-framed window in the tiny front room.

"Look," she said, aiming an index finger not down at the driveway, where the cop car still sat, but into the distance.

The *far* distance. From up here you could see all the way across Carrying Place Cove, down to Route 190, where it curved into town. And *on* Route 190 sped a car with a flashing cherry-red beacon on its dashboard.

We scrambled for the stairs and hurried down them.

"That's Bob Arnold," I gasped, "or I'll eat my hat."

"Oh, you betcha," Ellie replied, hustling down the second-floor hall, past one dark bedroom doorway after another. "And if he finds us here . . . ," Ellie went on as she raced ahead of me down the final staircase.

Right. It didn't bear thinking about. Bob was our friend, but that didn't mean he'd let us off scot-free. And tampering with anything that might turn out to be evidence—even when it had *already* been tampered with by investigators—was a pretty big deal, or at least it seemed so to me now that we'd done it.

A car crunched on the gravel outside. I leapt down the last

stairs, rounded the newel post at a gallop, and sprinted for the kitchen, where we'd come in.

The hallway's massive old bookcases, fragile knickknack tables, and assorted other obstacles—an elephant-leg umbrella holder, a green glass ashtray in a brass stand, a doorstop shaped like a bulldog—all tried to trip me, but the sound of a car door slamming out front spurred me on. Until . . .

By now, my eyes had adjusted to the dimness in here; it's why I hadn't already done a face-plant on the hall carpet, and why I spotted the orange manila envelope half hidden where it must've fallen behind the old cast-iron radiator.

I snatched it up, folding it awkwardly to stuff it into my pocket, and kept running until I caught up with Ellie, then followed her out the door. Together we scampered across the lawn to crouch at the orchard's back corner.

Downhill toward the front of the house, flashlight beams stabbed among the apple trees: Bob and the deputy, I guessed.

"Are they looking for us?" Ellie quietly wondered aloud.

"No," I said, my heart still thudding, "they're hunting for Easter eggs. Who *would* they be looking for, if not—"

Wait a minute.

"Ellie, that flash of light that we saw on the third floor, before we went in . . . I know you felt sure about what it was at the time, but *could* it have been—"

The flashlights turned our way. I got ready to run. If they came any nearer . . .

"I did notice," she said thoughtfully, "that when I was in the front room, I could see all the way to where you stood in the back room."

Right, because the doorways were directly opposite each other. Which meant that light from the *back* room could've shone right through to the . . .

"The deputy saw it," I said, realizing what had happened. "It wasn't a reflection from his headlights, like we thought. It was the light bulb in Alvin's office. It went on at the rear of the house, but it was visible from the front, as well."

I took a breath. "That's why the deputy called Bob Arnold, I'll bet. He saw the light, walked around out here, and found that kitchen door unlocked, then figured he'd better get Bob's okay before he went inside."

Meanwhile, a hundred bucks said both those cops were going to walk the whole length of the orchard fence line, all the way to the back corner.

Where they'd find us.

"Come on," I murmured as, staying low, I crept backward toward the overgrown brush and saplings at the yard's rear, then into them.

Unfortunately, though, the next thing I backed into was a barberry bush, whose thorns made my own rear feel like a pincushion. With *pins* in it . . . *Ouch.*

"Jake?" Ellie whispered urgently from somewhere.

The flashlights turned back toward the house.

"Here I am," I replied. But then, once I'd un-thorned the seat of my pants, I realized that whoever had been in the house earlier might now be hiding out here in this thicket.

With us. Still, now that Bob and his deputy were gone, we could skedaddle and—I hoped—avoid trouble. Thinking this, I stuck my hand in my pocket.

"Oh, no." The manila envelope was gone. I checked my other pockets. Nada, as Sam would've put it.

Then I spotted the faint, pale rectangle lying among a row of faded geraniums planted along the porch's front. The plants were too low and too skimpy to try hiding anything among them which I guessed must be why Bob and his deputy hadn't bothered poking their flashlight beams into them.

So they'd missed finding the envelope. As I watched, Bob

climbed the porch steps and pushed the door open cautiously with the end of his flashlight, while the deputy went on around to the front of the house again.

I looked at the envelope, nestled so cozily among the neglected plants, then at the distance across the yard and at Bob's backside, now disappearing into the kitchen's gloom. I could see his flashlight moving around in there.

Then, like a blessing from above, those streaming clouds covered the moon once more and the night got a lot darker all of a sudden. Meanwhile, Bob's flashlight flickered upstairs, and the deputy was still on the other side of the house.

No time like the present . . . After shoving myself back out through the brambles and thorns, heedless of the blood transfusion I would need on account of them, I took off downhill across the yard.

If I was right, somebody had found that envelope inside the house, maybe up in Alvin's office. But then in a mad dash to get out of there—on account of us, probably—they'd dropped it. And if whatever was in that envelope was important enough to break in there and steal it, I wanted a look at it.

Thinking this, I'd nearly reached the geranium border when my sneakered foot skidded on wet grass—of course the lawn had been getting watered regularly, or it would never survive the drought we were having—and flew up into the air. The other foot followed; instants later, the rest of me hit the ground hard. When I could see through the pain again, I found myself lying facedown among the geraniums, with my nose pressed up against more chicken wire, placed there to block any wild critters from setting up housekeeping under the porch.

Unfortunately for this plan, a hole gaped in the chicken wire, but luckily, no critters came out through it to see what was going on.

In the house, though, things weren't so quiet suddenly. First,

Bob Arnold shouted; then came the sounds of a scuffle. Finally, the porch door flew open, and footsteps thudded across the porch.

"Stop," Bob yelled as a dark shape hurtled over me. After leaping from the porch to the lawn, the shape took off running toward the orchard.

Bob emerged from the house, then stopped to radio that deputy, who appeared momentarily and headed for the orchard while Bob called for more help, standing there on the porch. If he looked down, he would see me. Correction: *When* he looked down . . . So I had to do *something* . . . and then I had it, I hoped.

Good old chicken wire, I thought, rolling myself against it testingly. Thin, flexible . . . and a bit rusty maybe? If I could just get myself through it, then I could roll underneath the porch and out of sight.

So as quietly as I could, I rolled again, harder this time, and the torn part of the chicken-wire barrier gave way all at once. That's why, instead of just tucking myself back out of Bob's view as I'd intended, I ended up way under there, in the animal-smelling dark.

Not only that, but somehow, I seemed also to be rolled up inside the chicken wire; like, so tightly that I couldn't move my arms. Or my legs. Or roll out of there, either, because a lot of sharp strand ends of that chicken wire stuck out, needlelike, mere centimeters from my throat.

I felt them when I swallowed, and if I moved, I thought I might get beheaded by them. Or halfway beheaded, which in practice I thought might be worse, or at least would last longer, before I stopped noticing the sensation altogether.

Above me a porch light snapped on. Then Bob's feet crossed the porch decking, moving away from me, and went down the steps. Meanwhile, that manila envelope still lay there in plain sight; all he had to do was look down to see it.

And all I could do was lie there, trying to figure out how to escape with my throat unslit.

At least it was dry under here. Through the gaps in the wire, I pushed my fingertips into soil parched to dust. That was good news, because it meant I wouldn't be stung to death by red ants, Eastport's most fearsome predators.

Too bad something else did enjoy extreme dryness: spiders. In the faint yellow glow seeping between the porch planks down into the crawl space beneath them, shapes moved. Skinny, long-leggity shapes. Eight leggity, to be precise, and lots of centipedes, the absolute leggitiest of all, plus a wasps' nest the size of a football, luckily abandoned, or at any rate, I hoped so.

But the worst thing of all was . . . Ye gods, it was a snake. A small one, to be sure, and not aggressive. If its slithering-away behavior was a clue. But maybe it was going to get its friends. They'd finish up what the spiders left, and when they got here, the centipedes would already be crawling in and out of my . . .

Oh, shut up, I scolded myself yet again. This whole night was trotting out every one of my phobias like in some creepy show-and-tell.

On the other hand, one thing wasn't my imagination: it was definitely getting harder for me to breathe down here, wrapped in chicken wire, with both my arms held tightly against my sides by the unyielding metal strands.

Pushing my fingers through the gaps in the wire, I tried pulling the whole swath down toward my feet while wiggling myself upward. This worked a little bit: after the wire nearly cut my fingers off, it moved enough so that at least the rusty strand ends weren't puncturing any of my favorite arteries. Or not at the moment, anyway.

Also, I'd heard no sounds from any nearby police officers for a while. So it seemed like now or never, a situation that was occurring way too frequently for my comfort lately, especially since I was pretty sure the tickling in my hair was either a spider or a centipede out on an exploratory mission to locate my most edible parts.

Unless it was a snake, a possibility I most definitely did not want to consider.

Besides, at the moment, I had a more important question to think about: Now or never *what*?

Four

At the moment I was nothing but a bundle tightly wrapped in a swath of old chicken wire, stuffed under a porch, in the dusty, critter-infested darkness. What I wanted was to get out of there, and to do that, I'd have to roll hard to the right, toward where I'd come in.

First, though, I'd need somehow to give myself momentum, or I might end up rolling only onto my stomach and getting stuck that way.

So . . . start with a quarter-turn to the left.

The flashlight I'd brought under here with me was wedged up uselessly under my armpit. When I turned, it beamed weakly over the tan, dusty earth underneath the porch.

Eep. As I turned a little more, though, the flashlight's yellowish glow lit up the face of a corpse. An *old* corpse, which seemed hideously to have been embalmed, as its facial skin was so smooth and artificial looking, and its hair as crisp and shiny as doll's hair.

Barely managing to repress a shriek, I flung my whole chicken wire–wrapped self very hard in the other direction, no longer needing more momentum. If I had to, I thought, I could levitate right out from under the porch, wire and all.

The gloom-filled, spider-infested . . .

Dead body–infested . . .

"*Gah*," I exhaled. The spirit was willing, but the flesh got me only over onto my right side, then stalled. Thick spiderwebs draped my face, clinging to my eyelashes and sticking to my lips, and going up my nose when I tried to breathe.

"Phoo!" I blew them away as well as I could. A couple of half-glimpsed creepy-crawlies skittered hastily away, too, but at least no spiders were in the web strands that entered my nostrils. I hoped.

Anyway, another roll sideways, fueled by the awful profile of that old corpse, which was not quite turned enough to look at me—*Not yet*, said an awful voice in my head—got me over onto my stomach . . . almost.

But not quite. A nail I hadn't noticed before stuck out from the plank above me, and while it didn't quite take out my appendix, it hooked itself securely in the chicken wire still wrapped very tightly around my midsection.

And all my other sections. So I was stuck. *Drat.* I could roll back the other way again, I supposed, and hope that move unhooked me somehow. But I really did have my heart set on at least some forwardliness; Ellie would be looking for me, for one thing, and besides, there was that corpse.

I wanted to get away from it, and I needed to find Ellie, and meanwhile, little thrills of near panic kept rippling up and down my spine, like someone playing a lot of off-key high notes very fast on a piano. But most of all . . .

Trapped. Oh, I really didn't like this at all, and there seemed to be nothing I could do about it, either. Behind me lay a corpse, while above me hung a bent nail that might just as well have been a boulder, in the blocking-the-exit department.

But before I gave up and started yelling for help, which

would get me out of here but also into Bob Arnold's squad car, I tried one last time. *Okay, now . . .*

Closing my mouth and eyes tightly and clenching my fists, I jerked my whole body yet again toward—I hoped—my only possible escape route. The chicken wire hooked on the nail that hung above me again, but this time I felt it give slightly. So I rolled back a little, then hurtled myself at it again. . . .

And again, until at last—with a faint metallic ping!—the wire strand that kept getting caught on the nail snapped suddenly. I just kept rolling, already planning to snatch that manila envelope up out of the geraniums as I skedaddled.

While leaving the dead guy behind, of course, if it even *was* a guy; the thing I'd confronted was so shrouded in years of dust, I couldn't tell.

After squeezing out from under the porch at last, gasping with relief while also terrified I might be spotted, I frantically wrestled the chicken wire off and scrambled into a crouch.

No one was in sight, but unwelcome company might show up at any instant.

So I should run. But the envelope I'd found had to contain something important if someone had gone to so much trouble to get it. And after what I'd been through tonight, I was not about to leave it behind if I could help it.

Thinking this, I heaved myself up straight and for a wonder did not fall (a) forward onto my face or (b) backward for an impromptu "skull vs. porch step" contest. Then, feeling pretty darned cocky after that little display of athleticism—the million or so times I'd stood up from a crouch with my grandson, Ephraim, in my arms was coming in handy—I flung the rolled-up tangle of chicken wire out into the dark yard, then turned as tires crunched the gravel out in front of the house. *Darn . . .*

Headlights shone briefly into the orchard and along the fence line as the car went around the driveway and stopped. A car door slammed. Footsteps crossed on the gravel. Bob Arnold had called in more deputies, it sounded like, to help look for whomever he'd nearly caught coming out of Alvin's house.

Standing in the gloom, I scanned the flattened geranium border. The men's voices stayed out front, but they wouldn't for long; Bob would station one of the deputies back here by the porch as soon as he'd brought them up to speed, I felt sure.

And that meant I didn't have much time, although I'd have liked getting brought up to speed, too. Like, who had been with us inside the house? Whoever it was had dropped the envelope in the dark hall without realizing it, probably . . .

Right, the envelope. I assumed the intruder we'd surprised must've found it in Alvin's office after tearing the place apart, but where the heck was it now?

Not where I'd spied it before, among the geraniums. So how had it disappeared and, more to the point, *where* had it . . . ?

I peered around, but by this time the clouds overhead had thickened even more. Foghorns moaned distantly, cool mist brushed my face, and I didn't dare use the flashlight. Still, I kept squinting around. It had been right here, so . . .

A hand seized my shoulder. "Eep," I said, jerking away.

"Shh. Come on." It was Ellie; my knees weakened with relief as she yanked me away from the porch. She hustled me along uphill through the dark backyard and into the stand of saplings bordering the rear of the property, where we'd come in.

"I thought they must've caught you. Or someone else had," Ellie whispered exasperatedly.

"Sorry. But, Ellie, I found a—"

Body. The word stuck in my throat as a picture of the desiccated remains rose in my mind. But even that wasn't the main thing occupying my thought processes right now.

Down at the house, Bob Arnold approached the porch. His flashlight beam probed the geranium bed, lingered around the place under the porch where the chicken wire had been.

There'd been no manila envelope among the geraniums or

anywhere near them. And I'd have noticed it for sure if it had been under the porch with me; my view of that area had been a little *too* good, as it turned out.

So there was only one conclusion I could come to: the envelope was gone. And the only way that could be true was if somebody else had found it and taken it.

After making our way slowly and painfully through darkness thickly furnished with thorny brush and ankle-snaring scrub trees, Ellie and I got back to the car and drove home without incident.

"Well, that didn't turn out the way I planned," she said finally, her hands gripping the steering wheel.

"Yeah," I exhaled. Facing up suddenly to a corpse under a porch hadn't been on my agenda, for sure.

"Do you think he spotted us?"

Bob Arnold, she meant. If he had, he wouldn't necessarily have bothered doing anything about it right that minute. After all, he knew where we lived.

"I don't know."

"Even if he didn't," Ellie berated herself, "I could've gotten us both killed. I should have known better than to drag you out on a wild—"

Right, like I hadn't done the same to her many times. "Hey, you didn't have to twist my arm. If I'd thought of it first, I'd have been under *your* window, agitating to—"

Well, not under her window. I'd have called or knocked on her door. Her husband, George Valentine, was working in Bangor all this week, and her daughter, Lee, was at a friend's house for a sleepover on account of no school tomorrow.

"I guess," she sighed and then fell into a silence, which I was glad to share. It's not every night I go out and find a body under a porch, and it's exhausting.

But I would tell her about it tomorrow, I decided as she

pulled over in front of my old house on Key Street, and I would break it to her then about the envelope I'd lost, too. She'd had enough for tonight; we both had.

"See you at the shop in the morning?" she asked.

I got out of the car, leaned back in through the passenger-side window. "Yep." Then: "We're alive, anyway," I said, hoping to coax a smile out of her.

It worked. "Yeah." A little laugh, even. But... "Jake, any minute I was sure I'd feel Bob Arnold's hand clamping down on my shoulder."

"Me too." Or someone else's hand. Someone worse.

But now wasn't the time to say that to her, either, so instead, I said again that I would see her tomorrow, and when I got inside the house, everybody was already in bed.

In the dim-lit kitchen, the air smelled like soapsuds and Comet scouring powder, courtesy of Bella's habitual late-night cleaning sprees. After dropping my jacket on a chairback, I put a mug of coffee into the microwave and buttered a hard roll for myself. Near-death experiences make me hungry.

I was at the kitchen table, with the coffee and roll, when Mika came in, dressed in a long, fuzzy pink robe and slippers and looking even more exhausted than I felt.

"Long day?" I asked sympathetically.

Her glossy black hair, still damp from her shower, moved prettily around her heart-shaped face as she nodded. "Yes. But mostly it was discouraging." She eyed my coffee, then began heating some for herself.

"Keep you awake," I cautioned, but not very forcefully. "Let people do what they want to" is my motto. Mostly.

She laughed unconvincingly. "Right, like I'm going to sleep." She sat across from me with her steaming cup. "On the other hand, maybe if I stay awake, I'll figure out what to do." She glanced up curiously at me. "You look like hell," she commented.

My turn to laugh. It wasn't Mika's usual style of remark. "I'll bet. But never mind me. What's got you still up and around? You ought to be comatose by now."

And with that, it all came pouring out of her. "Sam says he doesn't know how long Billy Breyer might be gone," she began worriedly. "Without him, Sam will probably have to give up some customers."

And the income associated with them, she meant.

"And if *that* happens, there's absolutely no question I'll need to go back to work even sooner than I planned."

The light dawned. "Mika, as far as money goes, you do know we'll all help tide you over until . . . ?"

She shook her head impatiently. "I do know it, we both do, and we appreciate it. But that's not the point." She paused. "I mean, thank you, of course." She dredged up a heavy sigh. "The point, like I said before, is that I'm not sure I'm fit to work. Or ever will be again." Pressing her hands to the sides of her head, she made a face. "And I don't know what to do about it. My brain has gone AWOL," she finished.

Like I'd told her before, I knew the feeling. For a while after Sam was born, I ran only the most basic routines and struggled with elementary concepts. I forgot how to add and subtract, for instance, which for me was a little like forgetting how to breathe.

"It's like there's a tiny Pac-Man in there, running around, eating brain cells," Mika said.

Yep. Luckily by the time Sam was weaned, I could do simple math, and soon I went back to my old completely illegal but eminently profitable employment: financial fixing for organized crooks, no questions asked. Or not out loud, anyway.

"Today I messed up a simple pie crust," said Mika sorrowfully, "and this afternoon I couldn't recall how to cream butter and sugar together." She sighed shakily. "The next thing I knew, I was crying into the dough again, and of course, that upset Ephraim."

"Oh, honey, take it a little easier on yourself. You've been doing only mom stuff since Doreen was born, so of course it'll take a bit of time to get back to your old self."

She was a fabulous mother, she adored those two kids, and I knew for a fact that she'd enjoyed every minute of the full-time motherhood experience she'd had so far.

Well, maybe not every *single* minute. But enough of them to wipe everything else out of her mind, that's for sure.

And now she wanted it all back.

Correction: *needed* it back.

"The thing is, I just found out there's a spot opening up at the technical school," she confided.

By this she meant the local community college, an absolute beacon of common-sense education for people who needed fewer obscure ancient languages and more career preparation included in their curriculum.

"Lecturer in the Food Sciences department," Mika went on, "where students get ready to enter the hospitality industry."

"Oh, I see," I said, understanding at last. *Yikes* . . . "So you don't just theoretically need your brains at some unspecified future date. You're on some kind of a deadline?"

"Yup. I'm right up against it, as they say around here. I've got the job if I want it. The school's already told me so. The question is, can I *do* the—"

Without warning, the kitchen light went on over our heads; we blinked in the glare.

"What's going on down here?" Bella demanded.

In a hairnet and flannel pj's, and with old, ragged tennis shoes flopping on her bare feet, Bella put her own mug into the microwave and pushed the button.

"For heaven's sake," she fussed as she got a tea bag from the canister, "it's nearly midnight. So what're you doing down here? You girls should be in . . ."

"Right." I got up, swaying a little. Now that the adrenaline had drained out of me, all I wanted was to lie down.

Sleep was probably out of the question, owing not only to the envelope I'd lost but also to the body I'd found, and even more to my not knowing what to do about it, since if I told Bob Arnold about it, then I'd have to tell him where I'd found it, wouldn't I?

Where, and what I was doing there . . . And then something else distracted me even more unhappily. In the harsh overhead light of the late-night kitchen, Bella's skin looked thin as waxed paper, and her bony hand trembled as she reached for a spoon.

The tremor was new, and it made me wonder suddenly who'd care for the children all day if—or, more likely, *when*—Mika went back to work. Nevertheless . . .

"Listen, what we were talking about before? It'll be fine," I assured my daughter-in-law yet again. "I promise."

Which might've been reckless. In addition to Mika's mental-focus difficulties, the child-care thing was a real problem, too, I'd just begun realizing, and it wasn't going to go away.

Or not by itself, at any rate. But Mika and those kids were the best things that had ever happened to Sam, and I loved her extravagantly. So when she looked up at me so gratefully and seemed to believe me so unquestioningly, I decided that Ellie wasn't the only one who could keep promises around here.

Come hell or high water, I resolved. But for now . . .

Exhaustion washed over me. If I really had to obsess over that dead body, I decided, I could do it lying down.

"I'm going to bed," I said.

To my surprise, I actually slept, and by eight the next morning, I was sitting in the WaCo Diner with a cup of coffee in front of me and a foursome of fishermen in the booth behind me, who were trading waterfront gossip while they shoveled down their bacon and eggs.

It wasn't the smell of fish that wafted from them, though; it was woodsmoke.

"Durn fires 're cuttin' into my fishin' time," said one. The grass fires, he meant. "I was out five ay-em this mornin,' hosin' down Tim Blankenships's garage roof so's the sparks from his hayfield didn't catch it."

"Ayuh," said one of the other fishermen. "When the wind's right, the smoke's so bad sometimes, we've got to close windows at home. All it's gonna take is one spark, and . . ."

So the fires were threatening houses now, I gathered. *Rain*, I prayed silently, but the forecast didn't call for any.

I glanced at the diner's entry, looking for Bob Arnold. I'd told him on the phone earlier that I wanted to meet him here, and he'd agreed to give me fifteen minutes.

He had not, however, agreed to be on time; probably the fires were slowing him down a lot, too. The better, I supposed, to rehearse what I had to say to him. But it still wouldn't be easy.

"Somethin' doesn't change, bad things are gonna happen," said one of the fishermen behind me, and a deep-voiced murmur of agreement went around their table.

No Bob yet. The waitress behind the long Formica counter waved the coffeepot at me, and I nodded, then on second thought decided to go for a plate of breakfast myself. My own kitchen had been a madhouse this morning, as usual, and for the kind of day I was expecting, I'd need fuel.

Rocket fuel, preferably, but the WaCo didn't have any of that, so I got fried eggs, toast, and a glass of tomato juice.

"Fine, dear," said the waitress with a smile, scribbling on her green pad. *Dee-yah*, the Maine way of saying it.

I smiled back at her, silently debating a shot of vodka in the tomato juice. But she hurried away before I could mention it. Then . . .

"Them gals might be littlish," came a voice from behind me again, "but they can haul a damn lobster trap."

Lobstah. And he must mean Helen and Anna; the Breyer sisters were the only young women working on boats this year.

"Yeah, but it takes two of 'em to do it," another of the guys argued in a reedy voice. "They ain't got the upper-body strength."

"You was a wimp, too, your first year," retorted the first guy, and laughter greeted this.

Then a third voice chimed in, low and gravelly, "At least them two ain't hangin' over the bow rail, unloading last night's boilermakers all morning, like some people I know."

More laughter.

"It's gonna be too bad if they can't crew no more, though," the first man said. "Work like bastids, the pair of 'em. Hell, you stick that hair o' theirs under a cap, you'd think they's men."

"'Cept they don't cuss. I got to admit, it makes a nice change," the first guy said.

"Havin' any women around at all makes a nice change for you," one of the other guys shot back. And then the talk turned to lobster bait—price, quality, availability—and I lost interest because Bob was making his way toward me, past the row of red leatherette stools at the counter, the seats all emptying now as the diner's morning rush dwindled.

"You will not believe this," he fumed, sliding in across from me and nodding at the waitress's offer of coffee.

All I wanted was to get this over with, so I didn't ask him what he meant. Instead, I opened my mouth to start telling him the story of last night: Ellie and me at Alvin's place, our activities inside the house, the missing manila envelope, and, of course, the long-dead body under the porch. . . .

Because, of course, I had to tell him. I couldn't *not* tell him. It was a dead person, for heaven's sake. But . . .

"We found another body at Alvin Carter's last night," Bob said before I could get a word out.

"You . . . you did?" Relief washed over me; now I didn't have to tell him about it. Or . . . did I?

A trickle of suspicion chilled my early enthusiasm for his announcement. "A body," I repeated slowly.

"Yeah. Under Alvin's back porch, of all places. Messed-up flower beds . . ."

Those geraniums, I realized.

The fishermen behind me paid their check and left.

"Bunch of torn-off varmint fencing under there . . ."

The gap in the chicken wire. Of course he'd have noticed.

"So we figured we ought to go ahead, have a look," said Bob. He eyed me carefully, watching for my reaction.

"Sounds right," I managed, keeping my voice even.

Because as I have mentioned, Bob may not look much like an effective police officer, what with his thinning blond hair, plump pink face, and general air of being the Pillsbury Doughboy's long-lost twin brother. But Bob could make a dead bird sing like a canary with that steely-blue gaze of his, and when that didn't work, he had a head swat guaranteed to shake loose the facts you might not have felt like mentioning.

Not only that, but he's also the kind of guy who can figure you out before *you* figure you out. For instance . . .

"You and Ellie wouldn't happen to have been out there last night, would you?" he asked.

And there it was, the direct question I'd been dreading. It meant that maybe he *had* seen us, and now he was waiting to find out if I would lie about it to his face.

"Um, actually . . . ," I began, wishing I'd never called him at all.

But just then Ellie walked in and spotted me. Her look as she strode past the counter toward us was so communicative, it was like she had a ticker tape streaming across her forehead.

Shut up, said the ticker tape directly to me in big red letters. *Just keep that fool mouth of yours . . .*

I clamped my lips shut; she nodded minutely. Then . . .

"Hi!" she greeted us cheerfully as she slid into the booth alongside me. "Bella told me you were here. What's going on?"

"Nothing much," I replied. "I was just about to tell Bob that I've hooked Billy Breyer up with a defense lawyer."

Bob's sparse blond eyebrows went up. But he didn't stop glancing from me to Ellie and back, and I could tell he was getting ready to ask questions we wouldn't like answering.

Fortunately, his cell phone chirped at him instead.

"Gotta go," he said after glancing at it. " 'Nother fire, out by the airport. Now, before I go, do I need to tell you two amateur snoops to cut it the hell out, whatever you're up to?"

"Oh, no," I said innocently, "we're not up to anything."

"Not at all," Ellie agreed, mild as a lamb.

But when he had gone . . . "*Amateur*," I burst out indignantly. "Just who does he think he's calling an amateur?" After all, Ellie and I weren't just local Eastport snoops. We were *well-known* local—

"Now, Jake." Ellie's coffee and blueberry muffin came; she'd ordered on the way in. "An amateur is someone who does something for the love of it." She buttered half the muffin. "And that's us. Also," she added before biting in, "he knows we were out there last night. What he said was a warning. You know it, and I know it."

She was right. But seeing my look, she reached across the table and patted my hand.

"Don't worry. If he meant to do anything official about our trespassing last night, he'd have done it already."

Trespassing and more . . . "I suppose," I agreed unhappily. It was no secret here in Eastport that Bob Arnold could smell the truth a hundred yards away. Probably he'd guessed, and then my face had confirmed it for him.

"But, Ellie," I said, "there's one other thing that . . ."

Because maybe I didn't have to tell Bob Arnold about the body under the porch—how *had* it gotten there, anyway, and more to the point, who'd made it dead, and why and when?— but I had to tell her.

"See, after we got separated last night . . . ," I began.

Listening as I told the whole story, she ate the other half of her muffin by tearing small pieces off it and popping them into her mouth.

"Huh," she commented when I'd finished. "An *old* body, you say. So maybe not connected to Alvin's death?"

"Mmm," I said, though in my admittedly *amateur* experience, two dead bodies discovered in the same location usually turned out to be more than, as my son, Sam, would put it, a coinky-dink.

We ate our breakfasts quietly for a little while, Ellie pitching in on finishing my toast. She liked the grape jelly in the little packets.

"In other news, I visited the girls again this morning," she said at last. "Anna and Helen."

"And?" It was eight thirty, and the diner was filling up again; when your day started at four in the morning, this was coffee-break time.

"And they're scared," Ellie replied.

Guys wearing plaid flannel shirts, bib overalls, and muck boots sat at the counter with other guys wearing gray Carhartt sweatshirts, tan canvas trousers, and the kind of steel-toed leather work boots that can double as bonking tools in a pinch.

"Not just scared of Prunia," Ellie elaborated. "They're worried to death because Billy's not home yet." She finished my toast. "He did get to call them and say he would be there overnight," she added, "but they figure it means he's going to be charged."

Which I thought was probably correct, unfortunately.

"I had to tell them," Ellie added, "that it's not a certainty, but it's definitely not out of the question."

I checked the clock that hung over the pass-through to the kitchen again. Nearly nine now, and it was time to open the Chocolate Moose.

"They're okay for today, though?" I asked as we went out. Billy's sisters, I meant.

Ellie nodded, but before she could say more, two ladies scurried across the street and over to us.

"Woo-hoo! Ellie and Jake!" they chorused.

Jane Whitley and Alice Green were the Dabney twins before they got married, and they still looked alike: blue-white hair, bright red lipstick, and broad smiles full of shiny white choppers that always made me think of those trick false teeth that clatter around on their own.

Grinning, they planted themselves before us. "We're on the contest committee," said Jane, producing a clipboard.

"And we want to make sure we can count on you two!" said Alice. "Go on, Jane. Get their signatures," she urged.

Their pastel pantsuits—one pink, one blue—must've dated from the 1970s. Ditto for the tan leather Hush Puppies shoes on their feet.

"Contest," I repeated stupidly. In the sky over our heads, a light plane circled; I wished I were on it.

"The cookie contest," Ellie reminded me quietly, and I recalled it with a shock. What with everything that had been happening lately, it had gone straight out of my mind, which I thought I might do also if I had to think about anything more.

Jane stuck out the clipboard. "Just sign right here, and you, too, Ellie."

Ellie obeyed, and then I did, scribbling my name on the next open line. For one thing, I was outnumbered, not to mention intimidated by so many white teeth gleaming at me all at once.

But as we quick-stepped down Water Street afterward . . . "I don't think we should really do it, though," said Ellie.

"What? Not enter the contest? But, Ellie, we just said we would, and we always . . ."

We cut through the parking lot across from the fish pier, where a dumpy little blue tugboat was tied, puffing smoke from its short, fat stack. Beyond it, on the water, the Campobello ferry trundled dutifully over the waves, headed for Canada.

"I know, I know," Ellie said. We passed by the hardware store, an antique shop, two art galleries, and . . . "We already signed up," she added. "But we could un-sign. And Mika could enter the contest instead."

And a law office, which reminded me again to call Mick Flaherty and let him know that it looked as if Billy Breyer was really in the soup, murder-wise, so he should get busy.

"I don't get it," I said as we reached the Chocolate Moose. Ellie turned the key, and we went in, the little silver bell over the door tinkling in the sweet-smelling silence.

"Why would Mika enter the contest in our place?" I went on, moving automatically into my morning routine: lights, fan, cash register, credit-card reader, radio, coffeepot.

Meanwhile, Ellie opened the kitchen: lights, oven, exhaust fan, and the baking sheets, for starters. Chocolate-chip cookie dough was chilling in the cooler, so she got that out and began covering the baking sheets with parchment.

"Mika needs to get her confidence back," she said as she worked. "Don't you think winning the Eastport Cookie-Baking Contest would give her a nice boost?"

"Maybe." In fact, it was not a bad idea. I took a paper towel and some spray cleaner to the glass-fronted display case. Its cooling motor was wheezing again, as if it had spent the night running uphill instead of sitting in a nice quiet shop.

"But how do we get her to do that?" I asked. "Enter the contest, I mean." I brushed a few crumbs from inside the case, wondering what was wrong with the cooler part and how to fix it. "Not to mention how we'd ever get *out* of the contest, now that we've told . . ."

Alice and Jane did not look at all favorably upon bakers who backed out, and Prunia abhorred such persons. And all three of them could get quite sniffy about it.

Ellie came out of the kitchen with a plate of mocha pound cake slices. "We'll just tell them, like it or lump it."

She slid the plate into the display case; behind sparkling glass, those cake slices looked scrumptious. But they weren't cool, and they weren't going to get cool, either, not until the compressor got fixed. So I would have to call Sam, and maybe he could . . .

"I mean, what are they going to do? Come to your house and shoot you?" Ellie added.

But this brought back to mind yet another thing I'd been worrying about; the question of exactly *where* Alvin Carter's death had occurred was starting to bug me.

"Ellie, when we were out there last night, didn't it look to you as if there was, like, a *trail* of . . ."

All those little yellow evidence-marker flags that the police investigators had placed definitely suggested this.

"Uh-huh," she answered quietly. "A trail of blood drops, I thought."

By now the first batch of cookies was in the oven, and that, along with the fresh coffee I'd just brewed, made the shop smell even more like heaven than before.

"And along with the stains on Billy's shirt . . . ," I said. *Stains* was putting it mildly. "It's just odd," I went on. "Because when you hit something with a—"

Right. A hatchet. I didn't want to think about it, much less picture it. Or say it.

But Ellie knew. "You're usually an arm's length away, aren't you?" she agreed musingly. "So you've got room to swing."

She went to the kitchen and returned carrying a chocolate pie decorated with whipped cream and candied violets, and put it into the display case, then grimaced at the too-warm temperature in there and took the pie back out.

"So how'd his shirt get all . . . ?"

"Precisely," I said. "But listen," I added, changing the subject, "about last night." I didn't want to, but I had to tell her about the manila envelope I'd found and lost at Alvin's the night before. Just then, though, she pressed the heel of her hand to her forehead exasperatedly.

"Oh, I can't believe I forgot—" She hurried into the kitchen, where she'd left her tote bag, and returned carrying it.

"Ellie, listen, what I need to tell you is—"

"Here!" After digging around in the bottom of the tote bag, she found something and fished it out. "Last night, when we were running, trying to get away, on the back lawn, by the geraniums, I glanced down and spied this."

"Oh, Ellie," I breathed as she held it up.

It was the manila envelope.

It wasn't until an hour after Ellie had pulled the envelope from her tote bag that we got a chance to open it. In between, fishermen from the docks wanting chocolate- and fruit-filled pastries came in, followed by downtown shop owners hungry for fresh ginger-chocolate biscotti, and they were interspersed with random customers from all over Eastport who wandered in, craving a taste of something sweet.

When they'd all gone, I sank back into a chair at one of the café tables, and Ellie emerged from the kitchen with a mixing bowl in which she was creaming together butter and sugar with a wooden spoon.

"Wow," she said. The display case looked like a plague of locusts had ravaged it, and the coffeepot was empty.

"I know. Just give me a minute." The manila envelope lay innocently before me on the café table. With my luck, it would contain old utility bills or something equally inconsequential.

But I was still itching to find out, because someone had thought it was important enough to go looking for in Alvin's house last night, and I wanted to know why.

"Go on," said Ellie, waving her wooden spoon at it.

The envelope was the kind that closes with a little string that you wrap around a paper disk. I unwound the string, pulled the flap up, and removed a thinnish sheaf of 8½ x 11 white paper, stapled together in one corner and folded into thirds.

Ellie watched from the kitchen doorway, with one eye on the stove, where chocolate was melting in a double boiler. "What is it?" she asked curiously.

"I don't know. I . . ." I unfolded the sheaf, flattened it on the tabletop, and turned it over to read it. "I, Alvin Carter, being of sound mind, blah-di-blah, et cetera and so forth . . ." I looked up. "It's Alvin's will."

It was dated just a week earlier, signed, and notarized. After scanning past a whole lot of *wherefores* and *therefores*, I got to the money paragraph. "Do hereby bequeath anything of any value remaining in my estate after settlement of all debts and obligations . . ."

At what came next, I stopped, blinked in disbelief, and read it again to be sure I wasn't imagining it. But I wasn't.

"Ellie, he left it all to Billy Breyer."

Her hand kept mechanically moving the wooden spoon, but she just stared. "That can't . . . Are you reading it right?"

"Yes. Oh, this is awful." Being set to profit from Alvin's death made Billy's tale of innocence much less plausible.

Then, before I could say anything more, Helen and Anna burst in, red cheeked and radiating boatloads of youthful good health, as usual, but not in cheerful moods, obviously.

Well, why should they be?

They flung their backpacks under one of the tables. "Can we stay here awhile?" Helen implored.

"Well, of course you can," I replied as Anna sank into a chair and put her hands to her head.

"She's so *nosy*," the girl complained. "When we got home from the IGA yesterday, she was already there, browsing through our closets and looking into the household checkbook."

While Ellie watched from outside, that would've been.

"Shaking her head and making those awful tsk-tsk noises," Helen interjected.

"Oh, dear," I commiserated, "That's terrible. But you just sit right there, now, and—"

"Jake," Ellie interrupted. "Can I see you in the kitchen, please?" Her tone was sweet, but her eyes said, *Urgent!* so I went at once.

"Let's say it's real," she began in low tones once we were far enough from the girls not to be overheard. "The will," I mean. D'you think there's anyone who could possibly tell us anything about it?"

I hadn't recognized the names of the will's witnesses or the notary's name on the document.

"I don't know. He wasn't very social. I don't know if he even had any friends. People he talked to, whom we could ask. Except . . ."

A thought hit me. Ellie too. Abruptly, she quit creaming the butter and sugar, and we both spoke at once.

"Mary Sipp," we said in unison. Alvin's housekeeper had apparently been grief-stricken over his death and had wept into her apron.

"I could be wrong," I said, "but I've heard enough about Mary Sipp to think she probably doesn't cry without something to cry about."

Ellie put down her mixing bowl, turned off the double boiler, and laid a sheet of waxed paper over the pastry dough she'd been preparing. Those fishermen had run us clean out of chocolate éclairs.

Then she got my jacket and bag and handed them to me. "Somebody needs to talk to Mary Sipp."

Right, I thought. "But what about you?" I asked.

Ellie's own jacket and bag were still on their hook, and she'd picked up the mixing bowl again.

"Somebody has to keep the shop open. Also, the girls don't want to go home to their aunt Prunia, and I don't blame them."

I got her keys out of her bag. Mine were at home, as was my car, but she'd parked her car out front before coming down to the diner earlier.

"You're right. We can't send those girls home to Prunia's tender care, can we?"

If she rummaged my closets, I'd last about five minutes before I was the one getting charged with murder. Which reminded me . . .

"Ellie, at least let them know not to worry about Billy's defense. The money for it, I mean."

Her brow lifted questioningly. She knew I couldn't pay; big old houses chock-full of extended families are expensive to run and maintain, and with winter coming soon and maybe Sam only semi-employed, ours could get even more so.

"Never mind. I'll tell you about it later," I said as I headed for the door, although I already knew that if I could help it, I definitely wouldn't.

Five

Back in the bad old days before I left Manhattan, Mick Flaherty was a prosecutor for the Southern District of New York. In that capacity, he specialized in mobsters' misdeeds, with an emphasis on their financial crimes.

At that time, he was always trying to get me to talk to him about what I knew on the subject, which I insisted to him was nothing, but it was actually plenty. Mick understood this, and he especially understood the part about that barrel in the East River.

As a result, he never got any info out of me. Fortunately, he never had reason to compel testimony from me, or things might have been different. Nowadays he lived in Maine and was writing a book called *Blood Money* about . . .

Yeah, you guessed it. So as I drove Ellie's Honda out of town—I'd had a bit of trouble starting it, but otherwise it was fine—I thought about what I could give Flaherty in return for his handling Billy's case. I had information he wanted that no one else could supply, because no one else knew it.

But the trouble with that idea was mobsters' legendarily

long memories. Or just as easily, some freelancer could try to curry favor with them by delivering me. Before I spilled any beans, I'd have to get Mick to find out how many of the old bad guys were still alive.

Because if a few of the original New York goodfellas were aboveground, pushing their aluminum walkers and peering malignantly through Coke bottle–thick trifocals, maybe Mick and I could still make a deal.

But maybe we couldn't, and as I sped across the curving causeway to the mainland, I decided not to worry about it yet. After all, I might not even need Mick Flaherty for very long: maybe it did look to the cops at first as if Billy had killed Alvin Carter, but once the whole story became known, the authorities would change their minds . . . wouldn't they?

Slowing through the Passamaquoddy community at Pleasant Point, I watched a young Native American man launch a birch canoe so lovely, it looked like it belonged in a museum.

Whatever the *whole story* turned out to be. That was why I was on my way to get more of it from Mary Sipp; for all I knew, she might have more information about Alvin's will, too.

Like why in the world it left everything to Billy Breyer. Now, if only I could recall just exactly where on Route 1 Alvin Carter's housekeeper lived.

Driving out of Pleasant Point, I passed between fields of grass and reeds burned black by the recent fires. Young men dug at the still-smoldering hot spots with shovels or doused them with hoses from a tanker truck idling nearby.

Rain, I thought prayerfully again, and at the intersection I waited for a loaded log truck and a flatbed piled high with stacked, strapped lobster traps to pass, then turned right.

I did remember that much, at any rate, and hadn't Bella Diamond pointed out the Sipps' driveway to me one time when we were driving out here, because she'd bought lamb chops at a farm stand there or something?

So I thought I'd recognize it and sped on uphill past the Farmers' Union store and the little white post office building, then over a bridge, beneath which Canada geese sailed tranquilly among the cattails.

Finally, after a half dozen miles of blacktop, I came to an unmarked dirt road leading off into the puckerbrush, which is what they call it around here after a lumber company clear-cuts the big, old trees and leaves the place alone for twenty years.

The land now was thick with youngish spruce trees, birch saplings, stump mounds, and brambles, lots and lots of thorny—

Well, never mind. I was pretty sure this was it as I drove in. But then the brush closed around me very thickly, and soon the road stopped.

"Humph," I said aloud, not worried yet. There'd been no warning sign, and only a massive old log lay across the road to block my way, and now that I was in here, of course there was no place to turn around, either. Still, I could just back out.

But first I thought I'd better eyeball the situation, so I turned off the ignition and got out of the car. The sky overhead was a clear, endless-looking blue, the air smelled like balsam pillows, and there were grasshoppers shrilling all around me.

"Well," I said, "here's a fine kettle of . . ." My words flew away into the motionless sunshine just as I realized that something was *moving* out in those brush thickets.

Something *big*.

"Uh, hello?"

Purposefully moving, and not only that, it was moving *toward me*.

Crunch. Crunch. Rustle. Crunch . . .

I got hastily back into the car, and now through the open driver's-side window, I spied the tops of some low red-leafed bushes swaying as they were shoved aside not far from my vehicle.

I rolled the window up. Nearby, leaves hung sparsely on the

bushes, revealing red berries gleaming in the sunshine like small individual droplets of bright blood.

There was still no chance of my turning around. But maybe I really could just back out; after all, I'd gotten in. By now the bushes had stopped their infernal rustling, but never mind, I didn't like the silence that followed, either.

So I put the car in reverse, turned to look back over my shoulder, and—

A man stood there, staring expressionlessly at me.

He was fortyish, maybe, with silver-threaded dark hair, thick dark eyebrows, and a square, stubbly jaw. Red flannel shirt, blue denim bibbed overalls . . .

In the city this would've been my cue to hit the horn and the speed dial together, while locking the car doors. But this was downeast Maine, where you could walk stark naked down Water Street with a diamond in your hands and nobody would harm you.

Besides, hadn't I seen this guy before? I was sure he was not just some dude who'd rolled in off the turnpike recently, and Mary Sipp's place was still around here somewhere, too.

So what the heck? Maybe this guy could help, and, anyway, there wasn't much he could do to me besides kill me and bury my body way out here where no one would ever find any of the parts of me that the coyotes didn't dig up. . . .

Stop that, I instructed myself firmly. *He heard you drive in. He's checking to see why. He's just some guy who happens to live around here, not Jack the Ripper.*

But that last idea wasn't very reassuring, either, so to stop myself from chickening out entirely, I shoved the car door open fast, swung my legs out determinedly . . .

And stopped, because standing there, growling at me, was a Rottweiler the size of a pony. Eyeing me sternly, he seemed to be trying to decide whether to eat me right now or have me for a snack later.

"Grr," the dog uttered from deep in his massive chest.

"Hi," I managed faintly. "G-good doggy."

The creature woofed scornfully in reply, as if to say that he was not now and never had been a "doggy." Then he took a measured step toward me, and another.

"Bingo," said the man, still standing behind the car, and the dog looked back alertly at him.

Bingo? What the heck kind of name is that for a slavering, ferocious—

"Bingo, come." The dog whirled around and dashed to the man's side. "Okay," the man called to me. "You can get out."

"Yeah, so *you* say," I grumbled. But I did it, and once I had, I could see that I'd been right, and that there was zero chance of my jockeying that car around to drive it out of here headfirst. I'd have to reverse all the way back to the main road.

Meanwhile, Bingo still looked none too friendly, and from the expression on his face, it seemed that the dog's master had not warmed up to me, either.

Also, now I noticed that he had a gun, a long-barreled shotgun, to be exact. My husband, Wade, would've known more about it just by looking at it, but Wade wasn't here, unfortunately.

Very unfortunately . . .

I found my voice. "This your land?"

He shook his head. The dog kept watching me. Sizing me up for steaks and chops, I supposed.

"Nope. Partridge hunting." *Pah-tritch.* The guy wore a many-pocketed khaki vest over the shirt—a hunting vest, I realized, faded and well used—and that made me feel a little better about him.

"I was looking for Mary Sipp's place." I started to raise my hands in the time-honored gesture of being lost, but I froze when the dog rumbled warningly.

"Bingo," the man admonished. "Cut it out. Go say hello to her, you old fool."

At his master's words, the dog's face transformed; pink tongue lolling, he bounded at me.

"Whoa!" I had time to exclaim before I landed on my back, with the dog clambering happily on top of me, slobbering warm, drooly kisses all over my face.

He was a whole lot of dog, as my father would've said, so this went on for a while, until he got tired of it, backed away, and then stood there stolidly so I could put my hand on his broad back to hoist myself up.

The man watched, a grudging smile playing across his rough features. "Mary Sipp, ey? What you want with her?"

I stepped closer, brushing myself off. The dog poked his massive snout into the weeds around the car. "It's a little hard to explain," I said. "But it started when a friend in Eastport got accused of murder, and . . ."

Maybe it was unwise, putting all my cards on the table that way. But when a man holding a shotgun stands in front of you, asking questions, your best bet is nearly always the truth.

"And I'm trying to help him out," I finished.

"You mean the kid who killed Alvin Carter?" The guy's face clouded.

Hmm, maybe I should've lied. His look wasn't encouraging. But in for a penny, et cetera . . .

"Yes. I don't think he did it, though."

He eyed me consideringly. Finally, "Yeah, I don't think he did it, either."

He whistled for Bingo, who whirled and came at a gallop. But it was a happy gallop, I thought, which is important when a dog that size is barreling at you.

The fellow broke open the shotgun and tucked the stock in between his side and his upper arm, bracing the barrel with his hand. I just stood there, unable to believe I'd heard right.

At last, I called stupidly, "You don't?" into the brush-and-sapling thicket that he and Bingo were vanishing into.

A harsh laugh floated back to me. That wasn't Bingo, I thought a little wildly. The guy's dark head poked out of the bushes again, followed by the rest of him.

His many-pocketed vest was stuffed full of partridges, I saw now. Small feathered beaks poked up, two from each pocket. So he didn't know just how to carry a shotgun safely; he knew how to use it.

I wasn't sure if that made me feel better or not. But there was no time to dither about it. He frowned impatiently, brushing a late-season mosquito away from his face.

"Come on, then," he said. "D'you want to talk to her or don't you?"

Through leaves heavily thinned by autumn, noon sunshine drenched the puckerbrush, warm enough to make me wish I'd left my jacket in the car. From where we began, it was a mile on sandy soil until we reached another dirt road, identical to the one I'd followed in here. But this one featured power poles and led to Mary Sipp's place, as I learned after trudging until my feet felt sore.

"Wow," I said, my fatigue disappearing as the dirt road opened up into a huge fenced grassy area bounded on all four sides by a weather-beaten asphalt driveway.

Goats looked up from inside the fence, then went back to their goaty doings. Bingo bounded away toward them but did not, I noticed, get too near; those little horns looked capable of doing a fair amount of doggy damage, and Bingo seemed smart.

Devon Sipp—that was the partridge-hunting guy's name, he'd told me it as we walked here, and Mary Sipp was his mother—led me around past a red-painted barn, a machinery shed, and a white board-and-batten chicken coop, plump, placid-looking red hens strutting around inside its wire enclosure.

"This looks wonderful," I told him sincerely. Dahlias and chrysanthemums bobbed bright, shaggy heads in the perennial garden, while beyond, in a grape arbor, ripe fruit shone dusty purple-black in the autumn sunshine.

The souped-up Dodge truck and the small tan sedan I'd seen at Alvin Carter's on the morning of his murder were both here, parked companionably side by side in the driveway. The whole place looked neat and well kept, despite the obvious low-money condition of its occupants. The rugs on the porch rail looked clean but threadbare. A windowpane in the shed was cardboard patched. The porch steps had been repaired recently, but with salvaged wood that was splintery and gray with age.

But everybody here was obviously trying hard to keep things reasonably together. Only the sight of the chicken wire stretched around the birds' yard made me shudder, the sudden snapshot of a long-dead somebody under a porch popping into my head momentarily.

Because what the heck had happened there, anyway, and to whom? Upon reflection, I had to hope it had something to do with Alvin's own death. The idea of two murderers lurching around his place one after another was just too much for my nervous system to handle.

"Come on. Ma's probably in the house," said Devon. "Now she's not workin' for Carter, she's gone back to getting her outdoor work all done before lunch."

Personally, I thought if I had this spread to care for, I'd be lucky to get my outdoor work finished before Christmas or possibly the next Fourth of July. But then I glimpsed a shape half-hidden in the doorway of a shed halfway down the driveway.

A *human* shape: shaggy gray hair, a heavy brow, a whiskery white face.

"Who's that?" I asked Devon.

By the time he turned, the figure had retreated into the dark interior of the shed. "Must be Butch. Ma lets him sleep down there. He helps with chores."

I kept watching, but Butch didn't reemerge while Devon led

me toward the house at the rear of the property. Beyond it lay more puckerbrush, a low, long swath of every possible autumn color, from yellow to maroon.

"And you? What do you do?" I asked, trying not to gawk at the house.

Built of weathered gray lumber, jutting out in every direction, it resembled an old wooden ship cobbled together from spare parts. Gables and porches and nonstandard-sized windows seemed to aim every whichaway, as Bella would've said. A taut clothesline with sheets billowing from it stretched across an upstairs balcony, while from a smaller line strung between two front porch pillars, faded Tibetan prayer flags fluttered like smaller sails.

"Me?" Devon said, answering my earlier question. "I do a little of this, a little of that. Whatever work I can get, I'll take."

The wooden screen door opened soundlessly. Inside, the cavernous hall paneled with beadboard smelled like lemon oil and beeswax and maybe a whiff of lavender.

Devon pulled the birds out of his jacket pockets and held them by their feet. "Ma?" he called. "You in here?"

At the sound, Mary Sipp came bustling through a doorway at the back of the house, wiping her pale, plump hands on a green-striped dish towel.

"Well, of course I am. Where else would I . . ." She paused. "Who's that?" she finished suspiciously, squinting.

Her steel-gray hair was cut aggressively short in a thick, curly fluff all around her head. In a blue gingham housedress, with a white bibbed apron around her generous middle, she looked more like an old-fashioned cookie jar come to life than the steel-booted, gun-toting gal I'd previously known only by reputation.

Devon strode toward her on an old red hall carpet whose nap had been worn away everywhere but around the edges. "Woman here wants to see you," he said.

I followed him. A brass-painted cast-iron radiator hunkered against one wall; opposite it hung a framed antique mirror with a bit of the silvering missing in one corner.

"Hey, look what I got!" He held up the birds.

At the sight of the birds, a stern look crossed Mary Sipp's face, but the twitch of a smile and the flour smudge on her nose spoiled the effect. "Very nice," she allowed. "You go pluck an' clean 'em and wash 'em out good, now, will you? And put 'em in the cooler."

"Yes, Ma, I will," he replied indulgently, then gestured me forward. "She don't bite," he told me. "She just likes people to think she does."

Harrumphing, she let him go by, meanwhile passing something white and floppy from one hand to the other. Despite her son's encouragement, I approached her cautiously, since her expression suggested she might hurl whatever she was holding at me.

Instead, she led me into a warm, bright kitchen that was full of the sharp-sweet smell of yeast bread baking. A pan of small dough mounds rising under ClingWrap awaited its own heat treatment.

Mary Sipp put the dough she'd been kneading on a floured cloth on the room's big marble-topped center island, popped the oven door open, and removed a dozen baked crescent rolls. Then, without a single wasted motion, she put the unbaked rolls in, set the oven timer, slid the baked rolls all at once onto a wire rack, and put the hot pan in the sink, then rinsed it with the sprayer so that steam billowed up from it before she turned to me.

And presto, she was done. "So," she said, "you must want to talk about him. Alvin Carter, that is, which I will, but only because that boy of yours seems very decent."

Sam, she meant, I supposed; a pulse of pride went through me. "Why, thank you. That's good of you to—"

"Thought it'd be the cops that'd be coming to ask," she went on, interrupting me. "Guess they still will be. You," she added, with a glance at me that might've been humorous, "can be my rehearsal."

She peeped at the oven temperature once more to be sure of it, then turned away, satisfied. "But the main thing I've got to say is that I'm sure the young Breyer fellow killed him. I knew he would be trouble the minute he . . ."

Uh-oh. She waved me to a wooden table by the low kitchen window. With two wooden straight chairs pulled up to it, salt and pepper and a napkin holder on the checked cloth at one end, I guessed it must be where she and Devon took their meals.

"Showed up," she finished, waving me to sit. Without asking, she poured coffee from an electric percolator and set the cup, a green cut-glass sugar bowl, and a matching cream pitcher before me.

Gratefully, I sat, stirred, and sipped, and then I felt my eyes snap open; that stuff could've powered a rocket ship. Meanwhile, she'd begun shaping her next batch of baking, first rolling the dough out into a thick sheet, then cutting triangles and rolling them up before curving them into crescents to place onto a pan.

Talking while she worked . . . "The boy was always acting so friendly, like Alvin was going to take some notice of him."

The baked rolls looked lovely. She saw me eyeing them. "Ain't frosted yet, but go ahead."

I got up and took one, then sat again and bit in while she went on. "Right from the start, he was always trying to get in good with the old man. The Breyer boy, that is, always smilin' and tryin' to make friendly conversation no matter how grouchy Alvin might be, what mean thing Alvin said to him."

Meanwhile, if anyone ever asks you what the food of the gods is, now you know that it's Mary Sipp's sweet rolls, warm from the oven. Chewing, I practically had an out-of-body experience. And, as she'd said, they weren't even frosted yet.

"Why was that so bad?" I asked when I could speak again. "For Billy to do, I mean," I added. Good *heavens* but those rolls were delicious.

Devon the partridge hunter reappeared, now dressed in a familiar brown uniform; suddenly I knew why I'd recognized him.

"Oh, you're the delivery guy," I blurted in surprise.

He grinned, showing white teeth. "UPS, at your service," he agreed. "And if I'm not mistaken, you live on Key Street—" He broke off as a wince creased his face. Mary Sipp caught it.

"You all right?" she asked with motherly concern.

The young man forced a smile, but it didn't reach his eyes. "Oh, yeah. Little indigestion." I could see he was trying not to elicit another spasm of whatever it was.

"Good meetin' you," he managed. "Find your way back to your car okay?" And when I said I could, he replied, "Okay, then. Gotta go. Birds're in the cooler, Ma. I might be home late."

Moments later the screen door slammed as Mary Sipp tut-tutted and shook her fluffy head. "Boy works more'n is healthy for him. Up to the mill in Baileyville most days early, evenings at the gas station in Perry." She slid the last batch of rolls into the oven. "Then on his days off, like today, if they call, he drives delivery."

I might've blinked. It was a far cry from Devon's claim of doing "this and that."

"So we're pretty all right for money, at least," she went on. "For now, at least."

"Must've been even better when you were working for Alvin, though."

The remark made her scowl. "Humph. S'pose so. He did always pay on time."

"And he was never . . . inappropriate with you?" Because the notion went through my head that grabby guys don't always pick their targets the way you might think.

She snorted. "Let's put it this way, I still carry my little friend." She reached into her apron pocket and pulled out the sweetest-looking little pearl-handled revolver, so cute I could almost forget how deadly it was.

Almost.

She put it back. "But no, he never gave me no trouble. I guess he knew better. Anyway, from what I hear, he liked 'em younger."

The oven timer buzzed again, and while she took the rolls out, the question I'd come to ask her kept racketing around in my head. But if I got too nosy, I felt sure she was well able to chase me out of her kitchen with that weapon she was packing.

Or even with just a broom. On the other hand . . .

Oh, the hell with it, I decided. "Mary, why were you crying right after Alvin's body was found? It doesn't sound as if you felt any affection for—"

She turned sharply to me. "No, I didn't. He was a nasty man, not even a clean person. Kicked the cat when he got the chance, so I kept it out in the kitchen with me."

That reminded me. What would happen to the animal? But she got to the subject before I raised it.

"I left a full feeder, plenty of water in the furnace room," she said. "Maybe I'll send Devon to get it." She shuddered expressively. "Myself, I never want to see the place again."

She removed the last baking sheet from the oven, slid the rolls it held onto a rack, and rinsed the tray at the sink. "Hell, you try lookin' out your kitchen window some morning, see some kid a-haulin' a dead body up the orchard lane, both of 'em all—" She broke off, ready to weep again just at the memory of it all, and I had to admit she had a point.

A short stack of household bills lay on the table where I sat.

I glanced over them idly, noticed that they had been opened and the envelopes discarded.

"Not that I cared about him personally," the murdered man's housekeeper went on as she sudsed a scrubbing sponge.

The bills weren't neatly squared up, just piled messily, so I could see some of them: propane, electricity. . . .

"All that money of his, you'd think it'd a-sweetened him up some, but no," Mary Sipp said, still working at the sink.

Her back was to me. I pushed a few of the bills aside so I could see more. Each of them, six in all, was marked *Past Due*.

"Do you have any idea who might get it all now?" I asked. "I mean, did he have any relatives or . . ."

I didn't want to tell her that at the moment, it looked to me as if Billy Breyer was Alvin's heir. She'd just slot that bit of info right into her theory of why Billy'd done it: out of anger *and* to get the money Alvin had left him.

"Not a single relation did he ever hear from while I was there," she said. "Nor any friends I knew of."

She had finished the washing-up and stood wiping her hands on a dish towel, rubbing it over her reddened skin with quick, angry-seeming movements. "I expect whatever's left after taxes and settling up, it'll go to the state." She rubbed her hands some more. "Although," she amended with a frown, "he did have one visitor pretty regular."

I got up. Her mood wasn't improving, and I wanted to be able to talk with her again if I needed to. After slapping the towel down, she turned sharply to me, hands on hips.

"Alvin Carter was the meanest man in Eastport," she declared, "and there's no mistake about that. He abused that Breyer boy terrible, always stomping around, criticizing and finding fault." Her voice lowered. "I think the boy was just bitin' back his anger all the time, while he acted so nice and friendly, until some straw or another finally broke the camel's back, and he snapped."

With a hatchet in his hands . . . It was one possible theory of the crime, just not the correct one. But a prosecutor would be able to argue it effectively.

Outside the window, the goats browsed within the fenced front-yard enclosure, while on the porch, Bingo watched them from a safe distance.

I thanked Mary Sipp for the refreshments and conversation and moved to go, steeling myself for the long trek through the puckerbrush. But when I stepped outside, the car that I'd left sitting at the end of the dirt road was parked by the house.

Devon must've put it there, even after I'd said I could find it. *Why?* I wondered.

That it gave him a chance to root through the glove box and storage pockets for more information about me crossed my mind. He wouldn't know it was Ellie's car. But whatever his reason, I'd left the keys in it, and they were there in the ignition now.

Mary Sipp stood inside the screen door. Making a show of finding my sunglasses and putting them on, I risked one last question. "That friend you mentioned who visited Alvin, who was it?" I looked over at her. "Because," I added hastily when she squinted dourly at me, "if there's a service for Alvin, I want to be sure they're invited."

Why arranging that might be my job, I didn't say, and luckily, she didn't ask. Instead . . .

"Service," she scoffed. "You mean like a funeral? Don't know who would go. And she wasn't no friend, neither. More like she thought she was his supervisor. Go out there, barge in, and try to boss him around." A snort punctuated this. "As if," she finished scornfully.

Out in the enclosure, one goat butted another. The target goat, unamused, lowered his horned head and planted his feet. Bingo leapt from the porch and ran down barking, and sud-

denly the whole goat gang was milling around and bleating unhappily.

"Oh Lord." Mary Sipp shoved open the screen door. "You
goats! You all simmer down now, and, Bingo, you get back
here."

It didn't sound calming, but it had the desired effect. Moments later she turned to me again, the dog at her side.

"Anyway, if there's a *service*"—she put a skeptical twist on
the word—"it's Prunia Devereaux you should tell about it,
though I doubt she'd go. The way those two fought, you'd
have thought they would—" She stopped, unsaid words hanging in the air.

"You'd have thought they would kill each other?" I asked
quietly.

Her lips tightened. "I never said that. And I never heard why
they fought, either. When Prunia came, they'd either go off in
her car for half the day or to the third floor. From there I'd hear
shouting, but not words."

The third floor, where all those papers had been. "How often
was this? And you've told the police about it, have you?"

"Couple times a week. Oftener lately. And I haven't told 'em
yet, but I will." Lips tight, she stared determinedly across the
yard, as if contemplating this. "I'm going in to see them in Bob
Arnold's office this afternoon. Bob's picking me up."

Super. So he'd hear about this visit.

She glanced over and seemed to read my face. "Devon said to
answer what they ask me, nothing more," she said. Not reas-
suringly, but she'd caught my drift. No fool she, as Bella would've
said.

"Yes, well, that's always good advice," I told Alvin's ex-
housekeeper as Bingo the Rottweiler pranced over to where
Ellie stood, his stubby tail wagging. I guessed he'd decided not
to eat me.

Even that didn't make me feel better, though, because I had

gone to a fair amount of trouble and had even assumed some risk to come out here and learn what Mary Sipp had to say.

And she'd been talkative, all right. Maybe *too* talkative.

But as far as I could tell, almost nothing she'd said made a lick of sense.

Back at the Chocolate Moose half an hour later, I sat at a café table while Ellie made a hot apple cider with a cinnamon stick in it.

"Mary Sipp lies like a rug," I said as she set the sweetly steaming cup in front of me. "I'm serious. I really can't tell what to believe out of her." I swallowed hot cider, let it remind me that some things in this world were still good. "Just for example, she says they're fine for money, but the bills on the kitchen table were all past due, and one was a shutoff notice."

Outside, a few late-season tourists in caps and unzipped bright fleece jackets strolled in the autumn sunshine, gazing at the old brick buildings, the wide, glittering bay, and the boats bobbing prettily at their moorings.

"She did not say one good word about Alvin," I went on, "and yet I didn't get the sense she disliked him particularly."

The wind had shifted, and the wildfire smoke had blown away from us for once. Across the bay, the houses on Campobello stood out clearly against a background of autumn-hued trees, all the outlines unmuddled by the haze we'd gotten used to.

"Huh," Ellie remarked thoughtfully. While I was gone, she'd baked a batch of our famous snickerdoodles; now she set one on a napkin in front of me.

But it didn't look right; snickerdoodles aren't darkish brown, unless you've burnt them. Cautiously, I bit in.

And immediately spit it out.

"Um. Ellie?"

She wasn't listening. "Helen and Anna will be here soon,"

she said, straightening the napkin holder and the little jar of toothpicks on the counter.

The snickerdoodle was . . . unusual. Not in a good way. "What did you put in these?"

"I told them they could study here," she went on as she gave the display case a quick wipe.

Oh, forget the snickerdoodle. "Ellie, why would Prunia be visiting Alvin Carter regularly and arguing with him? What did they have to argue about, I wonder?"

I dropped the remaining bit of cookie on my napkin, got a glass of water from the kitchen, and drank it. No sense wasting cider on palate cleansing, and what *was* that flavor in the snicker-doodle, anyway?

"I didn't realize Alvin and Prunia even knew one another," said Ellie, just as the silver bell over the door jingled and Anna and Helen Breyer blew in like a small storm, in a whirl of coats, caps, bags, and general unhappiness.

Their pretty young faces were full of woe, and the sound of rebellion was plain in their voices as they both spoke at once.

"Oh!" Helen exhaled in a gust of outrage. "I don't believe it. She can't *do* this! Not any of this . . . can she?"

"She can't," Anna said stoutly. "We'll petition the court or something. We'll say she's *ruining* our whole *lives.*"

Considering the number of teenaged girls who think some-one is ruining their whole life, I doubted the court would listen. But nothing their aunt Prunia had said or done lately made me feel very confident of her benevolence, and Mary Sipp's report about Prunia, even though suspect, agreed with my impression.

"She's forbidden us to go fishing *at all*, and if we don't fish, we'll never get our boat," Helen complained, plopping down at one of the café tables.

"*And* she went up to the school and got us taken off the lacrosse team," Anna added. "It's not *ladylike*, according to her. It's not nice." She put a vicious twist on the word *nice.*

Spying the snickerdoodle remnant on my napkin, Anna first

glanced at me with raised eyebrows for permission, then plucked the remnant up and nibbled at it. *"And she says she's taking us to Bangor on Saturdays from now on for deportment lessons, if you can imagine anything so stupid,"* she said.

"How to drink tea, which fork to use, and all that. Yuck," Helen said.

Ellie brought coffee while Anna tactfully got rid of the snickerdoodle remnant, squishing it into the napkin and dropping it in the trash without quite wrinkling her nose.

"And if you don't do what she says?" Ellie inquired mildly as she set the coffee mugs down.

"She'll stop helping pay our bills," Anna replied with a heavy sigh. "She's already not going to pay for Billy to have a lawyer. Says he can get a public defender."

All of this Ellie and I knew already, though the girls didn't realize it. But there was more.

"She says he's guilty," Helen added hotly. "Says his whole story doesn't make sense. I mean about him trying to help, and that's how he got all messed up with Alvin Carter's . . . well . . ."

Right then I'd have enjoyed swatting dear old Aunt Prunia with a rolled-up newspaper. The fat *Sunday Times*, preferably, numerous times about the face and head.

Ellie clearly felt the same. "I mean, imagine saying a thing like that to a pair of teenagers about their brother. What's that woman thinking?"

We were out in the kitchen while the girls devoured peanut-butter sandwiches and drank milk. Prunia had put them on a diet, too, we learned, because, as she'd said, they were both too "husky" to attract boyfriends.

They were both, I assure you, perfectly fine just the way they were. Luckily, we always had bread in the shop, and peanut butter for the cookies that had chocolate kisses pressed into their tops. Which reminded me as I pulled my jacket back on . . .

"Ellie, those snickerdoodles. They're . . ."

She made a face. "Awful, aren't they?"

I wouldn't have put it that way. But since she had . . . "They look fine, I guess, but I'm afraid the taste is a little . . . um . . . What's in them, anyway? Coffee?"

Something had turned them brown, but whatever the flavors were, they'd somehow canceled each other out, so that now the cookies tasted like nothing but sugary Crisco.

"Cocoa powder," she confessed. "Because listen, I haven't had a chance to tell you, but Mika was here earlier, while you were gone. And she asked if I thought Lee might be old enough to babysit regularly." Ellie's own daughter, Lee, she meant. "And when I said not yet, but maybe next year . . ."

Yeah, twelve was probably still a little too young; not for Ephraim, maybe, but Doreen was still an infant.

"She sat right out there at one of the café tables and cried. Just sobbed," Ellie said.

I stopped, with my bag in my hands. "I don't get it. Bella will babysit when Mika goes back to work. She'll insist. You know she'll be stubborn about it." I took a breath. "And, anyway, what's that got to do with a weird ingredient like cocoa powder? Which, by the way, you added why again?"

By now I thought maybe those snickerdoodles had something else in them. LSD, maybe, or some other brain-scrambling drug.

Ellie walked me to the shop door; the little bell rang as I opened it. "Bella takes naps every morning and afternoon," she said. "Mika says so."

"Really?" I hadn't known that. But then, I wasn't home during the day, usually, and Mika was.

"And she's having some trouble with the stairs," Ellie added, stepping outside with me. "Going up and down them, I mean."

I hadn't known that, either. A pang of mingled guilt and concern went through me.

"But the worst thing is that Mika's still so shaky about going back to work at all," said Ellie. Then she went on, "When she wasn't crying too hard to be able to talk, she said maybe the child-care problem means she should just forget about the job at the college, that she's no good at any of that stuff anymore, anyway, so—" Ellie stopped, sighed helplessly. "Jake, that's what she was really so upset about, I'm sure of it."

Ellie was right; Mika could find another sitter, or if Sam ended up being out of work over the winter, he could mind the kids.

And I had no doubt Bella could help. She would insist. The real trouble was that Mika was so worried about her old life being lost to her that even a minor obstacle to getting it back upset her way more than was warranted.

"The poor thing," Ellie said. "But I think we can help."

"And your plan is?" I asked absently, my attention caught suddenly by movement across the street.

It was Bella, just then climbing the steps leading from the uneven sidewalk up into Waggie's, Eastport's pet supply store.

Frizzy hair, bony arms, a cloth housedress, ankle socks, and moccasins . . . And as Ellie had said, Bella was having trouble with steps. Clutching the handrail, she hauled herself up the final step and paused, gathering herself.

"Instead of us," Ellie was saying as Bella finally got through Waggie's door.

"What?" I said, turning back to Ellie. But then I got it: the cocoa powder. "You're testing snickerdoodle variations, aren't you? To find out what works."

And what didn't. The one I'd sampled, for instance.

"So first, you find out what *does* work . . . ," I went on.

Chocolate syrup? Chocolate chips? Or just plain melted chocolate? There had to be something. . . .

"Then you give her some strong hints, once you've come up with the bare bones of a recipe?" I added.

Because that way, Mika could develop the recipe herself but not have to work her way down a lot of blind alleys first.

"Right. She'll do all the actual recipe creating," said Ellie.

Which would be no small thing. Adding chocolate syrup to a cookie recipe, for instance, would require adjusting somehow for the extra liquid: more flour, fewer eggs, or whatever. And that meant tinkering with the spices and the leavening, too, and perhaps with the oven's heat. It could all get pretty tricky.

But persuading Mika to get involved would be the real trick, and I didn't have time now to hear how Ellie planned to do that.

Also, just then the bell in the clock tower behind our building bonged noon, and in response, my stomach growled audibly. I hadn't eaten anything—well, nothing really edible—since the sweet roll in Mary Sipp's kitchen earlier in the day, and I'd had a very strenuous morning.

As if in reply to the distress call my stomach had sent, Ellie thrust a white paper bakery bag at me. It held a thick peanut-butter sandwich and a half-pint of milk from the drinks cooler.

Well, I didn't quite fall down and kiss Ellie's feet, but it was close.

"You didn't ask Mary Sipp why, though?" she said. "About the will, I mean. Why Alvin might've chosen Billy to inherit, of all people."

"No," I said distractedly as Bella came back out of the shop. She made it down the steps without trouble and went off down the street with her net shopping bag over her arm. "No, by then, I was so unsure of what I could believe out of Mary Sipp."

Nothing, basically.

"And then it occurred to me that if she didn't already know about Billy being in the will, I didn't want to tell her," I added.

"If he really is in it," Ellie put in. "After all, anyone can print something up, forge dates and signatures and so on."

Of course, she was right. But there were two sides to that idea: people could say *Billy* had forged it, then had killed Alvin so he could profit from . . .

Oh, my head was starting to hurt.

"Eat your sandwich," Ellie said wisely, seeing my face. "And . . . where are you going?"

I opened her car door. I still had the keys. "I'll be back shortly," I said as I got in. I started the car and rolled down the window. "And I will eat that lunch, don't worry," I added.

I set the white paper bag on the passenger seat.

"But right now, I've got a bone to pick with Prunia Devereaux."

Several bones, actually.

Six

"Mind your own business," Prunia said snippily, turning away to snap another white-sheet tablecloth over another long table.

I'd found her in the Unitarian church hall on Shackford Street, where in a few days the baking-contest results would be announced and the entries would be devoured, along with a little light lunch.

To that end, punch bowls, coffee urns, and electric teakettles were already lined up on a sideboard that usually held stacks of inspirational literature and copies of the *Sing Your Peace* songbook.

"I don't see what concern any of this is of yours," she added, moving to the next long table.

A dozen of them remained to cover. With their chairs, they just about filled the hall, whose walls were punctuated by old stained-glass windows. In an earlier life, the church had been home to a Catholic parish, and since it was pricey to remove and replace such large windows, the stained glass had stayed.

"Prunia, those girls aren't old enough to be on diets," I said.

Nobody's old enough, in my opinion, other than possibly for medical reasons. I went on, "Why, their brains aren't even fully formed yet, and their bodies *need* . . ."

Vitamins. Trace elements. Calories. For heaven's sake, they were active young women. And yes, even fat calories.

Prunia snapped out another tablecloth. "Humph. So *you* say. I suppose they need to be racketing around out on the water, too, messing about in filthy boats and getting friendly with all those *rough men*."

She made it sound as if Eastport's fishermen were a bunch of degenerates, and since I knew very well that they weren't, this may have heated up my temper even more.

But instead of exploding, I bit back my reply, and I took a deep breath, and I definitely didn't tell that rhymes-with-*witch* Prunia Devereaux just exactly where she could stick all her silly ideas about . . .

Anyway, what I *did* say was this: "Now, Prunia, think about it a minute. They're growing girls. Don't be so hard on them. Don't take them off their sports teams, at least."

She shot a suspicious glance at me, probably wondering where I'd heard this last part. That our shop was the girls' hide-out was not yet on her list of things she'd have to put a stop to, primarily because she didn't know about it.

I covered my tracks hastily. "I mean, I know you don't want them charging around a muddy playing field, behaving like roughnecks and getting all sweaty, but—"

This unwelcome notion distracted her from the earlier one, as I'd hoped. "I most certainly am going to take them off!" she cut in sharply.

Glaring, she turned to the task of arranging the main baking-contest table, where the final judging would occur. On it stood place cards, centerpieces of bright autumn foliage in wicker harvest baskets, and china plates.

Prunia began putting paper doilies onto the china plates,

spinning them one by one like miniature Frisbees with quick, angry little flicks of her wrist. I wondered what she would say if I told her that Billy was set to inherit from Alvin Carter.

Although not, of course, if Billy were to be convicted of Alvin's murder.

But that's not why I'd come.

"If you take the girls off their lacrosse teams, they'll lose their phys ed credits for the semester," I said. "Anna might even graduate too late to go to college next year, like you're probably planning."

"Humph," Prunia uttered. "Don't know why you think that. Girls don't need college. They need manners and charm, decent habits and a good appearance, not foolish books."

I couldn't believe what I was hearing. "Prunia . . ."

She quick-stepped away from me, got her sweater and purse, and returned with them over her arm. "But they will both need to graduate and find work as soon as possible," she added grudgingly. "I'm not going to help them out forever. So they'd better not lose credits, I suppose."

Luckily, she didn't ask me how I knew one missed semester of phys ed could delay a diploma, because I'd made it up.

"Do you know if anyone's heard from Billy again?" I asked as we left the hall and crossed the front lawn to the sidewalk.

Tight lipped, Prunia shook her head. "I don't think they let you gab on the phone all day when you're in jail," she said.

"He's not in jail yet," I pointed out. There were hearings and proceedings and court dates still to come, a lot of them, before a trial would even begin to be planned. "Well, I mean, he's there," I amended. "But not charged with any crime. He's being questioned, but not . . ."

"Not yet," Prunia said darkly and stalked off down the sidewalk, away from me, leaving me to wonder if she was just being unpleasant, as usual, or if she knew something I didn't.

I walked the other way, toward the Chocolate Moose, feeling discouraged by the results of my morning's sleuthing. Mary Sipp lied—but about which things, I couldn't be sure—and Prunia played her cards very close to the breast.

And I'd have loved to try more things, but I didn't know whom else to talk to or what else to do.

All of which meant that a guy like Billy Breyer, who'd been found with the victim's blood on him and who'd then been discovered to be that very same victim's legal heir . . .

Well, as Sam would've put it, the way things were going, it seemed to me that guy might just be fusterclucked.

"That makes no sense whatsoever," said Ellie when I told her Prunia's ideas about education for girls.

When I'd got back to the store, Helen and Anna had gone up to the library to use the computers.

"I hope they're not pricing bus tickets to California," Ellie had said only half jokingly.

She slid another snickerdoodle batch out of the oven now—chocolate-chip ones this time—and heavens, weren't they ugly, even before they began wrinkling as they cooled.

That's what they are supposed to do, by the way. It's a feature of this cookie: the crispy outside plus the inside's gentle yielding to the tooth.

What snickerdoodles are not supposed to be, though, are small brown puddle shapes punctuated by unfortunate-looking burnt-chocolate upwellings. In fact, none of the things those cookies resembled bear polite mention, so I won't mention them. Also, they tasted funny.

"What's Prunia think her nieces will do, anyway? Marry rich?" Ellie said, sliding the cookies onto a rack and the hot baking sheet into the sink.

"I don't know." I dropped the rest of the terrible, no-good, very bad snickerdoodle I'd tried into the trash and poured out the last of the coffee from the pot behind the front counter.

The thickish black liquid looked and smelled awful, but after that cookie, I'd have washed out my mouth with crankcase oil just to get rid of the oily, vaguely chocolate-flavored residue on my tongue.

"Not that I've got anything against beauty. Or manners or charm or any of the other fine qualities Prunia seems to set so much store by," said Ellie. "But the girls need a way to make a living." She shot a stream of steaming-hot water from the sink sprayer against the baking sheet, then dried her hands on a clean dish towel. "And before you say, 'They won't be able to fish when they get too old, and *then* what will they do?' just look at all the men who are still doing it. Into their seventies, even."

Ellie was right; I would have said it. Fishing was hard, hard work. Old men did it, and some women, too, but I'd wish for easier lives for the girls. Prunia would, too, maybe. But she was going about it all wrong; you wouldn't argue me out of that.

Meanwhile, Ellie had one of those chocolate-chip snickerdoodles in her hand. It was, of course, part of her plan to get Mika cheered up, although how she was going to get Mika into the baking contest at all still mystified me.

Now Ellie bit into the snickerdoodle, chewed thoughtfully, then chewed some more, possibly in an attempt to avoid having to swallow any of it. But finally, she did get it to go down and then reached hastily for my cup.

"Oh, dear heaven, that's awful," she managed at last. "But maybe we could dip them in something?"

A layer of chocolate improves almost anything. But she was already shaking her head at her own idea.

"Not these cookies, though. The flavor of the shortening in the recipe, along with those chocolate chips . . ." She finished with a communicative little shudder, then changed the subject. "Anyway, did you ask Prunia about visiting Alvin?"

"No," I said. "First of all, like I mentioned, I'm not sure

what to believe out of Mary Sipp. But mainly, if Prunia did visit Alvin, I don't want her knowing we're aware of it. I paused. "Or that we're snooping around at all, really, come to think of it." Because, for one thing, Prunia might do something nasty to the girls on account of it.

Ellie tossed her remaining bite of cookie into the trash, then did the right thing by dumping the rest of the batch, too.

"It was the Crisco," she pronounced, dusting her hands together over the bin.

That's the thing that sets snickerdoodles apart from other cookies, you see: no butter. Crisco makes the wrinkle happen and gives the cookies their familiar, distinctive tang. But it just didn't play nicely with chocolate, or not so far, anyway.

"Anyway, I called Mika and gave her a few ideas to work with," Ellie said.

So Mika could do test batches, she meant, in my oven at home.

"Suggested some different spices and so on," Ellie said. "I told her it would save us time if she'd try a few of them."

That made sense. If any of the test batches seemed to be worth perfecting further, Mika could go on working with them until she had a recipe she'd developed herself. One, I mean, that she could enter in the upcoming cookie contest. It was just the "getting her to do so" part that still stumped me.

Meanwhile, Ellie had finished her cleanup and stood gazing out our front window at the golden September midafternoon, with the blue bay glittering in it.

"I did have one other idea," she said slowly.

Out on the docks, men hoisted strapped-together stacks of wire lobster traps into the beds of their pickup trucks. On boats, dragging gear was being erected, the heavy scaffoldings and massive cable winches glinting dully in the slanting sun.

She continued. "I'm not sure it's even worth bothering with, but—"

Down the bay, dark clouds mounded on the southern horizon. By my watch, it was somehow already four o'clock.

"Ellie," I interrupted, "what if we can't? Figure out who else could've killed Alvin Carter, I mean."

Because no matter how Billy Breyer had ended up in it, Alvin's will was just too good a murder motive for prosecutors, and maybe even a jury, to ignore. His prints were on the weapon, and he'd had opportunity, as well, arriving at the Carter place before anyone else on the fatal morning.

I said as much while Ellie shepherded me out of the shop.

She paused to turn the key in the lock. "Actually, I've been wondering that myself."

Faint whiffs of wildfire smoke still drifted in the warm afternoon air, but now little wisps of fog were drifting in off the water, too, though the sky overhead was still blue.

"And the truth is," she went on as I followed her to her car, "I'm also suddenly feeling more uncertain about the whole thing."

I slid into the passenger seat; she got behind the wheel and settled herself. "Because?" I asked.

Sighing, she laid both hands on the steering wheel. "For one thing, the suspects we've found so far are useless."

She backed the car out of its parking spot at the curb in front of the Moose. "First, we don't know what the housekeeper Mary Sipp's real story is."

Pulling away down Water Street, past the post office and the long, white, red-roofed Coast Guard station, which overlooked the water, she went on. "But it seems to me that being short of money would give her more reason to want her employer alive rather than dead."

That made sense: dead guys hardly ever need housekeepers. Meanwhile, Ellie was driving us in the opposite direction from my house, but honestly, I was too tired and discouraged to care.

"I don't know what her son, Devon, contributes, or even if he does," I said. "But from the pile of past-due bills I saw on her kitchen table, it's not enough. She needed that paycheck."

We drove on up Water Street, toward the north end of Moose Island, past old sea captains' houses whose carriage barns had been turned into rental units with postage-stamp terraces and white-painted window boxes. But the summer people were mostly gone now, and bright fallen leaves covered the terraces.

"Prunia's mean enough," I said, abandoning Mary Sipp as a suspect for the moment. "She could've killed Alvin."

"But she's tiny," Ellie pointed out. We reached Cape Avenue, then turned left toward Hillside Cemetery as Ellie went on. "I doubt she could reach Alvin's head, even with a hatchet."

Darn, she was right. Also, there was the business of that other body, under Alvin's porch. Could she have killed whoever that was, too?

"Assuming she could grip the handle hard enough to swing a hatchet that way in the first place," Ellie added.

I must've looked puzzled.

"Prunia's hands," Ellie explained, frowning at the numbers on the houses we were passing, ranch-style homes interspersed with cottages and small prefabs. "She's got arthritic fingers, red and lumpy," she said.

I hadn't noticed. Trust Ellie to pick up on this. "Oh," I said, feeling even more discouraged than before. "But look," I went on, knowing I was grasping at straws, "what if Prunia knew Billy was Alvin's heir, killed Alvin—I don't know how she managed, but she did it—then framed Billy somehow, and . . . ?"

"The operative word," Ellie said drily, still scanning the house numbers, "being *somehow*. Also, I don't see how she would benefit. She's not named in the will, is she?"

Correct. There was no mechanism that I knew of for her to inherit in his place. Heck, I wasn't sure that Prunia had even known Billy was Alvin's beneficiary.

"But, Ellie, if it wasn't Billy or Prunia or Mary Sipp, then who *do* we think . . ."

"Did it," I was about to say, but before I could, she'd pulled up in front of the last house on Cape Avenue.

"Okay," she exhaled. "Here we are."

The *here* was unimpressive: a single-story, gray-shingled dwelling of no particular style, one long, low-roofed rectangle with a big front picture window, iron-railed front steps, and a slant-roofed side shed, which I thought might be an added-on bathroom.

Beyond lay Hillside Cemetery, an acre and a half of two-century-old slate or granite headstones leaning this way and that under maples whose autumn leaves flamed yellow and red.

"So?" I queried Ellie when I'd dragged my gaze back from them.

In reply, she sighed, then turned off the car's ignition. "I knew Alvin had a different housekeeper, and probably even several, before Mary Sipp," she said. "There were stories about how unpleasant he was to them, remember?"

Sure, I did.

"So someone else was there in the house with him every day not all that long ago," Ellie remarked. "And whoever it was might've heard things, seen things . . ."

I scanned the house again and found it not quite so unremarkable as I'd thought at first.

Upon closer inspection, the place looked amateurishly built, slapped together out of salvaged material—mismatched windows, PVC-pipe gutters and downspouts. And the iron railings were leaking rust onto the stacked concrete-block front steps.

Ellie spoke again. "Anyway, while you were out earlier, of course I got to thinking."

Oh, of course she had.

"And on a whim, I called Ardeth Jones down at the jobs bank and asked if they'd ever matched a job seeker with Alvin. And she said yes, not recently, but . . ."

If I'd been the one to ask, they'd have told me that this information was confidential. But I was "from away," as people still like to say around here, while Ellie had gone to school with Ardeth, had been in Scouts and on the high school soccer team with her. And in Eastport, that made a difference.

"And that person, Alvin's housekeeper before Mary Sipp, still lives here?"

Ellie nodded emphatically. "*Right* here," she said, angling her head toward the house.

A curtain twitch at the front window caught my eye, but when I blinked, I saw it was only a cat perched on the sill inside.

Ellie opened her car door. "Let's go knock," she said.

"But he wasn't home," I reported at the dinner table that night. "Which was odd, because the door was open and a pair of men's shoes were right there on the front step, as it . . ."

Across from me, Mika paused when a spoonful of carrot soup was halfway to her mouth. "Well, that hardly seems fair." She then ate the spoonful and blinked. Bella's recipe featured plenty of ginger and garlic.

"You think he might know something, though?" Sam asked. He had finished his own soup and was already working on the fried haddock, fresh coleslaw, and hash-browned garden potatoes with fresh parsley that we were having.

"Even if he did, why would he tell you?" Bella put in bluntly, presiding from the table's other end. Wade usually sat there but he was working late on a freighter that had lost all its steering power coming in through Head Harbor Passage.

"Actually, we meant to tell him the story and throw ourselves on his mercy," I confessed.

Sam looked glum. He'd had a long day trying to do his own job and Billy's, too, and the effort hadn't gone well.

"Mercy, huh? Like that ever works," he commented, and from his high-chair little Ephraim crowed delightedly.

"Work! Work! Work!" he yelled, pounding his spoon on the tray.

A look of strained patience may have flitted briefly across my face. I'd had a long day, also.

"I'll take him," Mika said, getting up, and before Sam could move to help, she'd slid her toddler son neatly up out of the high chair and bundled the giggling child under her arm.

When they'd left the room, my dad looked up from his fish and potatoes. For a man in his eighties, he had a fine appetite and excellent digestion, the latter because he gave it, as he said, plenty of exercise.

Now he picked up his glassful of beer, sipped delicately from it, and spoke. "Oh, he was home, all right."

With the ruby stud in his earlobe and his long gray hair tied back in that leather thong, he looked like an aging hippie who'd never given up on peace, love, and rock 'n' roll. Which he hadn't. Also, he was too old to have been a hippie. But he'd appreciated them and he was also the shrewdest man I'd ever met. That was why he was here with us tonight, instead of in a federal prison for the crime of murdering my mother.

Which he hadn't done, either, but that's another story.

"What?" I said, confused, and he smiled sweetly at me.

Oh, come on, his eyes teased.

"You mean—" I began, then stopped, because of course . . . "You think Perry Wilson saw us coming," I said.

Sam listened carefully. He wanted—*needed*—Billy Breyer to be exonerated. It meant the difference between building the promising small business he'd worked so hard on . . . or losing it.

"You think he just didn't want to talk to us," I asked my father, "because . . . ?"

He looked wise, which on him was not exactly a stretch. I'd described the curtain twitch in the window. A cat, maybe.

But maybe not.

"Who knows why?" my dad said. "But people do things for reasons."

Like not answering their doors. Or like killing Alvin Carter? Whatever it was, I had the strong feeling that if my father was right, Perry Wilson's reason for avoiding us would turn out to be a doozy.

"I don't see why—" Sam began, sounding frustrated, but a knock at the porch door interrupted him, and he got up to answer it.

"This all sounds messy," my father said, eyeing me kindly as Sam spoke in low tones with whoever was out there.

"It'll get messier if I can't fix it," I replied glumly.

A young man accused of a murder he didn't commit, two girls whose futures were about to be ruined, Sam and Mika's life upended . . .

Sam came in with the visitor, a pale, slender young man with pink-rimmed blue eyes and a thick shock of hair so blond that it was nearly white.

"Hello," he muttered, looking up briefly at us, then returning his gaze to the old kitchen's scuffed hardwood floor.

"This is Perry Wilson," Sam said, and I recognized him now. I'd seen him around town, walking, always alone.

And yes, it did turn out to be a doozy.

His eyebrows were nearly white, too, and so were his lashes. He reminded me of a skittish rabbit. But he was on a mission and determined to complete it.

"You were at my house," he said. I'd taken him out onto the porch, where he seemed more comfortable. "At my front door," he added. His thin, pale arms where they stuck out of his sweater cuffs were covered in scratches, I saw, like he'd been shoving his way through thorns.

Bella had put the two wicker chairs out so she and my dad could relax and watch the world go by, but instead, I had this bundle of nerves seated beside me, here, looking as if any moment he might jump up and scamper away.

"Yes, I was," I responded gently.

When he'd come inside the house, he'd been wearing a blue ball cap with the Red Sox insignia on it; now he turned the cap in his hands, as if the motion of his fingers might help keep him safe.

"I guess you didn't want to see me. Or my friend Ellie."

Who is, by the way, the least threatening-looking person you could meet. Only when you got to know her a bit, you might decide she's not all sugar and cream, as Bella would've said.

"I don't like people coming into my house," he explained in a near whisper. "Or me going in theirs," he added, by way of explaining his current unease.

"I see. But you knew who we were?" I asked. "And you came over here tonight because . . . ?"

He was not an unattractive man: clean, decently dressed, recently shaven, shoes—I recognized them—in good repair, and so on. Even his face probably looked ordinary most of the time.

But right now it twitched with anxiety. "You're those nosy ones, when somebody around here gets killed," he said.

"Those nosy ones" wasn't the way I'd have put it, but it covered the basics, I guessed.

"The old man died. I worked for him once, so you came to me. Questions, I guess," he added, and I nodded at this.

He had a way of boiling things down, I'd grant him that. "Well, yes," I allowed.

And I'd have tried small talk first, but he'd brought the subject of Alvin's death up, hadn't he? *Questions.* I pitched him an easy one.

"You did work for Alvin Carter, then, before—"

"Yes," he said, cutting me off, rocking back and forth in his wicker chair, making it squeak faintly.

Back in the bad old days, Sam would do the same when he

was trying not to have a tantrum. Sometimes it worked. But sometimes it didn't.

"Perry," I said quietly, and he stopped rocking, looking embarrassed. "Perry, would you like to walk around the block with me? I feel like I could use a little exercise."

Actually, I felt like falling down onto my bed and not moving for a year or so, but at my words Perry jumped up. So I fetched my sweater, and we set off in the dark, surrounded by what was becoming the familiar smell of vegetation burning somewhere nearby.

"So what was that like?" I asked Perry when we'd gotten to the corner of Key Street. "Working for Alvin Carter, I mean."

He'd relaxed somewhat once we got moving, but his face in the streetlights' yellow glow still looked pinched with worry.

At my question, his shoulders moved in a shrug under his jacket. That was when I noticed he was not the proverbial skinny weakling I'd assumed he was, but rather a lean, decently well-muscled person. Only his nervousness had made him seem fragile to me.

"It was okay," he said as we turned toward Washington Street. "I cleaned his house. Did laundry. Cooked some. And he paid me." Another shrug. "That was it. We never had problems, me with him or him with me."

He didn't sound quite so certain about that part. I let the silence lengthen as we crossed Washington Street together and started up the short, steep hill toward the high school.

Halfway up, he finally spoke again, which was good, because by then I was too out of breath to do so. "I mean, he got cross with me sometimes, sure. Thought I should use a different scouring powder, more bleach, whatever."

"Uh-huh." But I still had the feeling there was more.

We headed downhill again, toward Hillside Cemetery, and then into it. I'd taken this route a hundred times in the dark, on a shortcut home from Ellie's, so I knew the way.

Perry spoke up again. "Anyway, it's been a long time since I worked for him. Years." He strode along with his hands in his pockets and his head up, much more at ease now that he was outdoors and walking.

"Two years," I noted gently, "and three months." It's what Ellie had learned from the jobs bank. "So why'd you quit the job?" I asked.

Around us, the graveyard spread out on both sides of High Street, studded with old headstones whose pale shapes glimmered in the glow of the solar-powered "memory lights" people had placed there.

Cape Avenue ended at the far edge of the cemetery's older side, where Civil War soldiers and eighteenth-century sea captains lay buried. I thought of asking Perry if he wanted to go that way, straight through to his house. But now he was answering my question, so I kept my feet moving and my lips zipped.

Not answering it fully, though. "Got tired of it, that's all," he said with another shrug.

And not necessarily honestly, either, which I felt from the way his voice cooled suddenly. His silence returned, too, and there was no more talk between us until at last we left the cemetery behind, happily for me, since by then it had occurred to me that a stroll among the dead with a guy who might be a viable murder suspect was not such a great idea.

"I had no reason to kill him, though, if that's what you meant," he added.

We turned onto Clark Street, where the houses had gardens and crab apple trees, raised beds in the yards, and trellises spreading on the sheds. A few late-season tomatoes still hung from the trellises, small dark red blobs glowing dully in the yard lights.

"It was," I said, "exactly what I meant."

No sense lying to him; this guy might be socially awkward, but he hadn't just fallen off the turnip truck, as Bella would have put it. He had seen me and Ellie at his house earlier, then had had himself a good, long think about it, deciding what to do. And then he'd come straight to me.

"No offense," I added. "But we are," I went on, "those snoopy ones, like you said."

Under a streetlight, the ghost of a smile twitched his thin lips. "That's okay. We all have our . . ."

"Flaws?" I suggested into the silence. "Obsessions?"

He shook his head. "When I left Alvin, we were on good terms, is all I wanted to say. And I haven't seen him since."

We turned onto Water Street and walked awhile without speaking back toward downtown. A thin rain began spitting fitfully out of the sky now, but only a drop here and there. Not enough to help anything. The smoke smell from earlier still hung in the night air, or it could be that something else had been burning. We never knew lately.

"Although," Perry amended, "I might have glimpsed him when I was out walking. I don't know. Anyway, you don't have to come all the way up the hill."

But I wanted to. I had one more question to ask, but not yet. At the top of the Cape Avenue hill, beyond the big stone pillars that marked the cemetery's rear entrance, the graveside lights I'd seen earlier still flickered wispily. But otherwise it was as dark as a tar pit in there.

"So listen," I said finally, as if the idea had just occurred to me, "when you worked for Alvin, did you ever see Prunia Devereaux with him? At his place or . . . ?"

Under the streetlight in front of his own house, Perry looked unsettled again. "The lady with the short white hair and the sour look on her face? Always busying around somewhere?"

Probably, he'd seen her on his walks, too.

He went on. "Because no, I never have. Seen her with Alvin, I mean. Why? Did she say I did?"

"No, she didn't say anything about you."

He really looked unnerved now, chewing his lip and braiding his pale fingers together nervously.

"I just thought when you worked there, she might've . . . but never mind," I added.

Frowning, he half turned toward his house, whose cozily glowing porch lamp made the place look better than it had in the daytime, all the cheap materials blurred in the soft light.

"Who had the job after you did?" I asked. "Mary Sipp? Or was there someone in between?"

When he looked at me again, his pale white face hung in the streetlight's pallid glow, his rabbity pink-rimmed eyes in shadow and his mouth a tight, bloodless line.

"I don't know," he blurted. "I don't know any more about any of it, or why you're even asking me all these questions. Now I have to go inside."

I eyed the house, dark except for the porch lamp. "You live alone here?"

He looked impatient, shrugging his jacket higher on his shoulders against the thickening rain. "Yes. My . . . my parents left me the place." And with that, he fled away up his front walk.

"Well, thanks," I called after him.

But he didn't answer, just fumbled with his key and went in, the door slamming and a lamp going on behind the curtains.

Then the porch light went out, and I turned alone to face Hillside Cemetery in the dark.

The last streetlight on Cape Avenue sent a thin glow past the old stone pillars looming on either side of the cemetery entrance. But it also made the spike-topped iron fences around the centuries-old family plots gleam wickedly.

Hurrying between them with my step firm and my head held stubbornly high, I wondered who those fences were meant to keep out. *Or in . . .*

Don't think that way, I told myself. But this night's trip through the land of the dearly departed felt very different from the ones that had led me from Ellie's warm, cheerful house to my own.

Overhead, dry leaves rustled together, sounding like a chorus of secret whispers, and all the anchors, crosses, and flowing-robed angels atop the old gravestones didn't help any. I clutched my sweater's collar to my throat with one hand and left the other one free to punch with, should this turn out to be necessary.

Not that I expected any of my so far theoretical attackers to have *bodies*, exactly . . .

Oh, will you stop that? Deep in the darkness now, the street-light far behind me and the graveside lights giving off a ghostly shimmer but no useful illumination . . .

And they are all still just exactly where they were when I first saw them, I told myself. *They are not moving, and they are* certainly *not floating*.

The smells of dust, old stones, and fallen leaves mingled with the sharp, damp tang of freshly dug earth, suddenly. Then, in the next instant, my right foot came down, expecting to land on the solid path just like last time, and kept going instead.

Going down, that is. Sliding roughly against the loose earth and small stones, I fell with a little shriek, grabbing blindly at roots, clumps of grass, anything. . . . Because what I'd done was I'd stepped into an open grave. Someone's funeral must be scheduled soon, so the cemetery crew had opened a resting place in expectation of filling it.

Filling it with Alvin, probably, I realized; I hadn't heard of anyone else around here dying lately. Not that this understanding did me much good. I'd seized an exposed tree root with my left hand, and all my other parts were still busy trying not to fall the rest of the way into the hole.

But even from where I was, I couldn't haul myself back up. If I shifted my grip on the tree root at all, I risked losing it altogether, and then my goose really would be cooked. Because once I fell all the way down there, I'd never get out by myself. Not until somebody cut through the graveyard on their own way somewhere would anybody find me. Unless . . .

All right now. Damn it. The scant drizzle of earlier had made the tree root slippery. Also, and much more importantly, as far as I was concerned, I was in an old graveyard at night, in the dark, and a killer was on the loose.

So get your act together, I told myself. But the hole's crumbling side slid away from me when I braced my foot against it, and the sound approaching from somewhere in the darkness was . . .

Footsteps. Coming closer . . . I peered sideways just as two white sneakers appeared out of the gloom. Suddenly, the bottom of the hole I was falling into seemed like the safest place on earth.

But I couldn't quite force my left hand to unclench from around that tree root, because if it happened *not* to be safe down there in the hole—say, if someone peered down into it at me—I'd have no way to escape.

So I hung motionless, shivering and cursing silently. The shoes kept still, too; their owner was *listening* for me.

Then: "Jake?"

Relief flooded me so suddenly that my whole body relaxed, and the next thing I knew, I was at the bottom of the grave hole. The wet, muddy, cold . . .

My hands felt around for something to push myself up with and splashed mud the consistency of icy pudding instead. Given the recent dry weather, the cemetery workers must have soaked the hole to keep the dust down, I realized.

"Wade?" I called weakly, barely managing not to blubber, I was so miserable. And relieved. It was my husband up there. "Oh, I'm so glad it's you!" I breathed.

And not some awful graveyard-wandering killer, I added

silently, *bent on adding a small-town snoop to his list of victims....*

"Hey. You okay?" Wade's face appeared over the edge of the hole, his brush-cut blond hair, blue-gray eyes, and craggy jaw all now illuminated by a battery lantern. He must've turned it on once he realized it was me down here, and not some awful graveyard-wandering whatever.

"Can you get me out?" I implored. Because a freshly dug grave may not seem so awfully deep when seen from above. But when you're in it, it's . . . Well, six feet really seems like plenty, is my considered opinion about it.

"Reach up," Wade said. He had taken off his jacket and was now lowering one heavy denim sleeve of it down to me like a rope. "Grab the sleeve. Use both hands," he told me, and now I noticed he did not sound at all like he was in a good mood.

But I did as he said, and sure enough, the rough denim gave my hands plenty to grasp, even though by now they were so cold, I almost couldn't feel my fingers.

Also, I was shivering so hard that I had to clamp my mouth shut to avoid biting my tongue, but finally, my shoes scrambled up over the edge, and Wade hauled me away from the hole and let me down before my knees buckled.

He crouched beside me. "Okay?"

I nodded, working on getting my breath back. When I had, I pushed myself up to a sitting position. "Yes, okay. Thanks."

After clambering to my feet, I let him guide me between the gravestones looming white by his lantern's light until at last we reached the street I'd walked on earlier with Perry, and we turned toward home.

"You haven't said yet why you came," I said when I could speak again without my teeth chattering. That he'd been looking for me was obvious, but why? And how'd he known to look here?

Under the high school's parking lot lights, he stopped. "Bella said you'd gone out with Perry, so I figured you might have taken this shortcut back from his place."

That answered my second question. Wade knew me well. But I knew him well, too, and now I didn't like the look on his face.

"What is it?" I asked, because it had just occurred to me that Wade hadn't known I was in trouble, and he wouldn't have come out here for no reason. So something must be . . .

His lips tightened. "Jake, we can't find your dad."

Seven

By the time we got home, every light in the place was on, the windows all glowing smearily through the cold mist that had begun falling again, as if to taunt us with its skimpiness.

"It just won't quite rain," Wade said as we climbed the porch steps. "And the stuff evaporates before it lands."

The dampish air smelled even more strongly of smoke than before. Wondering uneasily about this, I trudged into the house, all drenched and filthy, only to find the whole family—except for my dad, of course—gathered in the kitchen.

"Oh!" cried Bella at the sight of me. "What did that awful young man do to you? I *knew* something was strange about—"

"Nothing," I told her gently, trying to calm her. "I'm fine. Perry didn't do anything to me."

Which was true. I'd fallen into that open grave all by myself. But that wasn't what really worried her, of course; she was distraught about my missing father.

"How far have you gotten?" I asked, pulling off my wet shoes and socks. He could be anywhere, but he did have usual haunts, and I imagined they'd have started with those.

"Pretty far down the list," Sam answered from the dining room, where he was working the phone. "I was about to go out."

"I'll do it," I said, going in to peer over his shoulder. On a yellow pad Sam had crossed off half a dozen possibilities: the firehouse, the snack bar at the gas station, the clubhouse at the ball field, where a barrel stove and some cast-off wooden deck chairs gave some of the old guys a place to hang out.

So I knew where not to look, anyway, and I had a couple of other places up my sleeve, too, ones I'd found him in before and, at his stern instruction, had never told anyone else about.

"You're sure you don't want company?" Wade asked when I paused at the back door.

I'd changed into dry clothes and equipped myself with a flashlight. "Thanks. But maybe you should try walking around the nearby neighborhood again, just in case."

If my dad had fallen or had had an attack of some kind, he might just be lying somewhere near home, unable to speak.

The thought made my heart thump and my legs feel liquid with fright. "I won't be gone long. And this time I won't be falling into any muddy holes."

Wade nodded in reply, all business. He was a good man to have around in an emergency. Or any other time, actually.

The pavement on Key Street gleamed slickly, reflecting my flashlight's glow, as I hurried downhill to Water Street and turned hopefully toward the breakwater. But no small figure was there on the dock or at the end of the fish pier.

Mist pooled in the lights around the boat basin, in it the shapes of men busily rigging up scalloping gear. No one else was there, either, though, or at the wooden picnic table in the shadows behind the hot dog stand.

But from the gloom came a familiar voice. "Hey."

I jumped at the sound, then spun around to glimpse him on the bench in the little cedar glade above the boat ramp.

"Dad, what're you doing here?" I hurried to him. "Are you all right? Why'd you take off so . . . ?"

He shifted to make room for me on the bench, patted my knee once I'd sat. "I'm fine. Just thinking, that's all." From below us, men called companionably to one another while they worked on their rigs. The drizzle had stopped again. "Gets a bit noisy back at home," he added gently. "For, you know, coherent thought."

"Yeah. It does." We sat in silence a little while. "But I should call and let them know you're okay," I said finally.

His earring glinted red in the dock lights. "Fine. I imagine your stepmother's tearing her hair. You'd think by now she'd be used to my evening stroll habit, wouldn't you?"

I didn't have the heart to reply that when a man is nearly ninety, no one gets used to him wandering off without saying where he's going, never mind how fit he is. Instead, I pulled out my phone and started punching in our number.

He put his hand on my arm. "Not yet." He was gazing at me intently. "Before we go home, are you up for more of a walk?"

My fatigue, not to mention all the aches and pains I was feeling after falling into an open grave, vanished as if by magic at his words. Not only did I badly want to know what my father was so thoughtful about, but I also knew just where I wanted to be while I learned it.

Five minutes later we were back on Cape Avenue, outside Perry's house. "The thing is," my dad said, "your stepmother is getting . . ."

"Tired," I finished his sentence for him.

The lamp still burned behind the curtains in Perry's picture window. The porch light now beamed a sickly yellow glow into the drifting mist.

"Yes." Neither one of us had wanted to say *old*. "And we need to find a way to tell her . . ."

"Right. She's a hard one to reason with sometimes."

His eyes twinkled, reflecting the streetlamp's glow. "I do believe you're correct. But . . ."

I sighed heavily. "We're working on it. Ellie and I, and Mika, too. But if Mika takes that job, Bella's going to want to take care of—"

"She can't." He said it flatly.

I glanced over at him, surprised.

"She'll never admit it. But it's going to be too much for her. I want to keep her around for as long as I can, you see, and if she . . ." His voice didn't break. Of course it didn't.

But I got the idea. My father didn't quite think that Bella walked on water, but he loved her so much that he fully expected she'd take two or three steps before she went down. And he was concerned about her.

"Anyway," he said to change the subject, having made it clear what he expected of me. To stop my housekeeper-slash-stepmother from exhausting herself. "Anyway, what's up here?" He waved across the street at Perry Wilson's house.

On our way here, I'd told him whose place it was, and about my little cemetery adventure while on my way home earlier.

"I don't know," I said now, "if he's just an unusual guy or he's got a guilty conscience."

"Hard to see what motive he'd have had," my dad said. I'd told him about Perry working for Alvin Carter, too. "It was too long ago, you'd think, for him to still be . . ."

"Holding a grudge about anything," I concluded his thought. "But there sure is something funny about him." And that body under the porch had been put there quite a while ago, too, maybe while Perry worked there.

A car turned onto Cape Avenue and came up the hill toward us. Together we stepped out of the glow of the streetlamp.

My dad watched the car. "Not ha-ha funny," he said as the car slowed.

A corner of one curtain in Perry's front window lifted, then fell down again.

"Nope," I said while the car pulled up to the curb across the street from where we stood and its headlights went off.

It was an old green Ford Galaxy that looked as if someone wiped it off with a chamois cloth every night. It was now parked near enough for me to see that it had good tires, working lights all the way around, and a recent inspection sticker.

"Somebody keeps it nice," murmured my dad a bit wistfully. Months earlier he'd given up driving entirely.

"Right," I replied softly. If I'd had to guess, I'd have said that the vehicle's upholstery was immaculate, too, and that the carpet was clean. I could practically smell the vinyl cleaner from here.

Because I knew whose vehicle this was . . .

"Wow," I breathed as the engine pinged, cooling in the night's damp chill.

Perry's front door opened, and he stepped out, then made a visor of his hand to peer at the new arrival. The cat I'd seen earlier dashed out past him and streaked off into the night.

Then a cap of white hair gleamed under the streetlamp as the driver made her way up to Perry's house and inside.

It was Prunia Devereaux.

"So much for him not wanting people in his house," I told Ellie in her car the next morning. Meaning Perry, of course.

"He just didn't want you in it," she noted, not taking her eyes off the road ahead.

After I'd finally gotten my dad home the night before, I'd asked Sam if he could fix our shop's display-case cooler, and he'd agreed, breaking off work on the old pickup truck he'd been rehabilitating for months out in our driveway.

Now, after his diagnostic visit to the Moose, we were on our way down to a salvage yard in Milbridge to pick up a part for the display-case cooler's compressor.

"He sure seemed to be expecting Prunia, though," I said. "I wonder what they were putting their heads together about."

"You and me both," said Ellie as we sped along the stretch of new blacktop on Route 1 south of Machias. "I mean, really. Talk about a pair of unlikely conspirators."

"That's for sure." Outside, the blueberry barrens spread out over the rolling hills on either side like a wine-colored blanket. "But so far she's the only one with even a theoretically decent motive," I said.

Framing Billy for Alvin's murder and then somehow getting control of Billy's inheritance herself, I meant.

"And if she was behind Alvin's murder somehow, she'd have needed help," I added. "But why pick Perry for her helper?"

Once we descended from the barrens, the narrow two-lane road ran between factory-built houses with lobster traps piled in the yards and through tiny settlements—store, post office, cemetery—with rushing streams dammed into millponds running through them, though the mills were all long gone.

Now that summer was nearly over, there was hardly any traffic. We took the turnoff through Cherryfield, where massive old mansions stood empty, on sale for pennies. Any money that had ever been around here was pretty much long gone, too.

"And Perry," Ellie said, "knew the layout of the place, not just inside but outside, too, like where the orchard was and probably where the tools were kept and so on."

Like, for instance, the hatchet . . .

On Cherryfield's Main Street, a two-story wooden general-store building; an old barbershop, with the red-and-white pole still outside; and a feed-and-grain emporium, whose elderly red-checked Purina poster remained tacked up to the front of the building, had all been turned into antique stores, none open at the moment.

"So maybe the two of them planned it together? But that still doesn't tell us why," Ellie mused aloud.

Correct. And I didn't see how Mary Sipp would have had any reason to hit Alvin in the head with a hatchet, either.

I told Ellie as much as we sped down the long Route 1A

straightaway flanking the old railroad bed, now missing rails and ties and transformed into a recreational trail.

"I mean, seriously, motive is a real problem, because it's not as if *Prunia* was set to inherit even if—" I stopped, struck by a new thought, as around us the land now sloped greenly down to a river, where geese floated, resting and eating before the next leg of their winter journey south.

Peering ahead, Ellie spotted the sign she was looking for, then slowed and turned in between two huge, ancient rose-bushes heavily loaded with shiny red rose hips the size of plums.

"Ellie," I said as we bumped up the grassy track. Stones rattled against the car's underside, and more rosebushes loomed on either side, their thorns dragging ear-piercingly along our fenders like fingernails on a blackboard. "Ellie, do you remember the date on that document? That will of Alvin's that named Billy as heir, when was it dated?"

She hit the brakes, but not on account of my question. Stretched across the road ahead of us was a chain-link gate with a stamped metal sign wired onto it.

KEEP OUT, the sign read, and after that came the usual hooey about trespassers being shot and survivors being shot again, et cetera. But numerous rusty bullet holes peppered the sign, as if to emphasize its sincerity.

"I thought you said he was expecting us?"

Ellie frowned at the chain link, while the thick, thorny rose branches crowded up to the car like something out of a horror film featuring plant monsters.

"He is. I called." She laid on the horn. I held my ears. Pretty rapidly, the racket brought somebody.

Some *things*, rather, and boy, wasn't I just having a bad run of canine luck lately? Bursting from the bushes, two dogs who looked just like wolves came flying up to the other side of the fence and flung themselves bodily at it, eyes crazed with—

"Skippy! Honey!" A young man of perhaps thirty, shaven-headed, sweating, and built like a refrigerator, appeared. His blue plaid shirt looked big as a picnic blanket, and his faded jeans, held up by red suspenders, were behemoth sized.

But when he swung open the gate and waved us in at last, I saw that there wasn't an ounce of fat on him, just muscle on arms like tree trunks and across his back.

His jaw was swollen, as if someone had punched him in it recently, but he seemed cheerful enough. "Sorry! Lost track of time . . . Go on up!" he called.

So we did, passing through the gate very slowly so as not to run over the dogs, who were running alongside us as if we were hot lunches being delivered.

Finally, the bushes and scrub trees thinned out and the salvage yard appeared.

"Wow," I breathed.

Several acres of cleared land spread before us, all of it covered with various kinds of scrap metal sorted into towering piles: car parts, trailers, bathtubs, household appliances, and who knew what else.

We could've ordered a new cooler-compressor part, but Sam knew what he wanted and Ellie had been here before, and after she'd talked to this guy, she'd insisted on coming because he had it right now, and because it was so much cheaper. Or so she'd said.

"Come on," she urged now, after parking the car by a heap of rusty hubcaps and getting out.

"But, Ellie, the . . ." "Dogs," I'd have finished, but Honey and Skippy were already all over her, planting their massive paws on her shoulders to cover her with kisses and running in happy circles afterward.

So I guessed they weren't vicious. "Oh," I said. "Well, in that case . . ."

I got out, too, and braced myself for an onslaught of canine affection, and by the time they got done with me, the salvage-yard guy had caught up with us.

After apologizing again for the gate and the dogs, the big bald guy led us into a rough wood-frame shack whose bareboard walls were completely covered with stamped metal signs. A small potbellied stove hunkered in one corner. A pair of bowling trophies stood on a shelf, with some sort of small framed document leaning between them. A massive mahogany desk and a vintage swivel chair, also huge, took up most of the rest of the room; and on the desk, atop an old leather-trimmed green blotter, was a kit I recognized, with a stamp and an ink pad. I'd had one of them myself once. It was a notary kit, and the framed document on the wall was the certificate of office, issued by the Maine State attorney general.

Also on the desk was a cardboard box, with what looked to me like an old piece of junk, but the sales slip wedged into the box said it was the part we'd come for. And between that and the notary kit . . .

I looked at Ellie. Her answering smile asked how I could have doubted that this trip was necessary, and now I understood that she was right.

"So," she said casually when she'd paid for the compressor part, "do you get very much notary business way out here?"

A notary stamp basically guarantees that the signatures on a document are legitimate, and that the signing happened in the notary's presence; it represents the notary official's sworn oath and is the "sealed" part in the phrase "signed, sealed, and delivered."

"Plenty of business," the guy replied. He touched his swollen jaw and winced. "Around here, and from other places, too."

The dogs wandered in and flopped to the floor. Luckily, the floorboards were solid. Somehow I seemed to be attracting huge dogs lately.

"People who don't want their neighbors finding out all their business," the big bald guy added with a wink, "they come to me instead of the notary in their own town, see?"

Ellie leaned down to pet one of the dogs. "Contracts, I suppose?" she said. "And . . . wills? I don't recall . . . Do notary public seals go on wills?"

"Oh, yeah. They definitely do."

The guy's certificate said his name was Clifton Ferrier. He walked us outside and stood surveying his domain, full to bursting with what would be junk unless you needed something from it—a vintage-car part, a claw-foot bathtub—and then it was a treasure trove.

"Had a guy from up your way, in fact. For a while he was here every few weeks. Changin' his will, changin' it again."

A light bulb went on in my head, and Ellie's smile widened as he turned with a grin.

"Kept his relatives' heads spinning, I guess, leavin' them stuff, snatchin' it away again if they made him mad."

"Alvin Carter?" I guessed aloud, watching the dogs amble off to sniff interestedly at Ellie's car.

"Why, yes, it was him." Clifton blinked in not entirely happy surprise that I'd deduced this. "I mean, I guess I shouldn't say. You are supposed to keep notary stuff confidential," he said. "But I hear he met up with trouble, so I guess one of those wills of his is going to come in handy to someone now."

"Actually, it was a hatchet he met up with. Sad thing. Who came here with him?"

Clifton glanced alertly at me, so, I thought, there was a quick brain inside that shiny bald head of his.

My own brain felt like a bowl of cold mush, but apparently two or three of its cells still worked. "I mean," I added swiftly, knowing the answer already, "he would've needed witnesses to get a document notarized, right?"

He fingered his swollen jaw again. Then: "Right. Now that you mention it, an older lady came with him, a little white-haired person. Real sharp tongue that lady had," he recalled.

Breaking off his remarks, he went out to the edge of the yard and called the big dogs off whatever they had cornered out among the scrap-metal heaps, then returned with the animals loping along behind him.

"But one witness ain't enough, you know," he went on. "You've got to have two of 'em, an' the lady didn't really want to if someone else could. So I called my two brothers in town, and they came out and put their names to the thing."

Ellie was busy strapping a seat belt around the compressor part in her car's backseat. Behind her, beyond the yard's rusty chain-link, yellow birch leaves fluttered against the blue sky.

"That was one time," I said. "But he made several wills, you said. Who witnessed those?"

I hoped I wasn't being too pushy, but maybe Alvin and Prunia had brought other witnesses with them on their subsequent visits, people from Eastport, whom I could ask about it.

Clifton's lips pursed consideringly as he frowned at the ground. "So, this matters, does it?"

Like I said, quick. "Yeah. Friend of mine is in trouble."

Deep sigh from the big bald guy in the overalls. "All right, you got me. First time, my brothers did the witnessing, like I said." He looked up at me. "But the truth is, after that I didn't bother dragging them over here. I just wrote their names where it said 'witness' myself." Another big sigh. "But keep that quiet, will you? If you can, I mean. 'Cause it's a big problem if people find out."

Yeah, he had that right. Doing what he said he'd done was exactly like committing perjury, just not in a courtroom; there would be fines and maybe even a jail sentence.

"And I might even lose my notary public license," he added.

Oh, you think? I wanted to scold him. Apparently, it wasn't *that* quick a brain, after all.

"I will if I can," I said. Because the last thing I wanted was for this guy to clam up on me now. "What about the white-haired lady you mentioned? Did she always come?"

Chastened, Clifton shook his head. "Just that first time. After that it was a young guy. I don't know his name."

Sure he didn't. But at this point I was guessing I did. "And do you remember the dates on any of those other wills or who their beneficiaries were?"

His answering look was troubled; he hadn't expected ever to be questioned about any of this, I guessed, and was wishing that he'd never mentioned any of it.

"No. None of my affair, so I didn't pay attention to what was in them at all, and I probably wouldn't remember if I had. But listen, really, if you could find a way to not . . ."

I moved toward the car. "Don't worry. I'm not going to say anything to anyone about you signing for your brothers."

Unless I have to, I added silently. Hey, he'd broken his promise; I reserved the right to break mine.

"You should see somebody for that tooth," I added, because of course that was what was wrong, and he nodded unhappily.

"Yeah. Got an appointment," he said, touching his jaw again.

Meanwhile, Ellie had finished making sure the compressor-part box wouldn't fly forward out of the backseat and take our heads off if she had to hit the brakes. Now she rested, seated on a stack of wooden pallets, with her face turned to the sun.

"So?" she asked as I approached.

A passel of crows eyed me sideways from a pile of old tires and then took off, cawing, as we got into the car. Once we were headed back down the driveway toward the road, I quickly filled Ellie in on what Clifton the salvage guy had told me.

"How'd you know?" I added. That this was where Alvin had come for his notarizing work, I meant.

"I didn't," she said, "but I thought it wouldn't be anyone in Eastport. To cut down on the gossip factor, you know?"

I certainly did. Gossip wasn't so much a bad habit in Eastport as it was a community sport.

"Yeah, I guess that makes sense," I said. "But what it all

means now is that we have to give the will that we found to Bob Arnold right away. We've kept it to ourselves too long."

Instead of going back through Cherryfield, the way we came, she drove through the town of Milbridge toward the low bridge over the river where it widened into Narraguagus Bay.

"You're right."

On one side of the bridge, the wide, flat bay stretched south, angling out into the Atlantic; on the other, masses of lily pads floated in the quiet shallows.

"Because when it comes out that Billy is Alvin's heir, it'll look bad for him, for sure." Which was why we'd hung on to the will. "But this business about Alvin making *lots* of wills, well, that means anyone who's named in one of them might be a suspect," Ellie went on.

Personally, I still thought being found at the scene with your fingerprints on the weapon, while also looking extremely guilty in the splash-and-splatter department, was vastly more damning than any last will and testament shenanigans that Alvin Carter could've devised.

But I didn't say so. It was too depressing.

"Which means we've got to tell him all about our being out there the other night. And that's not all," she continued.

"Yeah," I replied glumly, my heart sinking, as I understood what she meant. It wasn't even the worst of it. "I guess it gets dark now around five thirty or so, am I right?" I asked unhappily.

Ellie nodded, zooming us through the series of sharp S turns east of the bridge. "So we should get there around then," she concluded.

There being Alvin Carter's place. Because at this point there was simply no help for it; we had to go back.

"I'll drive by before then, check to see that the coast is clear," she added.

"Okay," I replied disconsolately as we zoomed through the

crossroads at Columbia Falls. A gas station, a grocery store, and a garden supply center went by; then we were in the thinly settled hinterlands once more.

"I know one thing," I said, contemplating the notion of another snooping expedition with negative enthusiasm.

Ellie glanced hopefully at me. "You do? What is it?"

"I know that I've never been more confused in my life." I stared out at the evergreen forest crowded up to both sides of the road. It looked just as thick and impenetrable as the problem we faced. "I mean, what're we even looking for?" I went on.

She nodded slowly, eyes on the road. "Yeah, I'm not certain, either."

We drove in silence for a while.

Then . . . "Okay," I said. "I'll make some excuse about not being home for dinner."

Now we were passing through Machias, with the college on a hill overlooking the little business district along the river, and after that it was forty more miles of narrow, sun-dappled blacktop through more trees until the turnoff to Eastport and the causeway onto the island.

"It's right there in front of our noses, though," I said as Ellie pulled into one of the angled parking spots in front of the Chocolate Moose.

On the bay, a cargo vessel the size of an ocean liner proceeded in stately fashion toward Head Harbor Passage, where it would turn toward open sea. The fitful showers of last night were gone; the mid-afternoon sky was mercilessly clear again.

"The answer to all this, I mean. We're close," I added.

"Yes, I'm sure you're right," Ellie murmured placatingly, not sounding convinced.

Me neither, actually. I was trying to encourage us. But as it turned out, I was righter than I knew. Even then we were too close for comfort.

We just didn't realize it yet.

* * *

Sam had been watching the shop for us. Now Ellie took over, while he took charge of the compressor part we'd fetched and I went looking for Bob Arnold.

I found him in his office. "Can I talk with you?"

I had Alvin's last will and testament with me, one of them, at any rate, and my big question now was, where were the rest of them?

Bob had just hung up the phone and was already on his way out the door. "Well, come on, then," he said.

In the parking lot he got into his squad car, waved at the passenger door, and I got in with him.

"Where you going?" I asked.

He swung us out onto Washington Street. "Nanny Wolcott, on Stevens Avenue. Says she's got a prowler, and can I take a look?" He blew a breath out. "But this is the third time I have been there, and she does not," he emphasized, "have prowlers."

On our way up Washington Street, I spotted Prunia Devereaux in her extremely clean little green car. She had pulled over to talk to Helen and Anna through the driver's-side window.

"What she *does* have," Bob went on exasperatedly as I half listened, distracted by what I was seeing, "is a cat. A large, orange, garbage can–invading . . ."

The girls carried bookbags and were on their way downhill; likely they were coming from the school's ball field and were on their way to the Chocolate Moose.

From behind the wheel, Prunia motioned for them to get into the car, urging them with quick, impatient gestures.

"So she's watchin' out for them while Billy's gone?" Bob commented, seeing this.

"If you can call it that," I said. The two girls glanced unhappily at one another and reluctantly did as they were told.

Bob looked thoughtful but said nothing more as we turned

into the little warren of residential streets behind the IGA. Nanny Wolcott, a retired Eastport schoolteacher, lived in a house entirely surrounded by high, dark green cedar trees that long ago must have been planted as a hedge.

He pulled up out front. The cedars looked menacing, like ancient guards. After climbing out of the squad car we made our way between them, breathing in the evergreens' sweet fragrance as we brushed against them.

"But if it makes her feel better," Bob said resignedly, meaning Nanny Wolcott, "I'll look again."

Inside the wall of pine-scented greenery, the air felt cool and still. We walked up the crazy-paved front walk, and he rapped sharply on the red-painted front door of the small stone cottage.

It opened at once. "Oh, Robert, thanks for coming."

Nanny Wolcott was a tall, long-faced woman with parchment skin and red hair threaded through with glints of silver. Her eyes, pale gray behind gold-rimmed glasses, were sharp and observant.

"No problem," Bob replied kindly. He really was a very good community police chief. "You two stay here, why don't you, and I'll have a look," he said and went off to investigate.

"And, Jake, so nice to see you again," she said, turning to me. "Would you like a cup of tea?"

We'd met often for disciplinary reasons back when Sam was in high school. He'd still been quite a hellion then, but she'd handled him with tact and delicacy, to which he'd responded.

Now whiffs of warm gingerbread wafted temptingly from the dim, quiet interior behind her, but I demurred.

"Bob has another stop after this one," I lied. I still hadn't told him why I needed to see him, and much as I dreaded it, I didn't want to delay the conversation any longer.

Nanny Wolcott nodded gravely. "He's so busy. I do hate to trouble him. But at night I keep hearing this terrible—" She stopped as, in the opening between the trees at the end of her front walk, she saw Perry Wilson stride by, looking neither to the right nor the left.

All the hairs on the back of my neck went up. What was he doing here? But Nanny just sighed, having recognized him, too, but for a different reason.

"Poor boy. He was a good child. Shy, you know, but very intelligent." She turned her gray eyes to me. "I taught him in school, him and his little sisters. Even then he was devoted to them, watched out for them everywhere."

Sisters? I'd never heard about any . . .

"But he was never the same after his folks died," she said sorrowfully. "He just withdrew into his grief, and he never came out, especially after the sisters grew up and moved away."

Just then Bob reappeared around the corner of the house, grimacing while holding at arm's length a big, struggling . . .

"Carmichael!" cried Nanny Wolcott happily. "You naughty cat. Oh, he's been missing for days. Wherever did you find him?"

The animal was the size of a cocker spaniel and the color of a tangerine, and its pink, snarling mouth was full of big, sharp-looking . . .

"Cat," Bob pronounced, shoving the hissing, squirming bundle of fury into Nanny Wolcott's arms, where it settled and purred while still throwing out angry glances at Bob.

"Trapped in the trash bin again," Bob said, brushing fur off himself. A ragged red scratch zigzagged across the back of his hand.

Nanny looked horrified. "Let me put some Mercurochrome on that."

He put up both hands, palms out, in a warding-off gesture. "No, no. Glad to find your prowler. You put old Carmichael on a leash, you could rent him out for crowd control."

And on that note, we left. Bob ignored his injury except for a comment about how Mercurochrome stings. He'd once had a guy swing a two-by-four at his head, making a sound like a home run being knocked out of the park when it connected, but he'd refused to pass out until after he'd cuffed the guy and put him in the squad car.

I was still pondering what Nanny Wolcott had said as we headed back downhill to Water Street, where, instead of turning in at the cop shop's parking lot entrance, he drove out onto the breakwater and parked.

The water spread out before us, dark blue and restless.

"So. What've you got to talk about that's so urgent?" he asked.

Yikes. This had *seemed* like a good idea. Now that I was here, though, suddenly what *really* seemed like a good idea was for me to jump off the breakwater right now and start swimming toward Portugal.

But . . . "Out with it," Bob said sternly. "Speak."

So I did. Alvin's house and our search through it the night of his murder. The intruder—besides us, I mean—in the house that same night. The porch, the second corpse, Mary Sipp's lies, and Perry's evasiveness.

"Or whatever it was," I said. "And finally, there's . . ." Alvin's will. Or one of them. I drew it out of my tote bag. "Guy in Milbridge says he notarized it. And several more."

Bob had listened with an increasingly sour but also very curious expression. The part about someone else with us in the house that night had seemed to interest him especially. When I got to the part about the multiple wills, though, and handed over the one I had found, Bob scowled.

"And, Bob, there's more." Because the heck with my promise. The fact that at least some of those wills weren't valid—on account of them being falsely notarized—might be important. So I shared this with him.

Bob looked up from the one will in his hands, having just

read the part about Billy Breyer inheriting from Alvin. "Oh, man. I don't care what kind of stamp this thing does or doesn't have on it. It's not going to help the kid."

At the end of the breakwater, some guys winched a pallet of lobster traps up off their boat's deck and onto the trailer of a flatbed truck. It was hard physical work, but they looked just as happy as little clams in their muck boots and overalls.

The way Helen and Anna would be, only right now they were probably out shopping with Prunia for nylon stockings and, God help us, even garter belts to hold the stockings up.

"But, Bob," I argued, "if there are lots of wills, anybody with their name in one of them might've thought—"

"If," he interrupted. "Because, first of all, we don't have any of them, do we? These other wills," he added skeptically.

I had to admit we didn't.

"And you say this notary guy, he faked the witness signatures on some of 'em?" If the guy would do that, his tone implied, why wouldn't he lie about other things?

Trust Bob to find the weak spot in an otherwise good argument; in his line of work, he heard so many lies that his BS detector was permanently set on high.

"Still," I said, trying again, "*if* there are . . ."

Down in the boat basin, some young recruits were learning how to dock the Coast Guard's big orange-and-black Zodiac boat. Much backing and forthing ensued, and while it was all going on, it struck me that I couldn't tell male recruits from females, all in their neat blue uniforms, black boots, and caps.

I went on. "It could be *any*—"

Bob made a scornful noise. "Doesn't matter about any other wills, anyway," he said, getting right to the point. "State cops hear about him being in one of 'em, they're gonna believe the obvious, that Billy did it for a payday." He took a breath. "That he killed Alvin Carter so he could inherit the money he thought Alvin was leaving to him. That'll be the story, mark my words."

"Even though the obvious isn't true," I said bleakly.

"Might not be," he corrected. "I mean, Jake, come on. If we didn't know Billy, he'd look guilty as sin, wouldn't he?"

He was right. "Yeah," I breathed, giving in, and he wasn't happy about it, either, obviously.

"All right," he said at last, putting the car in gear. "I guess better late than never."

Me giving him the will, he meant, and telling him about (a) it and (b) the rest of what Ellie and I had done.

As he drove off the breakwater, the fellows who'd been winching the traps up off the boat now moved speedily around the flatbed, strapping them down. One guy was limping. Another one's hand was bandaged. You could fish for a living all your life and never get hurt, or on the morning of your first day on the water, a fouled cable might take your arm off. Or you could drown. It all made me think about Anna and Helen again, and Bob seemed to catch my thought.

"Those girls all set where they are for the time being?" he asked as we passed the red-roofed Coast Guard station and the hot dog stand.

"I think so," I said and explained what was going on between them and their aunt. "I don't think she can *make* them move in with her," I added. "Or at least not until there's a family court hearing that says so."

He turned left off the breakwater, toward the Chocolate Moose. "She'd have to petition for the hearing first, too," he said. "That'll give 'em a little time at least."

Cool, clear air and sunshine the color of champagne made the Water Street storefronts resemble an old postcard picture. When the light was right, I half expected to see horse-drawn carriages with elaborately dressed ladies in them, doing their downtown shopping.

"You don't think he did it, either, do you?" I ventured.

Billy, I meant. Because, for one thing, Bob was being awfully nice about stuff he could've arrested me for on the spot: trespassing, tampering with a crime scene, withholding evidence. The list just went on and on.

Frowning, he pulled into a parking spot in front of the Moose and switched off the ignition. "No. I don't think he did it," he replied. "But I'm damned if I've got a single, solitary idea of how I'd convince anybody else of that." He turned to me. "Because do you know what the kid says happened? The rest of the story he wants people to believe?"

"Other than that he's innocent, and that he got messed up while trying to help Alvin? No. What?"

Through the Chocolate Moose's front window, I could see Ellie at the cash register, ringing up two customers. Helen and Anna were not at their usual table. Probably they were still somewhere with Prunia, poor things. Next thing you knew, she'd be demanding that they wear girdles.

But my attention snapped back to Bob when he began telling me what Billy was saying to his interrogators in Augusta, and when he got finished, I knew even more of the unpleasant murder-scene details than before.

Plus one large inescapable fact.

The kid was in much worse trouble than I'd thought.

And, unfortunately, so was I.

Eight

"Wait a minute. Perry Wilson has sisters, too?" Ellie asked that night, in a whisper. Like Billy Breyer, she meant.

"Yep," I whispered back.

It was eight in the evening, four hours after I'd had my conversation with Bob Arnold, and we were hunched down in the weeds out behind Alvin Carter's house.

"Two of 'em, according to Nanny Wolcott," I said. "But I don't see what they'd have to do with any of this. They don't even live in Eastport anymore."

We'd approached Alvin's place from the rear, via a narrow trail through some undeveloped city acreage that Ellie had known about from her childhood.

And by "trail," I mean the hilly, thorny, ankle-twisting, "low branch taking your head off" kind, not the gently sloping, gravel-paved, and clearly signposted variety, which I so strongly preferred.

Nevertheless, we struggled forward, squinching ourselves between crowded-together tree trunks and cringing away from dry bark-growing moss that felt way too much like human hair in the woodsy darkness.

"So do you think Perry was following you when you saw him at Nanny Wolcott's place?" Ellie asked.

"I'm not sure how he could've been," I said regretfully. I mean, couldn't someone besides Billy do something that was flat-out suspicious around here for a change? But no . . . "I think he was just out walking, like he often is," I added, "and happened to be there when I was."

Downhill from us, Alvin's big old white house, with its many gables, dormers, and pointy-topped turrets, rose ghostly in the gloom.

"So," I went on, "I happened to glean some utterly useless information about him from his old teacher. That he wasn't an only child."

We crept cautiously out from the weeds and brush and began circling the edge of the back lawn. "And what's this about Alvin?" she asked. "You were telling me, but then . . ."

Right. While we drove here, I'd gotten through the Perry Wilson part of my report, but once we got into the woods behind Alvin's property, the rest of the story had been delayed by a sudden pratfall (mine), followed by a "sneaker meets exposed tree root" face-plant (also mine), and a whole lot of hoisting and helping (by Ellie, of me).

Now we sprinted down the lawn to Alvin's porch and scampered up onto it and crouched side by side, with our backs against the clapboards under the windows.

"Jake?" she pressed. "What *about* . . . ?"

Yeah, Alvin, and what I'd learned from Bob. "You sure you want to hear this? It's . . . gruesome."

Her reply came patiently. "Jake, I'm out here with you in the dark, getting ready to trespass in a dead man's house."

"Good point." I nodded. She was pretty intrepid. "You know what killed the cat, though, right?"

Speaking of which, I wanted to check on the cat we'd seen out here before. Who knew if Devon Sipp really was coming to care for it, as his mother had said?

Ellie elbowed me. "Let's get this over with. You can tell me the Alvin thing while we're breaking and entering."

We crossed the porch—at least I didn't have to go under there this time, I hoped, but of course I stumbled over a basket of split stove kindling, which I'd somehow missed bumbling into the last time I was here—and tried the door. This time it was locked securely. But the latch on one of the porch windows was loose; when I pushed up hard, the latch screws popped out of the old wood.

"Oops," I said, raising the window so Ellie could climb in, then clambering after her.

Moments after I landed on the hardwood floor inside, Ellie was already on her way to the front stairway, but when she saw me heading for the kitchen, she turned and followed me to the low-ceilinged room, which had been Mary Sipp's domain.

"Anyway," I began as I spotted what I was hoping to see: fresh water in a large bowl, a tinfoil tray well filled with kibble, and a well-cared-for sandbox on sheets of newspaper. "Anyway, Bob said Billy told the state cops in Augusta that Alvin didn't die where he fell," I went on.

And hadn't my heart just sunk about a mile when I heard that? Because how would Billy know unless he'd seen it happen, and how would he have seen it happen if he hadn't—

"But wait, there's more." I yanked open the cabinet under the sink and discovered more cat food, plus a large bag of sand for the litter box. "Billy says he arrived here, heard a groan, followed the sound, and found Alvin with the weapon still in his cranium."

"Ohh," Ellie breathed, appalled.

With my conscience clear about the welfare of the feline for now, I went on, "But even that's not the worst of it."

Or the least believable, I could have added. Still, it was what Billy had said.

"When Billy found Alvin, Alvin wasn't dead. Instead, Alvin pulled himself up somehow and began to chase Billy, and when he did, Billy panicked and ran," I revealed.

Which you never knew, we still might have to do that, tonight, too; panic and run, I mean. I glanced out the kitchen window but saw no cop cars, probing flashlight beams, or other hints that we'd better do it pronto, though. So . . .

"While he was running," I went on, "Billy glanced back and saw Alvin staggering after him and swinging the hatchet."

"Ye gods. Tell me you're kidding."

"Nope."

We left the kitchen, where there was plenty of cat equipment but no cat, and headed up the front-hall stairs.

"When Billy got to the driveway and looked back once more, Alvin had fallen, and this time he wasn't moving." I paused on the stairs, thinking about what Billy said had happened next, and whether I'd have had the courage he'd had.

"And then Billy went back," I said. We'd reached the first stairway landing. Only one more flight to go. I hauled in a breath. "He picked Alvin up, carried him in his arms back to the driveway, and tried to do first aid. Then Sam showed up and called Bob Arnold."

"And that," Ellie said as she quick-stepped ahead of me up the second flight of stairs while I was still only halfway down the hall towards it, "is how Billy got himself covered with Alvin's . . ."

"Right. By trying to save Alvin's life."

At the top of the second flight of stairs, she stopped. The door leading up out of the staircase was closed.

It had been open when we left it.

"Ellie."

She'd opened the door at the top of the stairs and stepped through it into the darkness beyond. I followed, suddenly much less certain than before that no one was here but us. In the gloom ahead, something moved; I was pretty sure it was her.

But not *completely.* "Ellie?"

Her flashlight snapped on. I'm sorry to report that just for that moment, I was too unnerved to remember to reach for mine. In the light reflecting off the walls, she angled her head toward the room Alvin Carter had used as his office.

"No wonder he'd disappear for so long," I said, repeating what Mary Sipp had told me. "Who'd want to be going up and down these stairs more than they had to?"

"Right." Ellie aimed her flashlight around some more. "I don't think anyone's up here now, though," she added.

We could hope, anyway, so we followed our flashlight beams into the room Alvin had used as a private office, away from the rest of the house.

"Wow," said Ellie, waving the flashlight around.

"No kidding," I echoed.

Alvin Carter's third-floor hideaway was still as bleak and barely furnished as ever, slant-ceilinged and leak-stained. I peered around and located the wooden filing cabinets that I'd seen last time we were up here. But this time the drawers were all closed.

Ellie started yanking them open again. The folders that had been scattered on the floor were now stuffed back inside. Meanwhile, surely the faint sounds coming from downstairs really were just my imagination . . . weren't they?

"Hey, Ellie?" I said finally. "It's getting later. Maybe we should wrap this up."

By the sullen yellow gleams of our flashlights, the room seemed to hide furtive shadows that might jump out suddenly at any minute. I didn't know what they'd do once they emerged, but I knew they'd do it to us.

Downstairs, the big old grandfather clock in the hall bonged hollowly; the hush that came afterward was worse, like a held breath.

Except, of course, that a held breath didn't have rustlings and thumpings in it, plus some other sound I couldn't identify. Suddenly it struck me that we were rifling through a dead man's papers while trespassing in his house late at night.

Which, if you've read any ghost stories, you know isn't the wisest activity, especially since I still had no idea how the *other* dead body had gotten (a) under the porch, where I'd found it, or (b) to be a dead body in the first place. And both these questions seemed very important to me again suddenly.

"Ellie?" I said. "Are you hearing . . . ?"

I didn't believe in ghosts, exactly, but considering our current situation and the creepy feeling now rippling up and down my spine, there was no point being stupid about it.

She stood motionless, listening.

Rustle, thump . . .

"I hear it now," she whispered. "I was making too much noise while I was sliding these file drawers in and out, but . . ."

Thump.

My heart lurched. "Let's get . . . ," I began.

"Right." She headed for the staircase door.

"*Out of here*," I finished, following her.

Oh, you betcha.

Down all those many stairs, along the shadowy hall, through the gloomy front parlor, and out the window once more, landing hard on the porch outside.

"Yikes," said Ellie when we had scampered across Alvin's back lawn, bushwhacked through the dark woods, and were safely in her car.

"No kidding," I panted.

We hadn't had time to talk; even I had made it along that trail so fast, you'd have thought I was a deft-footed woodland creature instead of a bumbling trespasser.

"Not that I was scared," I said, leaning back against the car seat.

Outside, the sky was clear, with a zillion stars sparkling in it and the moon rising in the east. Ellie eased her car back out onto the road but didn't turn toward home; instead we were headed for the causeway to the mainland. I didn't know why. But for now, just not being in Alvin's house was such an improvement, I didn't care.

"Me neither," she declared. "Not scared, I mean." But I noticed her hands were tight on the steering wheel.

"Uh, where are we going?" I opened the thermos she'd brought along, drank hot coffee, and passed it to her.

She tipped it back one-handed, then spoke. "Well, while we were in there, it occurred to me that maybe Mary Sipp might have a motive, after all."

By now we were over the causeway, pulling up to the corner of Route 1. Fresh smoke hung in the night air. There must be another brush fire somewhere nearby, I realized uneasily.

"What if Alvin told her *she* was going to inherit? You said that she's got money troubles. Maybe they're worse than you think," Ellie said. At the intersection she turned right, headed north. "So I just want to see her place for myself," she added.

Which made sense, I supposed. "But Prunia..." I began. "Has been showing up in all the wrong places," I would've gone on, but Ellie kept talking.

"As for the method," she mused, "if I know Sam, then that hatchet started out in Alvin's toolshed, where it belonged."

She knew Sam well.

"So anyone could've grabbed it if they knew where it was," she continued. "Which Mary Sipp would have. Because what do you want to bet that she's the one who split all that stove kindling we saw in the basket on Alvin's porch?"

I had to admit she was right about that part, too. "Alvin didn't, that's for sure."

He'd have thought it beneath him. And Sam wouldn't have; he'd long ago made it clear to his customers that their firewood was their own affair, and not on his list of provided services.

Outside, the night went by: moonlit fields, dark forests, the occasional headlights passing in the other direction. I cracked the window open, and the woodsy perfume of evergreens floated in, minus the smoke smell now.

"And when we get there?" I asked, because when Ellie wanted a look at a place, she usually wanted more, like, for instance, to go inside, and I'd had enough of that for one evening.

"I'm not sure," she admitted. "But George is still working in Bangor, Lee's fine on her own for a while yet tonight, and if I'm not mistaken, Wade's gone out on the water again. So no one's home, watching the clock for your return?"

Not that Wade did this, exactly; still, I understood what she meant.

"Yes, but—" I started to say, then ducked abruptly as some big night bird, an owl, maybe, sailed low across the road, its wings' undersides flashing white in our high beams.

Ellie didn't flinch, but her tone sharpened. "Look, Jake, if we don't get Billy out of trouble, you'll be in it."

Drat. I'd been hoping not to talk about this.

"Don't try denying it," she added. "I know that lawyer you called to help Billy wants something in return."

Mick Flaherty, she meant. I'd been trying not to think about him. Ellie slowed as a porcupine waddled out of a ditch and began trundling across the road ahead of us.

"I can guess *what* he wants," she said.

I'd complained about Mick wanting information from me before, and without getting specific, I'd let her know my worries were no joke.

"But that's not going to happen," she went on determinedly. "Helen and Anna aren't going to live with Prunia, and you're not going to have to talk to that nosy lawyer, because Billy is not going to *need* a lawyer, not as long as *I* . . ."

She did get very protective of me sometimes, and the truth was, I didn't mind. Besides, she was right.

"Okay," I gave in. "We'll go look at the Sipps' place."

Despite my trying to feel cavalier about it, the idea of blabbing bad stuff about guys whose nephews were now running the organizations I'd worked for made my heart race unpleasantly. So if there was some way of avoiding a tell-all interview with Mick Flaherty, I was down with it, as Sam would've said.

"Go slower, please," I said, squinting out the window. At night it was hard to tell the dirt tracks leading off road from random spaces where old trees had fallen.

"The thing is, though . . . ," I said as I peered into the gloom. At last I spotted the bare, sandy opening between the trees. Ellie turned in, and the car slowed as the tires hit soft soil and shimmied a little in it.

"The thing about Mary Sipp's place is, there's another dog. A big one," I emphasized.

In the moonlight, the car rolled to a halt where I'd parked the first time I was here. When Ellie turned it off, I hoped hard that it would start again, but it was too late to worry about that.

We got out cautiously and closed the car doors quietly. The Sipps' big dog, Bingo, had been fine when Devon was here with it, but I wasn't sure about otherwise.

"I know about the dog," said Ellie, not sounding bothered. "You mentioned it." She swung the tote bag she'd pulled from the car's backseat at me; the bag was bulging with something.

"Venison steaks," she replied to my look. "From my freezer. They'd been in there since last fall."

And now it was deer season again, so George would bring a new supply home soon, making these steaks superfluous.

"Nice work," I said, realizing she must've been planning this all along. "So that stuff about you realizing just now that Mary Sipp might have a motive was a lot of . . ."

"Hooey," I didn't say, but she heard it.

"Um," she replied, caught. "Maybe I did think of it earlier. I can't remember," she added evasively.

Yeah, right. She just hadn't wanted to tell me about her plan to come out here until it was too late for me to veto it. But at this point, we might as well go through with it, and the good news was that the meat pieces were mostly still frozen, so it would take a while for even Bingo to dismantle them. And during that time, he would not be dismantling us . . . I hoped.

"So does her son live here with her?" Ellie asked.

Around us dry leaves rustled softly in a light breeze that was springing up.

Sure, that's what they are. Just dry leaves.

"I think so. But he might not be here now. He works a lot."

"Hope he took his dog with him, then," said Ellie, holding aside some whippy saplings so I could pass. Then . . . "Jake? What's that moving around back there in the bushes?"

So she'd heard it, too. "Just wind, I think."

She laughed softly. "Or a bear."

The rustling sounds were gradually getting louder.

"I think that bag of deer steaks you brought would probably . . ."

"Distract even a bear," I'd have finished. Also, bears didn't eat people, or not around here, anyway. But I didn't say any of it, because just then, a very large animal did appear, bursting out of the brush, with a snarl like a buzz saw, to plant four huge paws on the path in front of me. Challengingly.

"Ellie?"

It was Bingo the dog, and he didn't look happy. *Hungry* was how he looked. And *confident.*

And *mad.*

"Nice doggy," I tried.

"Grr," said Bingo, stepping toward us, stiff legged, and that's when Ellie tossed one of the deer steaks.

"Here you go, buddy," she said in that hearty, "I'm the human and I'm in charge" voice that is supposed to be good to use on dogs.

Good for *what?* was my big question. "Ellie," I said shakily. "More meat. Lots and lots more."

The dog shouldered me aside, his wiry tan fur scrubbing my forearm, and I heard a yell.

Not Ellie's voice, but *whose?* The question's importance paled, though, as the dog turned and looked at me, swallowed his mouthful of venison, and advanced on me again.

Apparently, he liked *fresh* meat.

"Eep," I said, backing away fast.

But as I did so, my heel hit something hard and stopped suddenly while the rest of me went on moving backward, and this was not a good combination at all. I flung my arms out, partly to catch my balance but mostly to fend off the dog, whose rapidly approaching teeth now resembled a whirring mechanism, like one you'd feed beef into to pulverize it into hamburger.

Which I guessed was about to be my fate. Falling, I felt the dog's breath on my face, and then the back of my head landed hard on something that was even harder.

And then the lights went out.

"Oohhh." Somebody was moaning. Me, I realized.

Opening my eyes, I blinked slowly. Which was a mistake. Quickly, I closed them again, but Bob Arnold splashed more water in my face, anyway.

"Rise and shine, kiddo," he said, not sounding happy.

I looked sideways. In the moonlit clearing where Bob had found us, Ellie sat on a stump with Bingo beside her. The dog looked content and not at all as if he wanted to devour me.

Getting devoured, though, was not my main worry just at that moment; getting arrested was.

"I knew it," fumed Bob, putting his hand in the middle of my back to help me sit up.

"Oof," I wheezed painfully. Who'd have known that slamming your skull into an exposed tree root is as effective as hitting it with a hammer, in the headache department?

The world turned woozily, and for a moment, it seemed I

might lose everything I'd ever eaten. But after a few deep breaths, it all settled . . . sort of.

Bob noticed. "Feeling better, are you?" he asked. Dirt and leaves stuck to his jacket, and his uniform pants were torn.

"Did the dog hurt you?" I whispered.

"Bingo," he replied disgustedly, "wouldn't hurt a flea." Oh, he looked irritated. "Dog wasn't attacking me. He was *licking* me," Bob added. "That's all he'd have done to you, too."

If you hadn't panicked, he added silently but scathingly.

"Oh," I whispered, biting my lip. "Well, but it *looked* . . ."

But Bob wasn't having any. Silently, he helped me the rest of the way up. All my blood rushed to my feet, and I did some deep knee bends to pump it upward again, then hobbled over to Ellie and sat beside her.

"You okay?" she whispered, and I nodded, causing what felt like crucial parts of my brain to shift dangerously.

"You?" I whispered back, and she indicated that she was fine, also, as Bob stomped up to us.

"You two," Bob fumed. "I *knew* you were up to something when I saw you driving out of Alvin Carter's place."

That got my attention. "You . . . you *followed* us?"

My already high opinion of Bob's surveillance skills went up a notch. But so did my anger level, and the various kinds of pain I was in failed to soften my reaction.

Plus, that head bump might've had something to do with it.

"What do you think you're doing," I began, "spying on two law-abiding . . . ?"

He shoved his hands in his pockets and just stood there for the minute or so that it took for me to ventilate the rest of my feelings on the matter, looking less impressed each time I raised another perfectly reasonable objection to his behavior.

"You done?" he asked when I'd run out of breath. "Because what I feel like doing now is tossing you both in the back of my squad car and hauling you off to jail."

My mouth snapped shut. Just this evening we'd committed

so many crimes, he'd have good reason to do exactly what he'd said.

"However," he said, frowning sternly at me, "the fact is, I wasn't following you as a cop. I was doing it as a friend, so I don't guess I'll pull any sort of switcheroo on you now."

"Uh, you guys?" Ellie put in. "The dog just took off."

I looked around, and sure enough, Bingo was gone.

"I think someone called him," Ellie said.

My feet started moving back toward the car even before she'd finished. Whoever had summoned the dog could be nearby, huddled among the bushes and small trees around us.

A branch hit me in the face as I hurried. In only a few moments, I'd veered off the rough trail, and in the now-waning moonlight, I felt a moment of panic. Thin, whippy birch saplings pressed up against me whichever way I looked.

"Jake!" Ellie whispered from a few yards away. But in what direction?

I turned uncertainly; then a pair of hands seized my arms from behind, and I bit back a startled yell. "Ellie," I said, turning, "don't scare me like—"

It wasn't Ellie.

"What the hell are you doing out here?" the man who'd just grabbed me by the arms demanded roughly.

Who the hell . . . ? My head spun. But after a moment I realized that it was the man Devon Sipp had called Butch, the fellow I'd seen lurking in the shed doorway the day before. Now his bushy-browed, scraggly-bearded face glowered down at me ferociously.

"Um . . . we . . . we were . . . ," I struggled to explain, and when I couldn't, he tightened his grip on my arms.

The smell of cherry pipe tobacco filled my head and sickened me. When Bob Arnold parted the brush surrounding us with both hands and peered through, relief nearly made my knees buckle.

"Well, well," Bob said pleasantly, but it was the kind of pleasant that sends a "Don't mess with me" signal. He'd snapped on his flashlight, its beam so bright white that it looked as if it could burn through steel. "Butch Bledsoe," he went on genially. "You know, Butch, we've got to quit meeting like this." Bob's tone suggested that, in fact, he was delighted to be meeting Butch like this, though I couldn't imagine why.

Butch, however, wasn't delighted. His overgrown eyebrows met frowningly over his narrowed eyes, which darted around, as if searching for some avenue of escape; and behind the wiry thicket of his unkempt facial hair, his lips clamped tightly together.

"Forget it," said Bob, as if reading Butch's mind. "You don't want to be rushing off before we've had a chance to talk."

Butch looked as if this was precisely what he wanted to be doing, but his sad-spaniel eyes said he knew better than to try.

Ellie appeared behind Bob. "What the heck is—"

"You still bunkin' up at the Sipps'?" Bob asked Butch, who nodded reluctantly. "Still runnin' those stolen vee-hickles down to New York, too?" Bledsoe's eyes widened and he shook his head energetically.

"Uh-huh," Bob replied, sounding skeptical. "On probation for 'em still, though, aren't you? Last I heard, you were."

"Yes." Butch's voice was surprisingly pleasant and his tone polite, as if behind the roughneck visage, there hid some mild-mannered college professor.

"Don't suppose you'd want to do me a favor," said Bob, his tone mildly calculating.

"Decide quick, will you?" I grumbled at Butch. " 'Cause it's getting cold out here."

Dark too. The moon, bright as a light bulb earlier, when it was overhead, now hung over the western horizon and soon would be setting.

Butch shrugged. "Guess I could maybe help you," he allowed. "Dependin' on what you wanted me to do."

Suddenly Bingo hurtled out of the brush again, panting happily. Apparently, the dog simply needed someone familiar to be around, because now that Butch was here, it was as if the Hound of the Baskervilles had suddenly decided to become a lapdog.

"I don't want much from you," Bob said. "Nothing you can't do as easy as fallin' off a log. Just a quiet little late-night tour of that farm you live on, that's all."

As he spoke, Bob herded us all back out onto the trail and got us moving along it.

"And while you're at it, you can tell us a little about the family there. Just to round out the picture a little," Bob said.

Butch's answering look was one of sullen resentment as we trudged back to Ellie's car. But his shrugs and mutters seemed to indicate that he would, in fact, do as Bob asked.

Bob's squad car was pulled in right behind Ellie's vehicle, and moments later we were all back out on the dark road, headed for the Sipps' property.

Nine

Approaching the house from the road gave a different view of it than I'd had the last time I was here. The barn stood at the foot of the driveway, shielded by a row of cedar trees that had grown together into a tall hedge.

We pulled in behind the barn and followed Butch inside it. The sweet smells of animal feed and clean straw filled my head, and the whole place felt peaceful, as if the warm exhaled breath of the creatures sleeping here had a kind of calming effect.

Butch switched on a hanging bulb, sending dim light high into the cavernous rafters of the barn and across the floor, which was bare wood except for an old carpet remnant spread in one corner. On the carpet stood a bed neatly made up with a plaid blanket and a striped pillow, a beat-up nightstand, and a lamp.

"See, at night we keep the critters inside." Butch waved an arm expansively around at the barn's vast-seeming interior. " 'Cause there's coyote, foxes, even a bobcat out here once in a while," he said.

In the barn's dim, deeper interior, I could make out woolly

sheep shapes. Soft snorts and a shuffle of hooved feet said we had woken the animals.

Bob looked impatient. I kept trying to catch his eye, wanting to know why, instead of hustling us home, he seemed to be assisting us in our snooping efforts all of a sudden.

I slid up alongside him as Butch led us out of the barn. The night was as quiet as a held breath.

"Why are *you* here, anyway?" I got the chance to ask Bob at last. "With us, I mean, instead of . . ."

We followed Butch uphill, toward the house, where a lamp glowed behind drawn curtains at a window upstairs. Then it went out.

" 'Cause you're right. There's something funny about all of this," Bob replied, keeping his voice low. "State cops think Billy's their guy, and they're getting no pushback at all. Nobody's saying different." He took a breath. "Except me. Who they talk to, but they do not listen to. And any minute the DA's gonna bring charges."

Ellie marched ahead of us, while Butch took the lead. "So?" I said.

"So," Bob went on quietly, "that kid's been a brick his whole life. Kept his dad from smacking his mom. He got smacked around himself for it plenty of times."

I could feel Ellie listening.

"Finally, the kid is left with two sisters, after an ordeal I wouldn't wish on my worst enemy." He paused. "So what's he go an' do, this kid?" Bob asked.

This time I answered. "He steps up to the plate, is what he does. Which is why I've been trying to *tell* you . . ."

"Yeah," said Bob ruefully. "I get it now. He's perfect for the crime . . . motive, method, opportunity, right?"

We'd reached the farmhouse, which glimmered faintly in what little moonlight remained.

"Right," I said. "But it doesn't fit. If he were the type to kill someone, which he's not, of course, but if he were, don't you think . . ."

"Yep. His old man would've bit the dust sooner. The kind of beatings he dished out, the kid had plenty of excuses. Instead, he waited until it was a matter of saving his sisters' lives."

I looked sideways at him. His round pink face wore the look of a man who had come to a realization. "Wait, so that's why you followed us tonight? So you could *help*?"

His chin lifted stubbornly. "Kid's wrong for it. But he's gonna get nailed for it. Nothin' I can do about it." Not officially, he meant, and then his voice changed. "Get down."

He put a hand atop my head, as if he were putting me in his squad car. I crouched reflexively. We were by the garage, amid the stiffened stems and dry leaves of what had been a small garden. The sweet, spicy scent of crushed lavender blossoms rose from beneath our feet.

"Did you see someone?" I whispered.

Bob was peering around the corner of the garage. "Anybody asks, I got a report of a prowler," he said quietly. "You were in the car with me when the call came in."

It's what we'd say to explain what we were doing here, he meant, if it turned out we had to. Meanwhile, his body had taken on the kind of stillness usually reserved for marble statues.

After stepping up very quietly behind him, I followed Bob's gaze to someone in the shadows on the porch: a man holding a long gun, a shotgun or a rifle, maybe, staring our way, as if some sixth sense had alerted him to intruders.

"Eep," I said softly as Ellie came silently up behind me.

"Sorry." She put a hand on my shoulder. "Is that Devon?"

Bob's night vision was better than mine. "Yup," he said.

"Where's Butch?" I whispered.

"Back at the barn."

Devon Sipp stepped off the porch just as Bingo leapt out of

the darkness at him, tail wagging madly. Luckily, the dog couldn't talk.

"Oh, so you're the one," said Devon, lowering his weapon. "Come on, then. Let's get in there, the both of us."

The dog followed Devon inside, the door shut, and a lock clicked. The light went on upstairs once more and after a minute went out again.

Bob straightened, his eyes still fixed on the dark house. A house with a dog in it, for Pete's sake, not to mention . . .

"That wasn't a gun. It was a cannon with a handle," I said.

I figured I'd give the idea of us being outgunned a try, even though it was unlikely to discourage Bob in the slightest.

And as I'd expected, it didn't.

"We're not going in there, are we?" I implored. "Tell me we're not."

"Yeah, no, maybe not." Bob crept ahead of me and Ellie. "But we're going to *look* in." While saying this, he gestured at the first-floor windows, which were low enough to the ground for us to do this.

Peering into the kitchen, I was glad to see Devon's weapon propped in a corner. Not the safest way of storing it, but at least it wasn't upstairs in his room with him, where he could take potshots at us from under the covers if he wanted to.

Oh, I hoped he didn't want to. What had started out seeming like a halfway decent idea—hey, if we had Bob Arnold with us, what could go wrong?—now felt spectacularly unwise.

"Over here," Bob said with a *Come quick* gesture.

Ellie and I hurried to where he was shining his flashlight into another window, the parlor's this time. The beam found a mirror hanging over the fireplace mantel and lit up the room. Sofa, lamps, an oversize tweed recliner facing a big TV, a big braided rug that clashed with the flowered wallpaper and striped curtains. The room was unfashionable, but it was clean and comfortable looking, and I didn't see any obvious murder-related items lying around. Unless . . .

"What's that?" I said. The window was open; I could see clearly through the gap, although the window was too high off the ground to climb in through. Apparently, the Sipps liked fresh air.

Bob aimed his flashlight where I pointed, at the recliner.

"Between the arm and the seat," I said. "Is that . . . ?"

A thickish sheaf of folded papers, with something written in big curly script at the top, poked up from alongside the chair's seat cushion.

Bob read the letters aloud in a whisper. "W-i—"

"It's a will, isn't it?" I cut in. "It's another of Alvin's dratted last will and—"

"Uh-oh," Bob breathed, snapping off his flashlight and backing away from the window fast. We hurried across the lawn.

A light in the kitchen went on, and I heard a refrigerator door open and close. Somebody was getting a late-night snack, I thought. Which meant they weren't asleep, the way I'd wanted, which meant I would really have liked to skedaddle pronto. But . . .

"I want to know who the beneficiary of that will is," Ellie said determinedly.

And I wanted to be the queen of France, but . . .

"I'm going in," she said.

Bob spoke up. "Oh, no you aren't. Lending you two a hand confidentially is one thing, but I surely didn't sign up to be an accessory to any crime. I'd like a look, too, but . . ."

Too late. She'd already slipped off into the darkness, back to the house. With a mild curse, Bob snapped on his big flashlight, prepared to go after her.

I stepped in front of him. "I'll go. You could go back down to the car and get it running while I corral her."

That way, in case *we* came running, possibly with an armed Devon Sipp right behind us, Bob would be ready to roll.

"Okay," he said grudgingly.

"*Jake!*" Ellie whispered from somewhere.

"Go," I told Bob. And then I made my way cautiously back across a lawn full of croquet hoops, a garden hose, a yard cart, a clothesline with clothespins clipped to it, and a lot of deer bones (femurs, I thought) all thoroughly Bingo-ized, judging by the extensively tooth-grooved look of them. It was a wonder we hadn't all broken our necks already.

"*Jake!*" The whisper came from near the house. I followed the faint sound until I came to a slanting cellar door that might just as well have had a THIS WAY IN sign on it.

So we lifted it. A damp, chilly basement smell drifted from the half dozen concrete steps beneath the door. Steps leading down . . .

We descended. A night-light, which someone had plugged into a heavy extension cord, glowed enough to let us walk around without knocking over the snow shovels and paint cans, garden tools and lawn carts stored down here.

"So listen," I said as we crept across the concrete floor toward a set of wooden steps leading up. "If by some chance we get caught in here, we'll say we were driving by, thought we saw a fire, heard someone scream, and had to get inside the house to help."

Because a prowler call would explain Bob's presence out in the yard, but not ours here in the basement. I could practically hear Ellie's eyes rolling, though.

"Uh-huh. And when we heard this scream, we ran up the steep driveway instead of driving up here because . . . ?"

Hmm, she was right. Bob's car was down by the barn. "Uh, to leave room for the fire trucks?"

Also, there was the little matter of Bob still being *in* his car, as well as our new friend Butch, who would have an entirely different tale to tell. . . .

Bottom line, we'd just have to *not* get caught, wouldn't we?

I aimed my flashlight at the cellar stairs while sweeping my arm back in an elegant gesture to suggest that Ellie precede me. "After you," I invited, and that's when my arm smacked into a pegboard, which I hadn't seen hanging there in the cellar gloom, and it had a lot of small tools on it, which I also hadn't seen.

And now many of them clattered to the concrete floor. For a couple of seconds, which felt more like a year to me, it sounded as if a pots-and-pans factory had exploded down there.

An instant later came the clickety-click of dog toenails on the hardwood floor above us. Sighing, Ellie gave me a look that was so patient, I knew what she really wanted to do was swat me, but instead, she dug quietly around in her tote bag. Then she scampered up the cellar steps, flung open the door at the top of the steps, tossed a frozen venison steak out into the hallway up there, then stepped out into the hallway herself.

"Hi, Bingo," she whispered, but I wondered if the dog had already alerted his master, who might right now be fetching the weapon he'd propped in the kitchen.

Probably Devon had used only bird shot to drop those partridges he'd bagged earlier, but I didn't much want a load of that in my backside, either.

So I waited, wondering first whether I might have to run and get Bob Arnold, then where Butch had gotten to, and finally whether he might betray us, even if the dog didn't. But after *that*, I gave in and climbed the steps myself—I couldn't stand not knowing where Ellie was another minute—and tripped over the dog in the hallway pretty much instantly and then over Ellie, too.

She was crouched down beside Bingo, who had a venison bone in his mouth and a grin drawn back around it, his tail sweeping the floor in slow, soundless wags.

"Now, Bingo," she told the dog nicely, "how about you take these yummy steaks and hang out in the cellar awhile, okay?"

She tossed the rest of the frozen meat chunks down the stairs. The dog trotted happily down after them, and she shut the door, trapping him down there.

"And now we," she said, hauling me up from where I'd landed when I tripped over her, "are going to go read the danged last will and testament of Alvin's and then get the heck out of here."

At least the getting-out part gave me something to look forward to. I swallowed hard and followed her.

The darkened parlor smelled like furniture polish. The braided rug I'd seen earlier covered most of the floor, a piano stood in the corner, and a jug of autumn flowers on the mantel was full of night-dimmed reds and yellows.

A propane heater stood in one corner, hooked to the kind of propane tank you'd use for a gas grill. The kind, I mean, that you aren't supposed to use in the house, and that you can exchange at the dollar store for a few bucks.

The whole setup made me think of the oil bill on the kitchen table, that this was what you would do if you couldn't pay for another delivery but the evenings were getting chilly.

"There," said Ellie as her flashlight beam picked out the sheaf of papers we'd seen through the window.

"Okay," I said when I'd snatched it up. "Now let's—"

But before I could finish, an unearthly moan echoed through the house. It sounded like some unhappy ghost had gotten stuck in a heating duct. *Ah-woo!*

"What *is* that?" Ellie whispered.

Then a loud thump came from upstairs, and I guessed it wasn't Mary Sipp turning over in bed.

"Bingo," I said, thinking aloud. He'd gotten tired of the bone, or maybe he was just lonesome; either way, he wanted out of that cellar and he wanted out now.

Meanwhile, the thump meant Devon Sipp was awake and alert and on his way down here. To get his gun, probably, so we had to hurry.

But we couldn't take the will we'd found along with us, or Devon would know someone had been here, and we *really* needed to know whose name was in it. In this new expression of his postmortem financial wishes, had Alvin Carter named his housekeeper, Mary Sipp, as his heir, or maybe Devon himself?

Not that it really mattered. Whoever it was, I just needed it not to be Billy, so that someone else could've had as good a motive for killing Alvin as Billy supposedly had.

Hastily, I unfolded the papers just as Ellie grabbed the back of my collar and yanked. "Come *on*," she whispered urgently, whereupon I took two quick steps back in the gloom and knocked over a footstool, which threw me off-balance.

But that wasn't all: Flailing for something to grab on to, I dropped the paperwork, slammed my hand down onto the keyboard of that damned piano and, with the back of my other hand, smacked the big vase of flowers on the fireplace mantel. The vase teetered briefly, then fell with a crash that surely woke any dead people in the vicinity. I teetered, too, struggling to keep my balance, until finally I collapsed into the sort of elaborate crash-down once performed only by trained vaudeville professionals.

A dark shape appeared in the parlor's arched doorway; I could just make out the shape of a pistol in its hand just as Ellie seized my collar again. But between getting gunned down or choked to death by my sweatshirt, I vastly preferred a third choice: that parlor window, which was still as open as it had been when I'd looked in here from outside ten minutes ago.

So I jerked sharply away from Ellie, scrambled up to my feet, and with my hand on her collar for a change, we hurtled through the aforementioned aperture just as the gun went off.

Miraculously unwounded, we hit the ground running and flew across the yard, then hauled ass, as my son, Sam, would've put it, downhill toward the barn.

"Is he coming?" Ellie gasped. Devon, she meant.

"Don't know," I managed. "He's not shooting. That's all I care about."

Well, not *all*.

"Ellie, I saw the will." Or enough of it, anyway.

She glanced back. "Where is it?"

"I dropped it." Yeah, I was good at that, wasn't I? I felt like kicking myself, but . . . "But I at least got a glimpse of it." And I'm good at glimpsing, as well, fortunately. "So I know . . ."

Our feet crunched the pea gravel in front of the barn door and along the big structure's side.

"You're not going to believe this after all the trouble we've gone to tonight," I puffed as I ran, "but in that version of the will . . ."

I stopped after we swung around the building's far corner. I hoped Bob would be there, ready and waiting. But he wasn't, and the spot where his car should've been was empty.

"Darn," I uttered softly as yet another hand seized my collar, and gosh, wasn't I tired of it. Spinning around, I was ready to pop somebody in the chops.

It was Bob, though, and when I saw him, I nearly fell into his arms, I was so relieved. The look in his eye did not encourage this, however, and neither did the crunching sound of someone coming down the gravel path behind us, not bothering to move stealthily.

"Go," Bob uttered flatly, hustling me forward, and suddenly I understood very deeply and personally just how he took drunk drivers into custody single-handed, spiriting them from behind the wheels of their vehicles into the backseat of his own as if levitating them by magic.

The squad car was pulled back into the bushes, where you really couldn't spot it unless you were back there, too. Ellie and I jumped in and had barely managed to get our seat belts on and fastened when Bob hurled himself behind the wheel, cranked the key, and sent that car rocketing out of its hiding place as if it was bound for a distant galaxy, set on warp speed.

"You can come back for your own car in the morning," he said as we sped down Route 1, past where Ellie and I had turned in.

No way was I about to argue with him.

"I don't know what possessed me," he berated himself. "I will," he added, "be lucky to keep my badge if this gets out."

But I knew what possessed him. He couldn't stand seeing Billy Breyer get his life ruined for something someone else had done, was what had possessed him.

I started to assure him that none of this would ever get talked about, but before I could get very far, he held up a silencing hand.

"No more breaking and entering," he commanded. "I get that you want to help Billy, and I do, too. He didn't kill Alvin any more than I did, but he's on the hook for it."

He glanced in the rearview and frowned; I peered around to look. Headlights glared behind us, coming on fast.

Bob swung suddenly into a gravel truck turnout, motioning for Ellie and me to hunker down in the backseat. After pulling to a stop, he thumbed his phone on, then propped it on the steering wheel in front of him, as if he was reading something on the screen.

But his eyes followed Devon's car as it sped by, not even slowing.

"So he didn't get a good look at Bob's car," Ellie said from where she crouched in the gloom beside me.

"Yeah, maybe," I replied sotto voce. Or maybe he'd glimpsed us, and he'd just had his suspicions confirmed. Devon didn't seem like the type to be playing it cool, but you never knew. Maybe he had hidden depths.

Then Ellie thought of something else.

"Who?" she demanded. "You said you read it, so in the will, whose name was . . ."

"No one's," I said bleakly. "It wasn't filled in."

It was just a blank form, in other words. Possibly, it was meaningful, but most likely, it was more of a blind alley.

"So this was," I added disconsolately, "a wasted trip."

"Well, we tried, anyway," said Ellie, sounding even more disappointed than I felt. This whole failed foray into Mary and Devon Sipp's house had been her idea, after all.

"Next time, we'll have to—"

But at this Bob hit the brakes, and the car's tires spit gravel as he turned to glower at us. "No," he said, his voice low and serious, as if he had a pair of real perps back here instead of Ellie and me.

"Now we're going back to Eastport," he said. "And it doesn't matter whose name was on some damned paper you found, because when we get there, you're going to drop all this."

What dropped, actually, was my jaw. "But, Bob, I thought—"

"Yeah, I know what you thought. But what I think is, sooner or later you're going to get shot."

"Burglars get holes in them more often than gets reported around here, and I don't want it happening to you," he added.

Small fires dotted the sweetgrass fields on both sides of the road through Pleasant Point, where men with water buckets and women with mops and brooms worked to extinguish them. Then we were on the causeway, and I got my voice back.

"But what about—"

"I'll still be working on all this, don't worry. But you two"— he glanced sternly in his rearview mirror at us again—"will not."

Ellie spoke up. "Okay, Bob. We're not making any progress, anyway. And you're right about the shotguns." She turned to me. "So we get it, Jake, don't we?"

"Oh, yes," I agreed, catching her drift. "We do."

Because what else could we say? Don't get me wrong. I loved Bob, and I respected him. But my honest reaction to his telling us to let go of this thing was, *In a pig's eye.* And I couldn't very well say that.

"So if you could just drop us both off at the Chocolate Moose," I went on, "Sam can come down and run Ellie home once we're done there."

Bob eyed me narrowly; I wasn't sure he'd bought it. But we pulled to the curb on Water Street, he popped the locks on the squad car's doors and let us out, and then he leaned out his window to say something more.

"I know," I told him before he could speak. "You mean it." About us terminating our snooping efforts, that is.

He just scowled in reply.

"And thanks," I added, "for saving our bacon out there."

Behind me, Ellie was letting herself in with her key. Someone was sitting at one of the tables, but I couldn't see who it was.

"Uh-huh," Bob said skeptically. "But next time, your bacon is getting tossed directly into the clink."

With that, he raised the car window and backed out of the spot, and I turned back toward the Chocolate Moose.

That's when I saw that it was Prunia Devereaux sitting in there, waiting for us.

"I've sent them away. It's none of your affair, I can't think why you've even involved yourselves, but if I don't tell you they're gone, I know you'll look for them."

Ellie and I stared as Prunia went on.

"You've neither of you a lick of sense. They're not wild animals, you know. Helen and Anna can't just raise themselves."

Out in the kitchen, Mika was wrangling another batch of test cookies off the baking sheet and onto a wire rack to cool. She'd let Prunia in to wait for us. She hadn't liked it, but Prunia had made a fuss.

Oh, of course she had.

"Where'd you send them?" I asked, thinking of the girls being yanked abruptly out of school and their activities, then stuck some strange place away from their friends. And worrying about their brother.

But . . . "Never you mind," Prunia answered darkly. "They're where they'll get what they need, is the important thing."

"And what's that?" Ellie inquired. "A weight-loss regimen? Fashion advice, maybe?" She took a calm breath. If you didn't know her well, you wouldn't know how angry she was. "Beauty tips? Dating advice? A solid awareness of how purely decorative they are," Ellie went on, "and how little they can really do in this world just because they're *girls*?"

Prunia had gotten up and was already halfway out the door. "I didn't come in here to ask for your permission," she went on. "I did it so you'd know they're gone and you can stop all your foolishness." She glared at each of us, even at Mika, who was peeking out of the kitchen at her. The little silver bell jangled hard as she slammed out the door.

Not long after, we finished putting the shop to rights and helped Mika clean up the kitchen. While we were working, a tow truck pulled up outside, with Ellie's car hooked to it. The operator lowered it gently and stuck his head in the shop door.

"I just was on my way into town with the truck when Bob Arnold called and asked me to haul this vehicle in here. Okay?"

As tired as we were, it was more than okay. We rewarded him with a bag of cookies, and he left Ellie's car in a parking spot. Finally, Ellie followed me and Mika outside and locked the shop door.

By now it was past ten in the evening, and on Water Street nothing moved but the cats who lived on the breakwater, eating bait and fish heads and glowering, yellow eyed, at passersby. In the car we were silent, slumped in that unhappy state where you're too tired to eat and too hungry to sleep. But when we got home, Ellie pulling into the driveway behind us, Bella slapped on her apron, ignoring our protests.

By the time we'd washed up, bacon, eggs, and toast had appeared, the toast slathered with Bella's homemade black-berry jam.

"There are," Bella observed out of nowhere as she watched us eat, "a lot of big, ripe rose hips out on Pleasant Street that the deer haven't gotten to yet."

I looked up from what little remained of the lumberjack's breakfast I'd just surrounded. "Really?" I said mildly.

Because Bella was no dope. She knew what Ellie and I had been up to, and now, for some reason, she thought there might be some sort of percentage in doing it on . . .

"Pleasant Street," I repeated while Mika rinsed our plates and Ellie tackled the frying pan.

"Yes." Bella brushed toast crumbs from the cutting board on the counter. "Perry Wilson's folks had a house down there, you know, before the . . . well . . . before the accident," she commented.

No one in Eastport believed it was an accident, but nothing had been done about it. Nothing could be. After all, when a man drives a car at high speed into a bridge abutment, you won't be questioning him about it, or his wife, either, if she's with him. Which she had been.

"And I do believe young Perry still owns the place," Bella went on innocently.

Now that the kitchen counters were all so clean that you could've performed skin grafts on them, Bella was polishing the toaster and wiping all the knobs on the cabinet doors.

Mika sat down, angling her head at our dervish of domestic cleanliness over there. She knew why Bella was making a show of her energy, too: to show us all how vigorous she still was. How capable of caring for children . . .

"So, Bella," I said carefully. It was past eleven o'clock. "Thank you for the supper. We really appreciate it." Nods all around acknowledged this. "But isn't it a little after your usual bedtime?" I questioned her mildly.

She turned, her look of exhaustion briefly unguarded. Then she caught herself. "Bedtime? Where did you get that silly idea?" But she flung her towel down like she was glad to be rid of it. "I'd better go see what your father's up to, though. He'll be fussing if I don't," she added, and a moment later, I heard her slow step climbing the stairs. We all did.

Mika let out a heavy sigh. "So you see," she said quietly, "the problem."

That if Mika took the community college job, as she hoped to do—if, that is, she felt she *could* do it—Bella would insist on babysitting. Oh, of course we saw. It was obvious, but still none of us knew what to do about it.

Then Ellie spoke. "And the snickerdoodles? For the contest?" she asked. "It's awful to bother you about them, I know. I'm sure they are the least of your . . ."

"Please"—Mika spread her hands in a warding-off gesture—"don't apologize. I was reluctant at first, but as it turns out, those cookies are the only things keeping me sane." She sat up alertly. "Let's go over what I've done so far," she added.

So there in the late-night kitchen, the three of us put our heads together over the snickerdoodle-and-chocolate combinations that Mika had tried, all promising but in the end all unsuccessful.

"Because the thing is," Mika said, "you can't just stir in, say, a half cup of chocolate chips. Or chocolate syrup or . . ."

"Or cocoa powder," Ellie chimed in. She knew all this already. "Or at least not without adjusting the amounts of all the other ingredients. So . . ."

I knew, too, but not nearly as well, so I just listened.

"So you take your best guess," Mika said enthusiastically. "But no matter what combination of ingredients I tried, I still couldn't get past the taste."

She shuddered expressively, and Ellie and I laughed. We'd learned, to our sorrow, that no matter how good they may be individually, some flavors go together and some don't. I mean, they *really* don't.

But then Mika frowned thoughtfully. "I still think there's a way, though, for some chocolate ingredient of *some* kind to make snickerdoodles even *better*."

"Good trick if you can manage it," Sam said, coming into the kitchen, wearing navy blue pajamas and a robe.

He kissed Mika, then grabbed a few cookies from the bag of failed snickerdoodle experiments she'd brought home. He bit into one, and a strange expression crossed his face.

"Mmm," he said, his gaze darting helplessly this way and that before lighting at last on the paper towels by the sink. Hastily, he crossed to it, then turned his back so we wouldn't see what he was doing with the chewed-up bite of cookie.

But we knew.

"Those are, um, interesting," he said when he finished washing the remaining bits down his throat with plenty of water. "Do we . . . ah, do we have a lot more of them?" He glanced around nervously, as if one of them might pounce on him and force him to ingest it.

"No," Mika said soothingly. "You're safe for now."

They really were so cute together. But when not much later their feet padded softly up the hall stairs together, my smile faded.

Ellie's too. "So," she said seriously. "This whole Prunia thing."

"Right," I agreed. "I wanted to ask so many questions! Why was she visiting Alvin Carter, taking him to make new wills, and what was she doing with Perry Wilson last night? Not to mention why she sent those two girls away so fast. Ellie, it's *weird*."

She frowned considering ly. "I think so, too. But there's no point asking questions when we can't trust her answers, and it seems to me, too, that the less she knows about what *we* know—or suspect—the better."

Still looking troubled, Ellie got ready to go. When she opened the porch door, the cool night air floated in on a breeze thinly threaded with woodsmoke, and a siren wah-wahed somewhere in the distance.

Something in the sound made me feel the seeming undoableness of our task. "Ellie, we've been at this and at this. And we're just not making any . . ."

"Headway," she finished for me. "I know." Under the porch light she made balling-together motions with her hands. "Nothing holds it all together. That's why—"

I'd already begun shaking my head. "No. We're not going on another snooping expedition," I said.

Because, for one thing, we kept nearly getting caught every time, and for another, we weren't getting anywhere with them.

"And that's why, starting now, we're taking a break from it all," Ellie said, surprising me more than somewhat.

I listened suspiciously as she went on.

"Tomorrow we're taking a nice picnic and some big plastic pails and Mika . . ."

I wasn't sure what kind of picnic could possibly involve big plastic pails. Also . . .

"Sam works at the Chocolate Moose for the day," she said, anticipating my first question. "And Bella watches the kids," she said. "Because, you know, I think Bella could use some more time on her own with those two children, don't you?" Ellie added mildly.

As I listened, I wondered yet again how my friend had packed so many brain cells into that perfectly normal-sized head of hers.

"You mean so she'll understand better how it'll be if she has them every day?" I asked.

"Right, and so when somebody else, like maybe some paid child-care person, ends up getting them, Bella will be fine with it. Even," Ellie added wisely, "if she says differently."

Honestly, why my friend Ellie hadn't yet gotten the Nobel Prize for common sense, I couldn't imagine.

"Meanwhile," she went on, "first thing tomorrow morning, *we* are going . . ."

Out on the dark street a pickup truck slowed, then turned in at our driveway. It was Wade, getting home from work.

"Rose-hip picking!" Ellie finished brightly, and with a wave at the arriving Wade, she went on down the front steps and across the street, heading for her car.

After watching her go, I stepped out onto the porch to greet Wade, who was just then getting out of his truck.

And that's when the explosion happened.

Ten

"Are you kidding me? Are you kidding me right now?"

Fists clenched furiously, Ellie stood, unhurt, on the sidewalk under a streetlamp, forty feet from her burning car. Orange flames shot up from what remained of the vehicle. Window glass lay in glittering bits all around it, and the doors had blown off.

Fire and police sirens were howling already from opposite ends of Eastport, and neighbors with their garden hoses were already out soaking tinder-dry front yards.

Ellie stomped around the car. It took a lot to make her really mad, but this stunt had done it.

"Somebody doesn't play nice," she said evenly, and from her, that tone of voice was definitely not a good sign.

It meant she was gathering steam.

"Someone wants me to be all scared," she said. "Oooh!" She shivered in mock fright. "Well, guess what?" Her voice hardened. "I sure hope you're happy!" she called out into the night.

Bob Arnold's squad car screamed up, and then a fire truck arrived from the other direction.

"Because you've gone and done it now!" Ellie called to no one. Well, actually, to someone. We just didn't know to whom.

Bob moved up beside me, while Wade, once he saw I was uninjured, went to talk to the fire personnel. Ellie was still fuming.

"She'd saved up a long time for that car," I told Bob.

He nodded thoughtfully. "Any problems with the vehicle that you know of?"

A laugh escaped me. "What, you think maybe it went up by spontaneous combustion?"

But I knew Bob didn't mean that; he was trying to find some non-homicidal reason why an ordinary car on a quiet street might go off like a bomb all of a sudden, and there wasn't one.

"She was having a little trouble starting it, that's all," I added.

Ellie had stopped yelling and now just stood watching the car burn. Wade went over to her.

But Bob wasn't yet done with me. "You listen to me, now," he said, his eyes on the firefighters with their foam sprayers billowing clouds of white stuff onto the vehicle. "You two are done with this whole business," he said. "If you didn't get it before, you have to now, do you understand?" He fixed me in his steely blue gaze, and as far as I could tell, there was nothing even remotely disobey-able in his look.

"Yes," I said, meaning it.

For the moment, anyway.

Loud bangs smacked my eardrums; I hadn't known car tires could explode. The vehicle's carcass, now a skeletonized hulk, sank defeatedly onto blackened rims.

Whatever Ellie had told Wade made him nod in agreement and walk over to join Bob and me.

"She okay?" I asked as Bob's phone rang and he backed away to answer.

Ellie's husband, George, was still away, her daughter, Lee, was most likely asleep by now—she was an extremely self-sufficient tween-ager, we all knew—and I couldn't imagine going home to a silent house after such an event.

"Yeah, she's . . . well . . . you know." Wade waved at the sullenly smoldering hulk slumped at the curb. "But she's handling it."

By now all the neighbors, not just the ones with dry lawns, stood outside in their pajamas, with their robes clutched tight against their throats, staring.

But things were winding down. Bob thumbed his phone off and returned to his squad car. Other vehicles, mostly belonging to the fire volunteers, began pulling out and driving away.

"Anyway, I told her she's staying with us tonight," said Wade, meaning Ellie, and since he did not at the moment resemble a man who would put up with any sort of argument whatsoever, I figured that much at least was settled. Then . . .

"What about you, though? Are *you* okay?" he asked.

Over the years Wade had gotten fairly used to us sticking our noses into places where they weren't welcome, but he drew the line at anyone getting hurt. Especially me.

"I'm fine." I led him toward our porch, where Sam, Mika, and Bella all blinked in disbelief.

"*Blew up!*" breathed Bella, her big grape-green eyes wide with shock.

Sam dropped an arm around her shoulders. "Everyone's fine," he told her soothingly. "No one's injured. Pretty soon there'll be a tow truck."

Smart boy. Telling Bella that all the cleanup was handled was a sure way to calm her. Then Ellie appeared, after giving the necessary vehicle information to Bob, and once we all got ourselves inside, she accepted a cup of tea, clean pajamas, and a new toothbrush.

Finally, I showed her to the tiny slant-ceilinged chamber behind the dining-room fireplace. What with all the people living in this house, there was no such thing any longer as a dedicated guest room.

"Oh, but I love it in here," she said as I bent my head to enter and tucked myself down onto the low footstool beside her. Damp strawberry blond curls clung to her forehead as she sat cross-legged on the narrow bed's patchwork quilt.

I handed her a towel. "Will you be able to sleep?" I asked.

We hadn't talked yet about what had happened or why. There wasn't much we could do about it tonight, anyway.

"I think so," she replied. "Bob said he'd take care of everything. Getting the car's remains off the street and so on."

She looked around at the snug little cubby where she'd be sleeping. A glass of milk and a flashlight stood on the floor by the bed; there was no room for a table in here.

"This is sweet. Thank you." She gave me a smile.

I smiled back at her. It had been a rough night, but for now we were safe and sound. After leaving the hobbit-high door to the little chamber ajar, I walked around the quiet house once more, checking doors and windows, then went upstairs and told Wade the whole story from start to finish.

The next morning my dad stopped me at the foot of the hall stairs.

"So, a little excitement," he remarked.

He was a master of understatement. "You could say that."

"Flatbed took the burnt car away."

I hadn't heard it, having finally gotten to sleep. We went down the hall toward the kitchen together.

"Think it was an accident?" He paused in the kitchen doorway.

"Nope." Because cars didn't just explode, did they? Just out of the blue like that? "If something hadn't gone wrong with whatever was wired to that ignition," I said, "Ellie would've been starting the car when it went off."

"Yup. Might want to keep your own car locked," he said.

He knew a lot about bombs and bomb making, having been in his youth a master of the craft.

"Here," he said, handing me a small plastic device with a button on one end. It appeared to be made from two TV remotes duct-taped together, and if I knew my dad, it probably was. "Use this to start your car, instead of the key," he said. "It's a remote switch. I wired it into your ignition system."

Like I say, a master.

"Stand back when you do it, though," he added unnecessarily. "Just in case."

Oh, you betcha. The first time, anyway. "Thanks," I said as we went into the kitchen, where Ephraim picked blueberries from his cereal with one chubby hand and flicked them across the table with the other.

One hit the back of Wade's newspaper with a milky splat, but Wade didn't flinch, being by now a hardened veteran of the multigenerational breakfast table.

My dad tucked into his rye crisps, cottage cheese, and slices of red tomato. Ellie buttered toast slices, added them to a plate of bacon and eggs, delivered the plate to me, and put hot coffee in front of me.

After last night, I thought just shooting it into a vein might work better, but after I applied myself to my cup in the normal way and to the good breakfast that Ellie had made for me, I felt halfway human.

"We still going rose-hip picking?" Mika asked, chewing her egg sandwich.

Despite what had happened the night before, she meant it, and that's my family in a nutshell.

"Oh, yes," Bella replied, putting two apples and a paring knife into the picnic basket she'd gotten from the hall closet.

In there already I recognized a quartet of wax paper–wrapped sausage rolls, some fat slices of cake, and—I blinked in surprise—

two splits of what looked very much like champagne, plus little clear plastic cups to drink it from.

"Just let me fill these thermos jugs with coffee," she said. The jeans and sweatshirt she wore were a sharp departure from her usual faded cotton housedress. "And then we can get going."

I hadn't thought Bella was coming along. After all, who'd be doing the babysitting? But as I began to say so, she shot me a look that could've fried more bacon and eggs, so I shut up about it.

"Don't you forget what I told you," said my dad, and Wade looked up from his newspaper.

He held an arm out; I got up and stepped into his embrace. The night before, he'd listened patiently to my story of all that had happened recently, asked appropriate questions, and offered one stern piece of advice: "Don't be alone with anybody."

It's those unwitnessed moments that'll get you in trouble, he knew, so no more strolling through the puckerbrush with guys like Devon Sipp, for instance, or taking late-night cemetery tours with Perry Wilson.

Not until I'd told him what we were doing this morning—and especially that we'd be together doing it—had he relented a little, and *Be careful,* was all the warning his pale blue-gray eyes conveyed now.

And then the four of us—me, Ellie, Mika, and Bella—were out the door, into a crisply brilliant fall morning, with orange leaves rustling in the maples and the chrysanthemums by the back porch beaming bright yellow in the slanting sunshine.

The air smelled faintly of gasoline and burnt rubber instead like grass fires for once. Feeling a little foolish—it really was a beautiful day—I pressed the button on my dad's remote gadget, and when (a) my car started and (b) nothing blew up in our faces, we all got in.

"So, Bella, why are you so set on rose-hip picking today?" Ellie wanted to know as we drove off down Key Street.

"It's the season for them," she replied shortly.

She had more reason than that; I could tell by the way she kept her lips pressed tightly together and her hands clasped in her lap. But she wasn't telling, or at least not yet, so I drove us along the waterfront to the beach access she'd been talking about the night before, where we parked and got out.

Up on the road, a long driveway led somewhere I couldn't see, but here a stony path from the parking area led between a high, grassy bluff and a granite outcropping that jutted out to the beach. On it we made our way between bleached, gnarly chunks of driftwood and lumpy swaths of dark green seaweed spread out on the sand like tangled yarn skeins.

"Heaven," Mika opined, spreading her arms wide to take in the blue water, white-topped waves, and the crying gulls wheeling overhead with the sun on their wings.

The smell was like cold salt water dosed with iodine, with a whiff of fish threaded through it. Even Bella softened when the shore perfume hit her. I put an arm companionably around her, and she walked alongside me to the water's edge.

There little waves foamed like lace. Bella leaned warmly against me, which surprised me, since ordinarily, she wasn't the least bit cuddly.

"So why did you bring us here?" I asked. "It's because of Perry Wilson somehow, isn't it?" I guessed.

But instead of answering, she slipped her shoes and socks off, handed the footwear to me, and waded in.

Behind us, Mika and Ellie had spread a blanket on the little beach and were weighing the red plaid fabric down at the corners with our bags and the picnic basket.

"My friends and I used to come here," Bella said, trudging back up through the soft sand toward me.

Her feet were already blue, and her calves were reddening from the frigid water. But she didn't seem to care. Back at the blanket, she sat to brush her feet off, then pulled her socks on. She had, I reminded myself, lived by this cold water all her life.

"We picked rose hips all along here back then, too," she said, waving up at the bluff's sharp slope rising behind us.

Beach roses, eight feet high and as lushly thick as jungle vegetation, grew all up and down the slope, creating a nearly solid wall of glossy green bushes bristling with viciously sharp thorns and loaded with shiny bright red fruit.

All four of us owned leather gloves, gifts from husbands who seemed to think steel-toed work boots were good gifts, too. And now that I'd plucked broken glass out of a window with the gloves on, and managed not to break any bones while dropping that very same window onto my fortunately steel-toe-booted foot, I tended to agree, but that's another story. As for this one . . .

"These rose hips are as big as golf balls," said Ellie as she snipped another stem-load of the fruit. One of the canvas tote bags we'd brought along was already nearly full.

Mika had been snipping fast and steadily, as well, but I could tell from the distant look in her dark eyes that she was thinking of something else.

"Did you hear from the college?" I guessed aloud quietly. "About the job?"

She nodded, brushing back the shiny black hair swinging in her face. "I start next week. If . . ." She angled her head toward Bella, who seemed thoroughly in her element here, moving confidently among the thorny bushes. "I'm afraid it'll break her heart when I get somebody else for the kids. I mean, she looks good here, but . . ."

It was true: Bella looked nimble as a mountain goat right now. But here in the sunshine at the edge of a saltwater bay, we all felt ten years younger, didn't we?

And besides, a pleasant couple of hours' worth of fresh air and exercise were not at all the same as a whole long day caring for an infant and a toddler. An *active* toddler . . . Heck, I'd had only one of them in my life, and that alone had nearly killed me.

"Sam?" I suggested.

He loved fatherhood and was fully capable of caring for his children. None of us worried about that. But . . .

"We've gone over our finances some more," said Mika. "If Billy's not back soon and Sam doesn't replace him, it looks like Sam will need to give up a third of his customers at least." She took a breath, her gloved hands moving efficiently with the snippers and her tote bag filling steadily. "And he says he *won't* replace Billy until he's *sure* Billy won't be back."

My own hands stopped moving. Back in the bad old days, Sam had got dragged in on drunk and disorderly charges so often that he'd started putting notches in his bed's wooden headboard each time it happened.

When he'd finally got sober, that bed looked like an army of beavers had gotten at it. But now he'd become a good father—and, it seemed, a very good friend to Billy Breyer.

A *loyal* friend . . .

"I see," I murmured to Mika, and the rose hips shimmered briefly through my proud tears. So I hadn't done it *all* wrong, apparently.

"*Which* means Sam will have to work full-time at whatever's left to try to make up for Billy not being there," Mika went on.

That took Sam out of the "taking care of the kids" picture, I realized. Just then Bella came over to us.

"D'you girls want to see something from the good old days?" she asked. "Right up there?"

She pointed toward the top of the bluff, where the corner of a red-tiled roof showed. A narrow path led up to the structure. This, I felt suddenly sure, was why Bella had brought us here.

A *steep* path. More thorny rosebushes, too.

Lots more.

*   *   *

Climbing the thorn-infested hill, I squinched myself together into the smallest shape humanly possible, trying not to get slashed, punctured, or both.

Unsuccessfully, I might add. *Ouch.*

"Bella?" She was right behind me, I could tell by the stomping and the huffing and puffing.

"What?" she wanted to know crossly, and speaking of various infestations, there seemed to be way more biting red ants than we needed around here. *Way* more.

Meanwhile, Ellie climbed on ahead of us, agile as a monkey and with her step full of a truly irritating amount of vim and vigor.

Seriously, people, keep all that radiantly well-oxygenated good health of yours at home, won't you? But I digress. "Bella, are you sure you know what's up there?"

"Of course I am."

Wincing, I licked a bleeding thorn scratch, while ahead of us Ellie hoisted herself up over the bluff's edge and vanished.

"Go on," Bella urged me impatiently, and not much later she helped me up over the edge by shoving me from behind, then scrambled up on her own and got to her feet. Not prettily, and not without effort, but she did it. Meanwhile, I sat there gasping and hoping that I didn't pass out.

"Hey, you guys!" Mika had made it over the bluff, too, and now she gestured for us to come see the rest of the building whose roof we'd glimpsed earlier.

Behind thick, overgrown masses of yellowing grass the place was nearly hidden from view. But parting the vegetation revealed a low, modern-looking structure with huge windows facing the water, a place that would've looked more at home on the California coast than it did on this easternmost stretch of coastline. Also, it looked as if it hadn't had so much as a gutter rehung or a dab of paint slapped onto it in at least forty years.

I spotted Mika on the long deck overlooking the bay. Bella and Ellie were just joining her there. I followed.

"Some view," I said, waving backward at the water and sky. A red-and-white tugboat putt-putted its way around the island's south end, toward the cargo port. Beyond, rafts of gulls lifted and settled.

But my companions weren't looking that way; instead, they bent over a heavily warped piece of plywood nailed over one of the house's big windows.

When I drew nearer, Ellie looked up at me. "The warp made a gap," she said.

"And there are skylights everywhere, so we can see in," said Mika as I bent to peek past the warped plywood into the house, then stepped back, with the hairs on my arms prickling.

It was dim in there, the skylights obscured by grime and decades of seagull droppings. But there was enough light to see that the walls were papered with newspaper clippings. And photographs, lots and lots of . . .

Ellie and I exchanged "Who knows?" glances and followed Bella around the side of the house, through more hip-high grass, until we came to a small door, which obviously led down into a cellar. A very old padlock, rusty in the extreme, secured the door to its frame. Bella contemplated it.

"I promised I'd never tell," she murmured, seemingly to herself. "And I never did. I've kept my promise for all these years. But now . . ."

My heart sank. Was this what she'd brought us here for? Because if she had, then never mind if she had a key; it wasn't going to work. The lock was too old, too neglected, too *rusty*. Maybe if you soaked it in lubricating oil, I thought, but even then, it probably wouldn't—

Bella reached out and, with housework-roughened fingertips, plucked the padlock hasp's big screws from their screw holes, rocking them around a little so they'd slip out of the rotten old wood more easily.

Then the lock's hasp came entirely away from the door, and the door opened, just as she'd known it would. This, then, was her secret, that she could get in here anytime she wished.

A stale damp-concrete smell floated out of the darkness. Bella snapped a flashlight on, ducked in through the low entrance.

"You planned this, didn't you?" I accused her as she waved the rest of us in. Cool dampness chilled my sun-warmed arms as I stepped through the doorway.

Faint shrug from Bella. "I told you my friends and I used to come here. One of them, Patty Montague, lived in this house before Perry's folks bought it."

We all went down; I glanced around a little nervously in the basement gloom, hoping there were no long-dead bodies down here. I'd made no progress in figuring out where the one under Alvin's porch had come from, and that made me wonder what large, obvious fact I was missing.

Meanwhile, just being here seemed to have given Bella new energy. Leading us up some wooden stairs, she went on, "But her folks fell on hard times, this place got foreclosed on, the city bought it, and there was talk of tearing it down. Making a park." With the view and the beach access, it would be a great one. "But the city didn't want to lose the property taxes," she said, "and at the last minute they sold to the Wilsons instead."

She pushed open a wooden door at the top of the stairs—its bottom edge scraped the floor with a harsh squeal—and revealed a gray rectangle of space. I stepped into it, Ellie aimed her flashlight past me, and then, with a sudden thudding of my heart, I leapt back, startled by the dozens and dozens of photographs tacked to the walls.

All of the same two girls . . .

A creepy feeling came over me. The pictures, some in color

and others in black and white, were mostly snapshots, but a few had been professionally taken: graduation portraits and so on. Tacked to the walls or taped. Some were newish; some faded and yellowing.

"Eek," Mika breathed softly from behind me.

"No kidding," I said, still staring.

Suddenly all I wanted was to get out of here as swiftly and efficiently as possible and then take a hot shower. But . . .

"Do I know them?" I wondered aloud.

Both girls were in their late teens or possibly their early twenties, blond, narrow faced, and thin lipped, with extremely pale skin and whitish eyelashes.

"They look like . . ." I said. Albino rabbits was what they resembled, with the kind of fair skin that burned to a crisp in ten minutes' worth of bright sunshine.

Gazing around wonderingly, Bella walked farther into the room, whose once modern Scandinavian-style furniture now looked like the stage set for a sixties sitcom: landline phone, tweedy upholstery . . . even the TV was built into a wooden console, along with a radio and turntable.

"We used to watch cartoons in here," Bella said, smiling distantly. "And even after Patty's family moved away, the rest of us used to sneak back in." Her smile faded. "I promised I'd never come in here with anyone else, though," she said, then turned to me.

"Anyway, the other day I came over here to check the rose-hip situation, to see if there were enough to make it worth us coming to pick them." Nostalgia softened her tone. "And, of course, once I was here, I couldn't resist trying to get a look inside the old house."

"I'm sorry? You climbed that hill by yourself?" I asked. Because doing it with the rest of us was one thing, but . . .

"Oh, no. There's a driveway. I just drove in and parked," she replied, and of course, at this news I didn't just throttle her.

Hey, I love steep, hot, thorny, exhausting, red ant–infested hills, and I wouldn't have wanted to avoid this one by coming up via the other, easier way . . .

"I didn't want anyone to see our car," she explained, and that confused me until . . .

Just then Ellie returned from checking the rest of the house. "So you saw all this?" she asked Bella, waving her hand around.

The girls' faces smiled from everywhere, even the ceiling. Bella nodded, biting her lip. "It's awful, isn't it?" she whispered.

It sure was, and my next thought was that somebody should warn those two girls, whoever they were. "I still don't get why you brought us here to see it, though," I said.

Bella looked stubborn. "Do you remember when Perry Wilson came to the door?" she asked.

"Yes," I answered slowly, "of course I do, but . . ."

Mika moved, wide eyed and tight lipped, toward the basement door, uncomfortable and wanting to get out of here right now. I always said she had good sense.

"And did you see his arms?" Bella demanded, as if something about them had been so obvious that even I must have noticed.

"I saw them, but I didn't really pay much attention to . . ." But then the light dawned. "They were scratched up, weren't they?"

I glanced down at my own arms. After that climb up through the roses, they looked as if cats had been attacking them. Just like Perry's. "You looked in here, saw this whole weird shrine, or whatever it is, and came home with scratches yourself."

She nodded slowly. "And that night, his arms were all clawed-looking. Plus, I felt like I'd seen a ghost, because here . . ." She waved a bony hand at the photographs. "Because you just tell me now," she demanded, "who do those girls remind you of, white eyelashes and all?"

Of course, I realized, it was Hilary and Jill Wilson. . . .

Perry Wilson's pale blond pair of long-gone, "never been heard from since" younger sisters.

Ten minutes later we were all down on the beach again. Getting out of that house had suddenly felt urgent to all of us, and we'd vamoosed.

"So they do really exist," I said, meaning the sisters in the photographs.

After our housebreaking adventure, we were hungry. Sitting on the blanket that Ellie and Mika had spread, we ate bread, butter, and cheese with plenty of mustard, washing the bites down with the hot milky coffee Bella had made for us.

Also, Mika had brought along some snickerdoodle pinwheel cookies with milk chocolate filling that she'd made as another test recipe for the contest, and the vigorous exercise and fresh air we'd all just had made them edible.

Sort of.

"The girls were homeschooled until eighth grade, but then they were sent away to a boarding school," I said.

It was what Nanny Wolcott had told me; I did not, I realized, know anything else about them. Heck, until now I hadn't been sure I believed in them.

Even Ellie had never heard of them. "I guess when you leave a place as a child, you don't leave much of a trace," she said.

Then Mika, who'd been gazing dreamily at the water while she listened, sat up sharply all at once. "I left my bag."

She searched around worriedly: on the blanket, under it, and on the seaweed-littered sand the blanket was spread on. "It's still in the house up there. I must have . . ." She got to her feet and headed for the path we'd recently descended. "You three wait here for me, and I'll just . . ."

"I'll go with you," Ellie said as she got up, brushing stray sand off herself, and then Bella decided she wanted one more look at the place, too, seeing as the others were going.

And I couldn't very well just sit here on the beach while they all labored up that steep hill again, could I? So the rosebushes got yet another chance at me, their thorns cutting brand-new lacerations across the old ones as I gasped and scrambled.

At the top of the bluff, we went into the house via the door Bella knew how to open, then headed upstairs just as before.

Only this time, someone was in there with us.

Mika grabbed her bag up off the table where she'd left it and moved back toward the cellar door again at once. "I don't care who those pictures are of," she said. "I just don't like them. I don't like this whole place a bit, and—"

I didn't like it, either, especially when a new voice demanded from the cellar, "Who's up there?" A man's voice.

Mika leapt forward, Ellie looked startled, and I was so shocked at the sound that I nearly fainted, even though after a moment I knew exactly whose voice it must be.

But Bella stood her ground, hands planted on her hips and her eyes narrowing in a way I thought boded ill for whoever was coming up the steps toward us. She glanced around, then grabbed a fireplace poker from the hearth and brandished it.

"Perry Wilson, you come up here right now, or I'll come down there after you," she threatened, and either Perry believed her or he was coming up the stairs, anyway, because he did it.

"What are you doing here?" he demanded to know when he'd emerged from the cellar stairs.

In his left hand he held a gun. Oh, of course he did. Why did everyone nowadays seem to need to have a—

"Never mind us. What're *you* doing here?" Bella demanded right back at him.

I'd been wondering how the person who'd put up all those photographs got in here to do it, and when Perry spoke again, I got my answer.

"I saw the lower door was open and came in that way to find out why," he replied. "Although ordinarily, I'd let myself in by the front door, with my key."

For his house-checking expedition today, he was wearing a preppy-looking yellow sweater, a white polo shirt, and khakis. Or maybe it was a photo-gazing trip. Above and around us all the pretty, pale blond girls grinned silently at us from their photographs, but the effect was like a chorus of screams.

Perry put the gun down on a small table, but when I eased toward it, he picked it up again. I still might be able to grab it if I could get to him before he shot me with it, I thought, and if it had been a .22, I might've tried. But it wasn't. It was bigger, and at this range, he'd have had trouble *not* hitting me.

"And all this?" I asked him instead. "These pictures of who- ever . . . *Are* they your sisters? I mean, what is this? Some sort of memory project or . . . ?"

"Yeah, that's them. Hilary and Jill." He let his gaze wander fondly among the photographs. "But I don't see them any- more. And I . . . I miss them," he said.

The remark took me aback. It was such a simple, relatable declaration. You miss someone, so you put their picture where you can see it, right? I mean, maybe the *way* he'd done it wasn't so understandable, but . . .

"Yes, well, I don't care," Mika declared. "I'm getting out of here."

Which was understandable, too. After a final, thoroughly creeped-out glance at the massive collage of girls' faces that Perry had created, she did just that, while Bella, Ellie, and I glanced at one another, all of us thinking the same thing. *Good idea.*

"Okay, then," I said, turning away from Perry toward where Mika had gone, hoping that Ellie and Bella would follow me.

All I wanted was for us to get out of here un-bullet-holed, and if we just matter-of-factly went ahead and did it, then—

The gun went off. The sudden thunderclap felt to me like a pipe bomb had exploded inside my head while my eardrums got smacked hard from the outside.

It wasn't good at all for the health of my brain cells, but it lit one hell of a fire under my fight-or-flight mechanism. I spun around so fast, I nearly twirled myself off the top cellar step.

But at the last instant I caught myself and flung my whole weight onto Perry Wilson instead and hauled him to the floor. "You lying little sack of . . ." I climbed up and knelt on him, grabbed him by the throat and shook him. "You *shot* at me!"

"Jake?"

Something touched my shoulder; I brushed it off.

"Jake! He's turning blue." It was Ellie leaning over me.

"What? Oh." I let go of Perry's throat.

Sometime when I wasn't looking, his hand had opened, releasing the pistol. I grabbed it and got up. Perry just lay there, his fingers tentatively touching the marks I'd squeezed into his neck.

"I dropped it," he whispered strickenly. "I didn't mean to shoot it at anyone. I just—"

"Oh, cry me a river. You could've killed one of us," I barked.

Above, a neat round hole had appeared in one of the blond girl's heads. Silent and wide-eyed, Perry stared at it in shock, maybe realizing what he'd almost done.

Ellie crouched by him. "Come on, Perry. Don't worry about it. No harm, no foul. Right, Jake?"

Bushwa, as my dad would've put it. But . . . "Uh, sure," I said. "No one's mad at you, Perry. We know it was an accident."

At this ridiculous lie, I could practically feel my nose growing. What I really wanted to do was punch him in his.

"Let's get out of here, though. There are too many . . ." The faces in the photographs stared at us, not pleasantly. "Eyes," I finished and beat it down those cellar steps and outside before anything else could happen.

Eleven

When we got him back to the beach, we sat Perry down on the blanket and fed him cookies and lemonade, plus a cheese sandwich and a dill pickle that nobody had wanted.

Gradually, he got back a little color and relaxed some, no longer looking as if he thought someone would hit him, which I still wanted to.

I'd given his gun to Ellie, who'd stuffed it into her small satchel. He hadn't even had the safety on, for heaven's sake.

"So, Perry, why don't you see your sisters anymore?" In real life, Ellie meant. Trust her to face right up to a subject.

He was watching the little red tugboat we'd seen earlier, now putt-putting back up the bay the way it had come. "What?" He blinked. "Oh. We're . . . estranged."

Then came silence; he stared across the water some more, until at last I couldn't help myself.

"Hey, Perry? How about I slap the taste out of your mouth? Since you're not using it for talking, I mean."

This focused him. "Huh? Well, since you put it that way . . ."

I got up and stood over him. "I do. Put it that way," I said quietly, feeling a dangerous calm spreading through me.

Because the flight part of my startle mechanism had settled down considerably by now, but the fight part was still ready to roll, and now Perry seemed to feel it, too.

"Okay. Well. It was all about my father, really," he began with a sigh. "He was an Eastport kid, married a girl from away."

"Because nobody here would have him?" Bella asked astutely, and he nodded. She did, I recalled, remember the old days.

"Yup. And they were smart not to," said Perry. "Long and short of it was, he hit my mom, and when I got big enough, he hit me, too."

Oh, man. "What about your sisters? Did they get hit?" I asked.

He shook his head slightly. "No. Prunia got them out of the house before they got big enough for him to start in on them."

Ellie turned, surprised. "Prunia? How would she know?"

"Oh, they were in a kids' group she helped out with," Perry replied, "and they got up the nerve to confide in her somehow."

So that was the connection: Prunia's long habit of service to the community, or, as my dad would've put it, do-gooding.

"They even lived with Prunia for a while, and after a few years, once our parents died and there was no danger from Dad anymore, they didn't want to come back," Perry said. Sitting cross-legged on the blanket, he looked down at his hands, which were resting limply in his lap. "Before the girls left, I got whipped for stuff they did."

Uh-oh. I had a feeling that Perry's story was about to get worse.

It did. "He'd get all sozzled, and I knew what was coming. So I'd march on in there and sass him real bad so he'd turn on me and leave them alone." A deep sigh escaped him. "I can," he added quietly, "show you the scars, if you don't believe me."

Oh, I believed him; we all did. The silence lengthened until . . .

"Perry, you did aim a gun at us, though," I said.

"And it went off, you dim-witted, butterfingered, dismal little dweeb of a . . . ," I wanted to add.

I bit my tongue instead. "Why," I asked him calmly, "did you even *have* a gun along with you if you were only . . ."

Generally, in Eastport you don't need a deadly weapon to protect yourself while you check on your vacant property. But then again, maybe he was a legitimate exception.

"Do I," he asked tiredly, "look like a powerful physical specimen to you?"

"No," I admitted, "you don't."

In fact, what he resembled most was a nervous rabbit: pink nose, red-rimmed and rapidly blinking eyes, anxious gaze. Plus, that hair . . . so pale, it was nearly white.

"If you come over here a few times," he began, and his wave said that by *over here*, he meant up there, to this house high on the bluff, "you see people." He paused. "Hanging out and passing around substances. The house isn't very visible from the street, you know. So it doesn't always feel safe."

I had noticed the long driveway leading in from the street but hadn't thought much about it.

"Not that I care about that," said Perry. "The substances, I mean."

Personally, I thought a few substances might do him a lot of good—prescribed ones, that is.

"Listen," I said, "don't take this the wrong way, but have you been missing any appointments lately? Like for any kind of counseling sessions or—" But then I stopped, having noticed that Ellie's small satchel was beside him on the blanket, and that somehow that annoying little gun of his had gotten back into his hand.

I glanced at Ellie. She'd noticed, too. Bella's eyes were closed at the moment, but from the alert way she sat with her bony hands planted in the sand, as if ready to shove herself up very suddenly if need be, I figured she must also be clued in.

"What bothered me when I'd come here was people looking for trouble," Perry said. "Like maybe to beat somebody up for fun."

He did indeed look like exactly the right target for this, and if we rushed him, I had no doubt we could immobilize him ourselves, just as I had up in the house. But while we were rushing him, and before we overpowered him, he could shoot at us again.

Deliberately this time, and as before, at such close range, he had little chance of missing. Now I noticed also how isolated we were here on the beach. With the bluff-and-granite book-ends jutting out at either end of the shallow inlet we sat by, we were really visible only from out on the water.

"You said your sisters didn't want to come back, but why?" Ellie asked carefully, hoping to distract him but at the same time not wanting to set him off.

Just not quite carefully enough. At the question, his face clouded with resentment.

"Not only do they not want to, but they don't have to come back here. They don't have to see me at all. The judge made that clear. I can't even call them on the phone. And that's just not right, that I shouldn't be able to . . ."

Our eyes met, Ellie's and mine. *Fascinating.*

But also scary.

"So they've got a no-contact order?" I asked as mildly and nonjudgmentally as I could. See *not wanting to set him off* above.

But those court orders for some people to stay away from other people didn't just get handed out like candy, I knew. Perry must've done something serious to get one issued against him.

His hand tightened fractionally on the gun. "They said I harassed them. Scared 'em, they said."

I understood. Heck, he was scaring me, and I wasn't even related to him.

"Perry?" I made my voice calm. "Hey, bud, gimme the weapon, why don't you?"

I held my hand out, palm up, still thinking he would let go of it. Instead, he smiled dreamily and put the gun to his head.

"Yeah, no, I don't think so," he murmured while the rest of the world went as still as a held breath.

"I love them, I protected them, and now neither one of them wants anything to do with me," he said, and pulled the trigger.

Perry proved me wrong about how close he could be to his intended target and still not hit it, fortunately for him.

Although it didn't hurt, either, that just as he fired the weapon, Bella's balled fist shot out like an unexpected snake striking and punched the gun so it flew from his grip.

After that, we'd have jumped him, but we didn't have to. He just sat there, shoulders slumped under the yellow sweater. A trickle of red ran down the side of his head, oozing from the place where the bullet had taken a divot from his scalp on its way by.

"Why don't they understand?" he asked mildly of nobody in particular. "I'm their *brother*. I'll *help* them. They have a *home* here."

Only we had heard the gunshot, probably; the granite outcroppings would have kept the report mostly down here on the beach. The gunpowder smell of a recently discharged firearm faded fast, as well.

Too bad my fury didn't. I wanted to shake him and shout at him, "You could have blown your fool brains out." "And, damn it, they'd have splattered all over me," I wanted to add.

But that approach wouldn't get more information out of him, and I wanted that even more.

"Perry, why was Prunia Devereaux at your house last night?" I asked.

His pale-lashed eyes blinked twice: *testing, testing.* He seemed surprised that they still worked; it seemed from his blank stare that his brain's whole internal operating system was in the process of rebooting. But then . . .

"Printer," he said. "I have one, connected to a computer. And she wanted to . . . posters?" he said. "For some contest."

A puzzled look crossed his face as he spied the gun where, punched out of his hand by Bella, it had landed near the water's edge and was now being engulfed by the incoming tide. Then a sudden awareness of what he'd just done seemed to come over him. "Uh, did I just try to . . . ?"

"Yeah." I take this stuff seriously. "You did. So maybe you should see somebody, Perry. You tried to hurt yourself. You want to try to get some help, I think."

Perry nodded slowly. "Yeah. You know," he said dazedly, "I think you might be right."

And owing to this and all the rest of what had happened so far, we were all pretty solemn as we gathered up our picnic gear and folded the blanket.

Especially me. I was going to have to get him to see someone, I realized, and preferably today. Maybe what he'd just done was only a gesture, not the real thing, but it saddled me with a responsibility that I hadn't been planning on either way.

It did not, however, disqualify me from doing what I did next. Feeling deeply, sincerely, sorry for people doesn't stop me from suspecting them, usually, when they merit suspicion.

"Perry, were you aware that before someone killed him, Alvin Brown had made you the beneficiary of his will?" I asked.

And yes, I did know that what I'd just said was a lie, but I wanted to see how he would react.

It wasn't the way I expected. "Oh, please," Perry sighed tiredly. "He did that to everyone. If he wanted something, he'd promise you something . . . usually that you'd inherit a fortune."

I felt my eyebrows go up at the arrival of this little bombshell. The question I'd thought might surprise and unnerve him didn't worry Perry at all, and not only that, if he was telling the truth, then it turned out he knew all about Alvin's "lots of wills" situation and cared not a single bit about it.

Meanwhile, we trudged up the sand together, Bella out front with the blanket and the picnic basket, then Mika and Ellie with two totes each full of shiny red rose hips, and finally Perry and me.

A bitter laugh escaped him. "He never actually delivered, though. The inheritance thing was because he wanted me to get the girls to come back and work for him."

Nearly getting his brains blown out really did seem to have loosened Perry up in the conversation department, I thought irreverently. On the other hand, he *had* missed his own head, which was either spectacularly bad shooting or pretty darned good theater.

"What do you mean, back?" I said. "Had they worked for him before?"

We stopped a little ways from the car, where the others were loading in our stuff. I stopped, rather; he didn't, until I put my hand on his arm to pause his robot-like gait.

"Perry, what happened?"

The others were waiting now, passing a lemonade jug around and talking quietly. We'd never opened the champagne, and I was glad.

I took Perry's arm and tugged gently on it, urging him forward. He hadn't answered my questions yet, but if I handled this next part right, I was pretty sure he would.

He was giving me the fragile, discombobulated act, and maybe it was sincere.

But maybe it wasn't.

"Get in the car, Perry," I said.

We were all silent on the way home, still shocked by what had nearly happened to Perry. I had even forgotten to use my dad's anti-car-bomb ignition gadget. Fortunately, it hadn't turned out to be necessary.

"Sit down, Perry," I said firmly when we'd gotten him home and into my kitchen.

Because the most important project for this afternoon was still a little story called "Perry Visits the Doctor." But first, I meant to get the rest of *his* story out of him. Luckily, at this point he seemed glad to be getting told what to do and was co-operative about doing it.

"Drink that down now," I said, putting a shot glass full of dandelion wine in front of him. Bella had made it in an earthenware crock, with sugar and raisins, a bushel of blossoms, and spring water so clear, you could see your future in it.

That wine looked like sunshine, tasted like Bristol Cream, and kicked like a mule—the trick is in aging it for a year—and I hoped it would kick-start Perry.

"So," I said, sitting across from him.

Bella and Ellie had gone down to the Chocolate Moose to open the shop so we might at least capture a little afternoon business, while Mika had gone upstairs to find Sam and the kids.

"So," said Perry before tipping back his glass and then looking around hopefully.

Oh, you betcha, I thought, filling the shot glass again. "Your

sisters went away. Rescued by Prunia, sent to school . . . That's
how she got them away from your abusive dad."

He nodded, a thin shock of blond hair falling across his narrow, unhappy-looking face. "That's right," he replied. "But once
they'd graduated," he said, repeating the tale resentfully, "they
didn't want to come and live at home again." He frowned.
"Where," he added stubbornly, "they belong."

I had the strong feeling that Perry's sisters probably knew a
lot more about where they belonged than he did. Also, if I ever
had to move in with Perry, I'd probably just walk east until my
hat floated instead.

Still, this was his story, not mine.

"You got them back for a while, though?" I asked. "Back
here in Eastport and living with you?" He must have; he'd said
they'd worked for Alvin.

While he considered his answer, from upstairs came the pat-
ter of little feet. *Thud-thud-thud!*

Tipping his head and smiling a little too sentimentally at this,
Perry nodded. "That's right."

Possibly his warm feelings about the stomping of little kids
were partly due to the fact that he'd already polished off his
second shot of truth serum, er, I mean liquid sunshine.

And of course, I did not want to seem inhospitable. "So then
what?" I asked, pouring again. "After they came home?"

I gave him a little extra wine since he liked it so much, and he
seemed to appreciate this.

"They wanted to work," he said sloppily. "In-shis . . . I
mean, insisted. And Prunia knew that Alvin was hiring. Cook
and . . . and a housekeeper, he wanted both. It was perfect for
them."

Huh. "What did they study in school?" I asked. Not, I was
guessing, cooking and housekeeping.

"Oh, college prep, both of them. Math, science . . ." He

waved a careless hand. "I don't know where they ever thought they'd use that stuff."

Right, he probably didn't. But I was betting they had.

I got out some wholemeal crackers and the Camembert that Bella had bought on sale at the IGA deli. Each year around now, when the summer people went home, you could eat like a Parisian until the fancy grub that had gotten stocked just for them ran out. Then the rest of us went back to Swiss and cheddar again.

"Try this," I said, setting a plate in front of him. I mean, what the heck? He was pleasantly sozzled, and there was no sense incapacitating the poor guy. He should eat something.

"So the girls didn't like the job you and Prunia found for them?" I asked.

He shook his head, chewing. "No. They thought they were too good for it, and they hated Alvin. So much so that to get out of it, they came up with a story about how he molested them."

He winced, remembering. "That he tried to corner them and kiss them, they said, or put his hands . . ." A red flush crept up his neck. He couldn't describe this part comfortably, I gathered, whether because he knew the girls' story was untrue . . . or because he knew it was true, I couldn't tell.

"Anyway, they left. The job *and* our house. Said they'd never come back. Went back to school in Bangor for their bachelor's degrees, they said." He made a face of disdain. "But you tell me, now, what's the use of that? The two of them living in an apartment, working as servers while they go to school . . . I tried persuading them, but . . ."

Harassing them, he meant. It's how no-contact orders get issued, and like I said, they don't get handed out easily.

"Anyway, I missed them," he said, "and when I couldn't talk to them, it was worse. So I put a few pictures of them up at the water-view house." Up on the bluff, where we'd just been, he meant. "And then a few more," he went on. "And I got in the habit of sitting there sometimes, looking at them and talking to them and . . ."

And before he knew it, he'd built himself a full-blown, no-kidding pathological obsession. I pictured him out there talking to a lot of photos, even doing the voices so they could talk back. . . .

Brr.

"If they'd just *listen* to me," he said, "if they'd just let me, I could make them *see* . . ."

Whether or not he'd been out murdering people lately, being made to see anything by Perry didn't sound like fun.

I touched my throat nervously, then got up. "Uh, Perry? Listen, I'm so glad we've had this little chat. But how about coming with me now?"

Because there was still that doctor's visit to attend to. As I may have mentioned, you don't fire a gun at your head—accurately or not so much—while I'm around and then get to skip the mandatory mental health checkup afterward.

Perry smiled owlishly at me, having had enough dandelion wine to make him agreeable without making him immovable. So I loaded him back into the car, drove to the clinic, and walked him inside without much difficulty.

Being there, though, was something else again. The busy waiting room was filled with coughing kids, crying infants, and right-to-the-end-of-their-very-last-nerve-looking moms, plus a few long-suffering elderly people.

Some patients were being ushered into the treatment rooms at one end of the room, and others into the dental clinic at the other end. I took one of the medical-unit nurses aside and explained what had happened, and she looked appropriately concerned.

"Call Prunia if you need any help," I told the nurse. "Or you can call me," I added reluctantly.

Perry gazed around, goggle-eyed; he'd had a lot of wine.

"Mr. Wilson?" said the nurse, inviting him to follow her, and after a moment he did.

Which left me there watching him vanish into the treatment area, and that's how I left him.

Half an hour later . . . "One more day, Mick. Please, you know how important it is to have . . ." I paused. "An attorney who eats nails for breakfast, broken glass for lunch, and prosecutors for dinner."

An attorney like him.

But . . . "Jake, I don't work for free, you know." Mick Flaherty's voice came patiently through the phone as I sat in the sun-splashed dining room of my old house, hoping the mid-afternoon brilliance streaming in might revive my brain.

"I mean, we had a deal," Mick said. "I defend this Breyer kid, who, by the way, have I mentioned lately that he couldn't look any more guilty if he wore a big sign around his neck that said 'Please convict me'?"

"I know." In the background of wherever Mick was right now, music was playing and ice clinked in what sounded like highball glasses.

"And, in return, you spill the beans on all that juicy stuff you've been keeping from me," Mick said. "The bad guys you worked for in the city, what they did and who they did it to."

Cut-crystal highball glasses, probably. Mick liked pricy bourbon. Meanwhile, I was having ginger ale with a shot of grape juice, served in a glass that had once held Smucker's.

"Those guys are all dead now, but they have offspring," I reminded him.

I already knew that Mick wanted his book to be stuffed full of previously untold stories, tales of the city's crime families and their deadly doings, of which there'd been plenty.

I, on the other hand, wanted to stay alive, with my house unincinerated and my own family un-terrorized, because remember those steel drums I told you about?

You can do a lot of things to those drums before they hit water, none of them pleasant.

"Mick. Please. There've been developments. Billy Breyer is going to get buried for this if you don't help."

Silence from Mick's end. Around me in the big old house, the sounds of cooking and laughing and crying and baby babbling went on, right along with the jangle of music coming out of the radio in the kitchen, making a joyful noise that I didn't want to have to put into the witness protection program.

"Okay," Mick gave in finally.

I let out a breath of relief. "Thank you, Mick. I—"

"I'll stay on it through the probable cause hearing, which, by the way, is happening today," he cut in. "And don't expect much to change on account of it. It just lets them keep on holding him in custody beyond these first forty-eight hours."

I didn't care about that, and I doubted Billy did, either. All I knew was that you don't go to a murder trial with anything but the highest-powered legal rifle you can find, because you get only one shot at it.

His tone changed. "Anyway, Jake, I'll do my best, you know that."

I did. It was why I wanted him.

"But my advice is that if you can do anything for this kid at your end, better do it fast. Once the actual trial machinery gets rolling . . ." His voice trailed off. "But once that happens, you'll have to find a way to pay me," was what he meant.

"I understand, Mick. Just another few days."

There was a communicative little ice clink from his glass while he noted the way I'd pushed my request from "one more day" to "a few." But then he relented. We went back a long way, Mick and me. "Okay, then, I'll get to work," he said and hung up.

Mika came in while I sat staring out the window afterward, watching the autumn sunshine dazzle through the yellow leaves of the maple trees in the backyard.

"Hello?" she ventured. As usual, she had the baby in the sling around her neck and little Ephraim attached to her apron by a chubby fist.

"Gammy!" He grinned through a mouthful of Weetabix, and I grinned back.

"I just wanted to tell you," Mika said, "I'll be here all afternoon, working on those cookies."

"Oh!" I got up. "Mika, you've got so much going on. If you don't want to . . ."

That cookie contest might've been insignificant in the big picture, but every year it got great publicity for the Chocolate Moose. And we *had* wanted to increase our large-order and catering business, which winning the contest would surely help.

So I still wanted us in the contest, but not if it meant more stress for Mika. "We can do it next year," I told her.

But in reply she shook her head, making that glossy, blunt-cut black hair of hers swing in the afternoon sunshine. "Oh, no you don't. I'm in it, and that's that." She didn't quite stomp her foot, but the effect was there. "And," she added, "we're going to win . . . I hope." A tinge of doubt softened her voice.

Darn. Ellie's original idea—to boost Mika's confidence by putting her in a position where she couldn't lose the cookie-baking contest—stood to backfire pretty spectacularly unless it turned out the way we'd planned. In that case it would've been better for us to stay out of it entirely, not try to influence things at all. Meanwhile:

"I've decided that mixing the chocolate into the batter won't work at all," Mika continued. "Not in any form."

"Yucky!" Ephraim agreed, waving the stuffed duck he was carrying. The baby crowed, grinning at it.

"I see," I said.

Upstairs, Bella ran the vacuum cleaner. Down here, in the parlor, my dad turned the TV on, cursed briefly and colorfully at the news, and turned the news off in favor of a YouTube video by a jazz guitarist he'd recently discovered named Stefan Joschi. Meanwhile, Wade was up in his workshop, cleaning a gun for a guy who was going to take it hunting when the season opened, and Sam was in the bathtub, singing loudly and tunelessly.

And happily. We all were. Despite our various troubles, for the moment, anyway, our general contentment floated through the big old house like the sweet smell of the fresh coffee burbling in Bella's percolator.

But then my phone rang.

"Perry's on the way to the hospital. Gunshot wound." It was Bob Arnold.

A fist of guilt punched me as I clutched the phone, and I heard myself babbling. "He must've had another gun . . . Oh, Bob, this is my fault. I should've stayed with him. I shouldn't have trusted that he'd be, I don't know, *prevented* somehow from—"

"Wait a minute. What're you talking about?" Bob sounded as if he'd had enough of this day already, and I knew how he felt.

"That Perry shot himself," I said. "He tried again, and I could have—"

"What? No. Jake, no, he didn't," said Bob.

"Could have what?" Bella wanted to know as she came into the dining room with a load of clean laundry in her arms.

"Jake," Bob repeated into the phone, "Perry didn't shoot himself. Somebody shot him."

By the time I got to Cape Street, the emergency vehicles were all gone and only Bob's squad car still stood in front of Perry

Wilson's house. From the front walk, Bob saw me drive up, but when I got out of the car and approached him, he waved me away from the conversation he was having on his phone.

"Prunia," he mouthed to me as he listened, rolling his eyes.

Her voice carried tinnily from the phone. "Get him some things he'll need," she was saying agitatedly.

A weight lifted off my heart. It sounded as if Perry might not be dead.

"Prunia, we don't know what he'll need," Bob responded, "or if he'll even . . ."

Survive. He didn't say it, but the word hung silently in the air, and the weight of guilt lowered painfully down onto me again.

I should have kept Perry at our house. I should have, I thought.

"I don't care," Prunia said stubbornly. "I'm going up there to that hospital, and when I do, I want to bring along his . . ."

She wanted to get into Perry's house, was what she wanted. Pondering this, I eased back toward an overgrown barberry hedge thickly speckled with bright red berries that ran along one side of Perry's yard.

Perry, after all, was not here. And neither was Prunia, or anyone else who might stop me. So . . .

The cemetery bounded the other side of the yard, and I doubted that anyone was watching me from there. I waited until Bob moved a bit farther away, then made my move along the hedge, through tangled forsythia bushes, to Perry's back deck and up onto it.

Glancing around nervously, I tried to look as if maybe I was selling something or canvassing for a political candidate. The difference was, I didn't knock, just turned the knob.

The door opened. I stepped inside and closed it behind me. A pang of guilt skewered me as I smelled the snack Perry must've been cooking for himself and expecting to enjoy. Pork and beans out of a can, I found when I reached the kitchen. Toast, already buttered, sat ready on a plate on the counter, with a fork lined up beside it. The beans, though, were burnt on the bottom of the saucepan.

The burner was turned off. It puzzled me until I realized that Bob or one of his deputies must already have been in here.

I backed out into the dim linoleum-floored hallway, where a wooden coat-tree, a cat's cleanly maintained sandbox, and a hook with what looked like a house key on it were the only features.

The cat streaked past me as I eased down the hall. It was a yellow tom with a jingle bell on its collar.

"Scat," I whispered, but it was already gone by the time I peeked into the dining room, where floral curtains and a massive corner hutch loaded with Hummel figurines made it look as if Perry's mother might still live here, at least in spirit.

The living room held the standard couch-and-two-recliners combo, plus a coffee table and a TV. Parting the front window's heavy draperies a millimeter, I saw Bob Arnold still talking on his cell phone while he walked toward his car.

My own car was still out there, too, so he'd know I was around here somewhere, and he'd be wondering where I'd gotten to. So I'd better hurry. As I made my way to the bedrooms the yellow cat came back and kept twining around my ankles.

One of the upstairs rooms held twin beds, two chests of drawers, and a dressing table with a three-panel mirror. The girls' room, I gathered.

The other bedroom was empty, and by that, I mean bare to the walls. Faded squares showed where pictures had been taken down; a pale area on the hardwood floor outlined where a rug had been. The closet stood open and empty except for a few vacant hangers. Drawn shades at the windows made the room look all right from the outside. But inside . . .

An unpleasant chill went through me. Someone had gone to a lot of trouble removing every trace of whoever had once slept in here. From Perry's revelations that morning, I guessed it must have been his parents' room.

The bath was as neat and clean as I expected from a guy like Perry; one thing I didn't suspect him of having was germs.

But there must be something to find in this house. Why else would Prunia want to get in so badly?

My step quickened. Perry's room, militarily neat. A linen closet, likewise. Finally, I looked into the last room at the end of the hall.

And got a surprise. Perry had said he had a printer, but this room was a fully equipped small-business office: desk, chair, lamp, laptop. A modem blinked behind the computer, and a ream of paper sat neatly beside the printer.

When I opened the laptop, its screen sprang to life, but it was password protected. I ducked to peer under the desk; that's where I kept my passwords, on sticky notes.

Just as I did so, I glimpsed movement outside the room's small window. It was Bob Arnold's head going by. He glanced in as he passed, but didn't see me poised frozenly and moved on.

I relaxed. But no luck under the desk. Cudgeling my brain for the names of Perry's sisters, I came up with them finally and tried the first one.

Jill . . . no luck. *Hilary* didn't work, either. But then . . . a wild guess. *Jilary*. Bingo. The laptop's screen opened to the project that Perry had been working on most recently.

"Oh, my . . . ," I heard myself exhale wonderingly, because displayed on the screen was one of those online legal forms that you can use if you want to try being your own lawyer. To make, for instance, your own perfectly legal last will and testament. This looked to me just like the other two that Alvin Carter had made before his death.

Clifton Ferrier had said he'd forged the witnesses' signatures, so I had to assume that at least some of Alvin's wills were invalid legally.

But if no one knew that, then the one with the most recent date on it would be accepted as legitimate by a probate court. And whoever was named in it would inherit Alvin's estate, which could end up being sizable.

So maybe Perry had thought he could lure his sisters back home if only he had a fortune to use as bait? I hadn't quite worked out the details of how he'd do it yet, but it was a better motive for murder than many I'd heard of.

Help commit a crime, get paid, perhaps handsomely, and—

"Jake, dammit, are you in here?" I jumped at the sound of Bob's voice and his heavy footsteps stomping down the hall.

"Yeah, I'm here." I closed the laptop quickly, stepped away from the desk. "Sorry, Bob, I couldn't help but . . ."

Snoop.

"Yeah, yeah. Come on, now. Get out of there." His arm made a sweeping motion as I exited the little office. "I swear, Jake, one of these days I'm going to . . ."

Drat, I thought. If there was more to find, I'd missed my chance by standing around woolgathering, as Bella would've said.

As I clattered down the stairs and hurried ahead of him toward the back door, I looked hard all around, but I didn't spy anything else that was interesting.

The cat meowed from the back hall. A full water bowl was in the kitchen, along with a supply of kibble, so I felt safe in leaving the animal here for now.

I mean, until I knew if Perry had survived getting shot. As I wondered about this again, Bob slammed the back door behind us.

"Bob, why did they even let Perry out of the clinic? Didn't they know he'd just tried to harm himself?"

"Yeah, well, that's not what he told them," Bob replied. "I've already talked to them. He said it was a joke, that you guys took him seriously, but he never intended to—" He stopped. "And on top of all that, he told them that he didn't know the gun was loaded," Bob said.

"None of which is true."

"Right, but they didn't know that, and, anyway, what were they supposed to do? Hog-tie him?"

"Yeah, no. And not that it would've done any good."

"Correct. Somebody could've found him at the clinic just as well as they did here."

His phone pinged. He looked down at it, turned, and slogged away from me across Perry's backyard. The scowl on his face told me something had happened, and I followed him for two reasons.

One, I wanted to know *what* had happened. And two . . . "Wait a minute, Bob. Don't you want to know what I found in Perry's—"

"No." He got in his car, gunned it to life.

I ran up to the open driver's-side window, leaned inside. "Bob, darn it, what's so urgent that you can't—"

He tossed his phone onto the car seat. "When Perry left here, he was conscious and looked like he might have a chance."

"Oh, no," I breathed as a bad suspicion struck me.

"Yep. Just now at the hospital, somebody took another shot at him. Hit him, too. I don't know yet how bad."

A minute ago, I'd had Perry pegged as the prime suspect in this little fiasco; the printer and the online wills had convinced me. The specific details of how he'd framed Billy Breyer didn't matter, only that he'd managed it, and his getting shot merely meant he'd had an accomplice.

Now, though . . .

"Jake," said Bob, "get your elbows out of my car window." *Or they'll get torn off when I hit the gas*, his look added.

So I did, and then he did, roaring away past the neighbors, who were still watching from their front porches.

As he went by, though, something else had already begun to make them look around uneasily as they frowned and sniffed.

Then I noticed it, too, the smell faint but identifiable.

Smoke.

Twelve

"Okay, Bella, take this," I said, pressing a pistol into her hands.

It was only a starter pistol, the kind they fire off at track meets to get the runners going. On my way home I'd stopped at the high school gym to borrow it, saying while crossing my fingers behind my back that Bob Arnold had sent me for it.

So, not lethal, but if you fired it off near me, it would certainly get me going, and that's what I hoped it would do to someone else if she needed it up at the hospital.

"All right," she said, accepting it, and listened carefully when I told her what I needed her to do at the hospital where Perry Wilson was.

"Say you're his aunt, he's your only living relative, that you absolutely must be with him," I told her.

Because someone had to guard him, obviously, and ordinarily, that somebody would wear a uniform and carry a service weapon. But between the time I'd left Perry's house and reached mine on the other side of Eastport just minutes later, every siren in the world had begun to howl.

Then the fire trucks took off, their own sirens wailing out a harmonizing note of distress, and all the ambulances and squad cars followed. A new fire burned somewhere nearby, I gathered.

Meanwhile, Wade was out on a tugboat, Sam was no doubt on one of the volunteer fire trucks already, and Mika was at the Moose, while my dad and the kids attended library story hour.

So Bella was all I had. I thought a moment while she pulled on a jacket.

"Tell them you promised his mother on her deathbed that if Perry was ever sick or hurt, you'd be there for him," I said.

Our regional hospital's nurses were sticklers for visiting rules at the best of times, and the more so, I expected, when somebody was shot. But that story I'd given Bella oughta get 'em right in the heartstrings, I thought.

"You probably won't even need the gun," I said. "Unless . . ."

"Unless whoever tried to hurt Perry Wilson before decides to try it again," Bella finished grimly, and she was right. It was unlikely, but it was possible.

Nevertheless, her big green eyes were clear and steady, and so was her hand as she tucked the weapon determinedly into her sweater pocket.

"I'd better go right away," she added, "or I might not be able to get across the causeway."

If the fire burned too near it, she meant. That was the direction the smoke seemed to be coming from, anyway, and the air was getting thick with it.

"Right. Take my car," I said, glancing outside nervously.

It would leave me carless, while Ellie's was just a cinder, but that couldn't be helped. Bella strode out of the house, her spine straight and her attitude dead serious. Maybe she was an old lady, her look said, but anyone trying to take advantage of that fact would get a surprise.

Once she'd gone, I called Ellie and brought her up to date on the printer I'd found at Perry's house and the interesting documents he'd been printing on it. Oh, and that he'd been shot, of course.

"And now with this new fire burning—" I began, but Ellie interrupted me.

"I just heard about it over the scanner. If they don't get a handle on it, they'll be closing the causeway soon, and then only fire trucks and so on can get through."

So Bella might not be able to. My heart sank. "Yeah, okay. So, listen, Ellie, how about if you go down and close the shop? Send Mika to the library with the kids and my dad." If there turned out to be evacuations, they'd be taken to safety, along with the kids. "And then—" I began.

But Ellie didn't need to hear more; what I'd said already was plenty. "Right, see you in five," she said and hung up.

Not much later Ellie and I were in the old vehicle Sam had been working on out in the driveway. It was a 1949 pickup truck with three on the floor, a bunged-up exhaust system, and barely any brakes. No inspection sticker, either, and no registration, which meant no plates. But it ran, and that was all I cared about at the moment.

Ellie felt around for a seat belt as we pulled out of the driveway, and then, to her surprise, she found one.

"Yeah, he has Mika riding with him sometimes," I explained the presence of the safety equipment. "If there'd been a way to put in airbags, he'd have done that, too," I added. He adored that girl, and considering who his dad had been, I thought that his devotion to her represented a huge triumph of nurture over nature.

Meanwhile, every volunteer vehicle in town—you could tell who they were by the flashing blue dashboard beacons—zoomed by as we made our way out Route 190 toward where smoke billowed.

Some of it was white, showing where water had already hit

flames and turned to steam. But a lot of it was black, evil-looking stuff, especially in areas where dry brush and old trees still burned merrily where they'd fallen.

"Ellie, is that black smoke doing what I think it is?"

"Yup. Spreading," she confirmed unhappily.

Ahead of us lay Pleasant Point, and Eastport was behind us. In the opposite lane from us, a few cars that had already been turned back at the causeway went by, the drivers looking alarmed or disgruntled or both.

Another volunteer firefighter roared up behind me. I touched the brakes, meaning to pull over for him, but the brakes on the vintage pickup truck had other ideas. The left one engaged. The right one didn't. As a result, the truck veered sharply into the opposite lane, directly into the path of yet another pickup, this one sporting a ram's-head hood ornament and having lots more pulling power than we had. Or, more to the point, pushing power, since that's what it was about to do to me and Ellie: push us.

"Yeeks," she said, bracing herself.

"Likewise, I'm sure," I replied as our left brake began smoking while the right one stayed stubbornly uninvolved.

But then suddenly it did grab hold, and this produced a whole new series of unpleasant maneuvers by the truck, which couldn't seem to decide if it wanted to land nose down in the ditch or in the bed of the opposing vehicle.

I gazed through the big pickup's tinted windshield and saw that its driver looked ready to jump out. I could only assume that his fingers were clamped around the steering wheel. Mine certainly were.

But then under my hands the wheel began straightening. Our vehicle's tires rolled back over to their own side of the road, seemingly on their own, while the other truck roared past with its horn blaring, like something out of a disaster movie.

And then it was over as fast as it had begun. Once both

brakes were working again, the steering straightened, and that was that.

But I still felt like I might throw up. All at once the idea of driving Sam's truck didn't seem so smart anymore, and I wondered what other deadly curveballs the old vehicle might try to pitch at us before the trip was done.

We'd reached the turn I wanted, though, so I took it.

Ellie sat up straight, frowning as she looked around. "Why're we going here?"

We were headed uphill toward the same small gravel turnaround that we'd parked in before, where the path through the woods to Alvin's house began. In daylight, the pretty country lane meandered through old pastures bounded by leaning fence posts with rusted barbed wire clinging to them. A sign listing the park rules sported so many bullet holes, you could've drained spaghetti with it.

I pulled over onto the gravel, and the old truck juddered to a stop. "Okay, think about this," I said, turning to Ellie.

The smoke here was gauze thin, drifting in wisps, but its smell was sharp, even though the vehicle's windows were closed.

I held up one finger. "First, Alvin goes on a will-making kick. He uses the promise of money to manipulate people, make them do what he wants. Or tries, anyway."

"Okay." Ellie watched monarch butterflies flutter prettily among the burst-open milkweed pods growing in the field nearby. But she was nodding. "Probably Mary Sipp was one of the first ones he tried it on, then. And after that maybe Perry? Or even his sisters, to get them to put up with . . ."

"Maybe. His early efforts couldn't have been too rewarding, though, because Mary Sipp wasn't a sucker for that kind of thing, and Perry already disliked Alvin too much to trust him, probably because Alvin really did make passes at Perry's sisters."

We got out of the truck. Sirens howled only a mile or so in

the distance as the wind shifted and smoke began blowing at us from the west.

"But it's not important who was first," I went on, "since in this situation, it's what comes last that counts. The date on the will is what makes it the valid one."

"Oh," Ellie said and went on nodding thoughtfully as we made our way to the forest path and then into the woods.

The *dark* woods. Towering pines, spruces, and tamaracks rose all around us, their needled branches blocking the sky.

"So let's say someone knew that," said Ellie, trudging beside me. Underfoot, the gravel thinned until the path was only pale dust snaking between parched-looking cinnamon ferns. "That Alvin was a little nuts on the subject of his own will, I mean," she added.

I was about to agree, but I tripped over an exposed tree root instead and pitched forward onto the path. This wouldn't have been so bad if when I landed, my forehead hadn't connected very forcefully with *another* tree root, this one as hard as granite.

Correction: it *was* granite, just root shaped. I pushed up onto my knees, watching the little drops of red blood plop onto the spot where I'd just nearly brained myself.

Ellie crouched beside me. "You all right?"

I touched my forehead. My fingers came away red. "Yeah, except for the hundred thousand brain cells I just killed."

Suddenly the woods around us felt darker and more silent than before. Smokier, too.

"Hey, let's get going." I made my feet move forward on the path: one-two, one-two.

Ouch-ouch. My head wasn't the only part of me that had hit the ground hard. But the smoke smell was getting stronger by the minute. Getting into Alvin's house was important, but getting out again afterward was starting to feel crucial, as well.

Crucial, and not exactly a sure thing, I thought. And by the time we'd made our way through the ankle-threatening tree roots, glistening poison-ivy patches, thickets of brambles whose thorns were as sharp as snake fangs, and the many other natural features with which this forested area was so well furnished, the idea that we might be in some sort of peril sank in even more.

We were twenty yards from Alvin's house now, but between us and it, pale flakes drifted down from the sky onto his lawn.

I caught one and tasted it. "Ash." It was floating on the breeze out of the west, from the fire nearby.

Ellie sighed, staring downhill at the house, which was just as unpainted, unkempt, and generally decrepit as the last time I'd been here.

It crossed my mind to wonder why Alvin hadn't taken better care of the place. On the other hand, maybe the work Sam and Billy had been doing was the first step in a plan of some kind?

But either way, Alvin's neglected maintenance schedule was the least of my worries right now. Much more striking to me was the way the smoke wasn't just wispy anymore. Thick gray fingers of it seemed to reach greedily out of the woods behind us as the smoke flooded between the trees.

"Okay, explain it to me," said Ellie, catching sight of the smoke.

Persuade her, she meant, not to beat it right out of here, instead of pursuing whatever harebrained plan I'd come up with, *which* I hadn't yet told her about, either.

We started across the lawn. "Okay. Think of it like a game of musical chairs. Sooner or later there'll be only one chair left," I told her.

We reached the back porch and climbed onto it. An unhappy memory of being under the porch, face-to-face with yet another dead body, assailed me briefly.

"But in *this* game," I went on, shoving the thought aside, "you *want* to be the last one standing."

That old corpse would get explained or it wouldn't, I'd decided, but I wasn't going to waste any more time worrying about it. For one thing, it just didn't seem *connected* to the rest of what was going on—no vanished or missing persons in anyone's past, no never-again-heard-from runaways or whatever—and for another . . .

Well, for another, I just couldn't figure it out, that's all; and meanwhile, somebody had fastened a padlock to the kitchen door since the last time we'd been here. The window I'd gotten us in through before was locked, too, via some tacked-in angle irons, which I wouldn't be able to remove without a claw hammer.

And, of course, I hadn't brought along a claw hammer.

"How about we check in Alvin's toolshed?" Ellie suggested sensibly.

But by that time I'd already wrapped my jacket around my hand and punched through a pane, a maneuver that turned out to be surprisingly difficult and not like in the movies at all.

Still, it worked, and what the heck, by the look of that smoke, the place was probably going to burn, anyway. I punched out the rest of the panes, clambered in, then helped Ellie climb through, as well.

Inside, she brushed glass bits off herself. "By 'last one standing,' you mean . . ."

"I mean if I'm right about what I'm thinking probably happened, we're going to find another of Alvin's wills somewhere in this house. Or it's supposed to be one, anyway . . ."

We hurried along the hall, where the wallpaper already seemed dingier and more out of style, the ceiling's plaster more mottled with patches of damp.

"You mean hidden somewhere?" Ellie wanted to know as we climbed the stairs.

"No. Out where it can be seen easily. But the point's not where, Ellie. It's when."

We'd reached the door to the third floor, but just as I was

about to poke my head through, a loud thud came from somewhere below us, followed by the tinkle of glass.

Well, my heart just about hopped right out of my chest and hotfooted it down the stairs.

But not Ellie's. "The window fell, is all. That we crawled through. We left the other sash pushed up, and it must've . . ."

"Oh." She was right. My heart crept back in between my ribs, where it belonged, and settled there.

"Anyway, whichever will the court decides that Alvin made last is the legitimate one, the one that'll get probated, and its named heir will inherit Alvin's estate," I said.

Alvin's third-floor office looked just the way we'd left it.

"Oh, I get it now," said Ellie. "Like when George's aunt died, they found two wills in her house. And you're right. The most recent will—the one with the most recent date on it, I mean—was the one the probate court went by."

"So," I said. "What if you wanted to fake one? You get to decide what date's on it. When would it be?"

"Why, just before the person's death, of course," said Ellie, looking out the high window.

"Correct. And you'd know when that was because . . . ?"

She frowned suddenly, turning back to me. "Because you'd killed them. So what works best for you would be first, you kill the person and *then* you put the will where it'll be found."

"Exactly. And as for Alvin's will, you'd expect to find it in his . . ."

She was already nodding. "In his desk. So that's why we're here. Because someone did this. Which means . . ."

I nodded, pleased. "Correct. If there is a will in this center drawer, whoever's named in it as Alvin Carter's heir is the one who killed him."

Which was a big if, actually. We'd already been through these drawers, so if a will was here it would have to have been put here recently. Suddenly, I felt extremely nervous about opening the drawer. Ellie glanced out again and looked as worried as I felt.

"Well, then, if it's there, you'd better find it and grab it quick," she said, "because I'd say we've got maybe five more minutes to get out of here. Because there's a fire, remember?"

"Huh?" I slid the desk drawer open slowly.

"Jake," Ellie said gently, "everything's burning out there. We're about to be crispy critters."

I followed her gaze. Outside, the air looked grimy with smoke, and a few bright, fluttery embers sailed terrifyingly in it, as if the fire must be rather nearby.

And this inspired me more than somewhat to hurry the heck up. The thing was either there or not. So I yanked the drawer open the rest of the way and shoved my hand to the back of it. Whereupon a thumbtack that had been lurking back there pierced my thumb.

Yowtch. But then . . . *Got it* . . . I pulled the object I'd finally located from the back of the desk drawer. As I'd expected, it was an envelope, one that hadn't been there the last time I'd looked. Which meant someone had put it there recently, and now all I had to do was open the envelope to find out whose name was on the papers inside it.

But before I had a chance to fold the envelope flap back and find out who dun it, something smacked the window glass hard. I whirled as Ellie put a finger on the pane. From the tiny feather stuck to it, I guessed it had been a bird.

Ellie touched my shoulder, then pointed. Behind the park's tall trees, smoke rose in columns. "It's scaring the birds out," she said.

It was scaring me, too. Time to go. I looked down at the envelope in my hand, sorely tempted.

Another bird hit the glass. We could open the envelope later, I decided.

"So you think Perry printed the fake will and Clifton filled in all the signatures, including Alvin's?" Ellie asked as we gathered ourselves to go.

The smoke looked like fog drifting. I stared another moment in wonder at it.

With, unfortunately, my back to the door of Alvin's office. But suddenly . . .

"Hello, ladies," said a voice from behind me.

A *familiar* voice.

But not, unfortunately, a friendly one.

He was still big, still bald, and still dressed in a blue plaid shirt and faded jeans with red suspenders.

But this time he had a gun, and it was aimed at us.

"Clifton," I said, and he nodded curtly, not nearly as pleasant as he'd seemed a few days ago, when we'd chatted while standing in his junkyard, as Ellie loaded the compressor part we'd bought from him into her car.

He had notarized Alvin's wills, the legitimate ones *and* the fake. I held up the one I'd found, now smeared with a bloody thumbprint thanks to the tack that had been in the drawer.

"You came to get this?" I asked.

It made sense. He had been here in town already—at the dentist's office inside the clinic, I realized belatedly now, where he'd seen Perry with me at the medical unit in the very same building and thought it was time to eliminate his no-longer-needed accomplice. And he had seen the fire threatening Alvin's house.

So he'd come to rescue the will he'd planted here, meaning to put it somewhere else later—among the burnt ruins of the house, maybe—since, after all, it couldn't do him any good if it was all burnt up.

Speaking of which, a faint orange glow now showed in the

fog above the treetops at the back of the house. It looked much more ominous than before, more *immediate*. And I could see from Ellie's pale, anxious face that she thought the same.

"So, Clifton," I said, trying for a casual tone, "what do you say we all just head on downstairs and talk this whole thing—"

"Nope." He raised the gun he was holding just enough to stop me in my tracks. "But don't worry," he added, glancing out at the ash bits flying past the window. "I won't let you suffer."

And you can call me crazy, but I found this just immensely unreassuring. First of all, I thought there might be a whole lot of suffering, oodles of it, in fact, in store, but more than that, I was concerned about when the suffering ended. Like, *why* it ended, and so on and so forth, as Bella would've said.

Ellie's gaze kept darting toward the doorway, but Clifton filled it completely; no way could we shove past his bulk even if he didn't shoot us first.

"Now, give me that," he said, reaching out with his other hand. When he moved, it was like an enormous boulder rolling.

Some of the big pieces of ash flying by the window glowed red. I imagined some entering through the downstairs window that we'd broken.

Flying and settling on things, *flammable* things . . .

"Oh, come on," he said when I refused to hand him the envelope. "You know sooner or later you're going to have to—"

In spite of all the sparks, though, my habit of really not liking to be told what I'll have to do shone through.

"Oh, yeah?" I sneered. "Who's gonna make me? You? *Pfft.*"

And I guess my fearless tone—not really, as I was quaking inside—must've surprised him enough that he didn't notice my arm coming up fast, my clenched fist still clutching the will now swinging back at the window behind me.

If Clifton got the document and then killed us and left us

here, he'd likely get away with the whole thing: the murder, the money, all of it.

So I tightened my fist, kept my wrist cocked inward so my arteries didn't get severed, and smashed my knuckles as hard as I could against the windowpane, the way I had downstairs. Whereupon the whole old, rickety window fell backward out of its frame, and the will went with it.

Fluttering whitely away in the thick, dark smoke . . .

"Jake?" Ellie said worriedly as the smoke billowed in, stinging and choking.

Panic stabbed me as smoke made my eyes stream, the tears hot and acrid tasting on my face. But it meant Clifton couldn't see, either, didn't it?

I flailed blindly about before I found Ellie's hand and gripped it and pulled her along as I crept toward where I hoped the door was. Clifton had been standing directly in the doorway a minute ago, but soon he'd be coming into the room to find us.

If we took it slow and quiet—and we were lucky—we could probably slip past him. But I could feel Ellie struggling not to cough, and I personally was trying very hard not to suffocate.

So, as you walked into the room, Alvin's big desk was directly in front of you. That meant the question was whether Clifton would go around it to the left or to the right.

And what the heck, I decided to split the difference. While still gripping Ellie's hand, I scrambled straight up onto the desk and over it, then out the door and down the stairs lickety-split, with Ellie clattering down right behind me.

By the time we got halfway down the first flight of stairs, though, he had figured it out and was thundering down the stairs, too. His size didn't hurt his speed, either; he was gaining on us.

Hurry, hurry . . . In the first-floor hall I shoved Ellie into a coat closet under the stairs, slipped in after her fast, and got the door closed just as heavy footsteps thumped angrily by.

"He must be rushing outside to try to find it," I said under my breath to Ellie. The document I'd flung out the window, I meant. With any luck, by now it had found one of those flaming embers and burned itself to a—

Hey, wait a minute. That wasn't right. That wasn't right at all, I realized suddenly. Releasing that document out into the smoky evening—somehow the rest of the afternoon had gone by, and now evening approached—had been a bonehead move.

Well, except for the part about distracting Clifton, which might just have saved our lives. But . . .

"Ellie!"

I felt above me for the hanging light-switch string that is found in every hallway coat closet in an old house, located it in the mothball-smelling dark, and pulled it. A light bulb went on. Ellie sat on a small bench under the closet's slanted ceiling, bent over and coughing.

"Ellie, we've got to—"

A roar of angry frustration came from somewhere outside the house as Clifton tried and failed to find what he was looking for.

"Okay." Ellie put her hand out, still coughing. "But what's the hurry? He's already—"

"Out," she'd have finished, but the point now was that we weren't. I wasn't 100 percent sure that I could hear fire crackling nearby, but I didn't very much like imagining that I could, either.

And not only that . . . "Ellie, if Clifton finds that will and destroys it, then he can just deny all this." I took a breath. "He can say he never faked a will naming himself as Alvin's beneficiary, never killed Alvin so he could plant the will and eventually get it put into effect . . . He can say he was never here at all, and that we're lying if we say he was."

"You're right . . . especially if Perry doesn't survive or doesn't *know* who shot him," Ellie agreed. "Then Clifton can just wash his hands of all this, can't he?" She was getting her wind back.

"Yup."

So now we had to find the darned thing again, so we could prove what we said . . . that is, if it even still existed, if it hadn't already been burned to ash.

We crept from the closet and made our way cautiously toward the kitchen. Like the rest of the house, it was evening shadowy in here now, but the stairway we'd descended was acting like a chimney, sucking smoke straight on up the stairs.

So we could breathe, sort of. And there was enough light to see a pile of clean dishcloths still stacked on the counter.

"Where'd that cat get to, do you suppose?" Ellie wondered aloud while I soaked the towels with water at the sink, then wrung them out.

"Outside, maybe. Here. Take some of these wet cloths. We might need them to breathe through when we get out there, too."

If we got out there. I could see flames through the kitchen window, stalled momentarily by the green lawn. But they wouldn't be stalled for long; that smoke still had embers in it, and they looked a lot bigger now, not just glowing but actively burning.

The missing cat peeked from behind the stove. "*There* you are," said Ellie.

A cloth shopping bag hung on a hook by the door. Ellie snatched it, then grabbed the poor cat by the nape of its neck and pulled. Twisting and squirming, yowling and clawing, into the bag the annoyed cat went, and then Ellie cinched the drawstrings.

"Nice work," I commented, not mentioning the blood now running freely down both her arms. We had more pressing worries.

"Clifton might still be out there," I warned as we hurried to the parlor, where we'd come in.

As Ellie had thought, the upper window sash had fallen. Its glass, scattered across the floor, crunched as we walked over it. I gave the remaining frame a hard yank with both hands, whereupon the whole structure fell to bits. I tossed the pieces aside. It was all going to be firewood in here soon, anyway.

"After you," I said, gesturing at the empty window hole, but Ellie hesitated.

"How come smoke's not pouring in anymore?" she wanted to know.

"Wind must've shifted," I said and stuck my head out.

And discovered just how unhappily correct I was. It had shifted, all right, so much so that now the small firebreak that the damp green grass had afforded was made irrelevant. The fire marched from an entirely new direction now, through the orchard straight toward us.

As I watched in horror, one gnarly old apple tree after another went up, torch-like. The fruit sizzled and popped, and the smell of apple crisp came drifting sweetly.

"Ellie," I said, scared to the bone suddenly. "Jump out this damned window hole, get clear of the house, and run down the driveway."

I glanced at the orchard again; more of it was blazing now than just a minute ago.

Ellie didn't move. "Do it now, Ellie," I said. "Don't stop to look back. I'll be right behind you."

Now the fire was much hotter and brighter, and the smoke smelled like applewood chips had been tossed onto a hot barbecue grill's glowing coals.

"Go!" I said again, and Ellie obeyed. Clearly, I had to get out of here now. Just not until after I'd checked out one last, unlikely hunch . . .

The parlor behind me was a smoky shambles. All the lamps

were blown over, the pictures were askew, and the scarf from the piano now dangled forlornly from the chandelier, blown up there by a hot gust.

Amidst the wreckage, I tossed pillows and swept curtains aside. That broken window's crash had happened *before* I had tossed the will out of the attic. . . . And it was before the wind had changed, too. Which meant that when the document fell to the level of these windows, it could have blown right back in here. . . .

Probably not, but I had to make sure. Right now it was the only evidence we had that Clifton had faked a document to make himself Alvin Carter's heir. It didn't prove he'd also killed Alvin, of course, but it gave him a great motive, and that meant that at least Billy Breyer wasn't the only suspect anymore.

Now, if I could just *find* the thing, assuming it was here at all. . . .

A soft tap-tapping, like sleet softly hitting a window, came from the other side of the house. Embers, I guessed unhappily, and not long after an ominous crackling started in the kitchen.

Which I was pretty sure meant the house was on fire . . . I gazed around wildly. *Damn it, where would I be if I were a fake will written for profit by a sly, murderous . . .*

There. Peeking out of a basket by the fireplace was a page of something. I snatched it, felt the rest of the pages come with the first one. It was the same will that I'd tossed out the attic window. I knew by the bloody thumbprint on it.

Oh, good for me, I thought, pleased that something had managed to work out right for a change.

Then I spun around suddenly and dove in the direction of the window hole as a cloud of orange flame billowed hugely and without warning down the hallway and into the parlor.

Yikes . . . The heat was astonishing, like that of a blowtorch aimed straight at me. The hairs on my arms prickled, and the inside of my nose didn't feel so good, either.

And now, on account of the sudden smoke, I couldn't find the window. . . . Fumbling and stumbling, I staggered blindly into a low footstool, then lurched headlong into the piano. Or something. Whatever it was, it was hard, and it hit me in the middle of my forehead and punched my nose, bloodying it. But I would find that window, damn it. I *would*—

"Jake!" Ellie's voice. "Are you still in there?"

I wanted to answer, but all I could do was cough.

"Jake!" She sounded desperate.

"Yeah," I yelled, but no sound came out. I was trying, but I couldn't breathe, so I couldn't answer.

And something was holding me down, too, so I couldn't move.

A trickle of panic iced my insides. This was bad. Suddenly, much faster than I'd realized, the thick, dark night filling my head meant that I was out of oxygen, and out of time.

A burst of sorrow filled me—*too late!*—and then a hand grabbed me. Something large and heavy was hauled off me. *Ouch.*

Then Ellie yanked me up, flung one arm over my shoulder and another around my waist, and dragged me over to where the window had been. I stuck my head out, gasped in the night air, and a well-aimed shove at my rear end had me tumbling the rest of the way out. After landing hard on the porch, I rolled, then struggled to my feet.

Ellie's shape showed in the window opening; behind her the flames leapt orange and yellow. I grabbed her hands, they came out through the opening, and the rest of her followed.

"Oof," she said, clambering to her feet, and then we took off down the gravel driveway together.

"Which is where I *said* you should go," I grumbled at her as we ran. " '*Away from the fire,*' I said, but did you go that way?"

"If I'd followed *your* instructions, right now *you'd* be . . ."

Yeah. Toast.

"Besides," she added, "when have you ever known me to follow any of your—"

Also yeah.

I kept glancing around as I ran, but saw no one. Finally, we reached the end of the long driveway, where it met the road. There was still no sign of the murderous Clifton Ferrier, last-will-and-testament forger and hatchet man par excellence.

But unless he'd simply fled—which he couldn't, could he? He had to get rid of us, or we'd be able to reveal his crimes—he was out here somewhere. And there were still lots of unburned trees and brush all around us, perfect for him to hide in. And ambush us from.

"We need to get off this road," I said.

If Clifton spotted us here, it might be the last time that anyone saw us. Meanwhile, I felt like a bagful of bones that had been run over two or three times by a steamroller, and Ellie was still bleeding down both arms from all the cat scratches.

Which reminded me. "Where . . . ?"

She pointed at her tote.

My mouth fell open. "You've been carrying it all along?"

I'd thought once she got the cat out of the house, she would let it loose. But never mind. Ahead of us the road stretched bleakly back toward town in the dark.

I felt like a duck in a shooting gallery. "Let's get over into the bushes."

But before we could do it, a car appeared, its headlights coming toward us through the thickening smoke.

Or no, a *truck* . . .

"Get ready to run," I said.

Because I could think of no reason why anyone would be here right now. But . . .

"Jake, it's not him," Ellie murmured.

It was Mary Sipp's big, shiny green pickup truck, the one I'd seen outside Alvin's house the day of his murder and in her own yard later. But Mary wasn't driving it. Instead, her son

Devon was at the wheel. When he'd reached us, he leaned out at us, wincing at the thickening smoke.

"Geez, what're you two doing out here?"

Relief washed over me; a ride out would vastly decrease our chances of getting turned into toast.

"Ma left some stuff of hers in the house. I was in Eastport when she called me about the fire," he said. "So I figured I'd see if I could rescue anything for her." He thought a moment. "Is the cat in the house still?"

I approached the truck, still clutching the fake will I'd rescued from Alvin's house in my right hand. "Yeah, we have . . ."

Ellie stayed back. She always was the smart one of us. But I'd gotten all the way up to within a few feet of the vehicle when the driver's-side door flew open and Devon jumped out.

After crossing to me in a couple of swift strides, he slung his arm around my neck. Also, suddenly he had a knife in his other hand. A big one, with a fat wooden handle and a blade edge so sharp, it seemed to be throwing off tiny sparks.

He dragged me to the truck and into it, shoving me ahead of him across the newly upholstered bench seat. "Tell her to get in here, too," he grated into my ear. And when I didn't . . . "This is a hunting knife," he growled. "I can slice through a deer's spine with it, and it'll cut through yours, too. So . . ." He jerked his arm tighter around my neck. "Tell her."

But I didn't have to. Grimly, she crossed in front of the jacked-up green pickup truck and climbed into the cab, shooting him a truly murderous look as she did so and still lugging the bagful of cat that she'd been carrying.

Now, as she put the bag on the floor, yellow flames began shooting out from between the trees lining the road. The very *flammable* trees, evergreens, whose pitchy sap would make them blaze up like torches . . .

Devon caught on to the approaching peril and, without hesitation or pause, slammed the truck into gear. After reversing wildly into Alvin's driveway, he peeled out, with the tires spitting gravel, and careened forward again, toward the main road and town.

At the corner the truck skidded to a halt just long enough to be sure a fire truck wasn't barreling toward us, then burned rubber again to make the turn. But he wasn't heading for Eastport to take us home. Instead, Devon swung the truck onto Route 190 toward the causeway and the mainland and, judging by the thick, dark smoke rising up against the evening sky, also toward the worst of the fires.

Meanwhile, I still had Alvin's will in my hand. So now I unfolded it, and of course, the document I'd pulled from Alvin's desk didn't name Clifton Ferrier as the will's beneficiary.

It named Devon Sipp instead.

Thirteen

As Mary Sipp's green pickup truck approached the causeway on Route 190, the whirling dashboard beacons from passing cop cars threw a weird pulsing glow into the smoke clouds, like lightning flaring.

Devon had taken his arm from around my neck, but he still held the knife in his fist, which was resting on his knee. He thought that was enough to keep me from leaping at him, I supposed.

And he was correct. "Listen," I told him, "I'm really not sure you want to drive right into all that—"

"Shut up." He twitched the knife on his knee so the blade glinted. "I want to hear from you, I'll ask questions, got it?"

I took a deep breath. "Got it," I said.

"Now, hand me those Tums on the dashboard," he said as his face twisted in pain, and when I obeyed, he bit two or three of the tablets off the end of the open roll of stomach remedies.

He was sweating, too, obviously in a lot of misery. But now that I wasn't so terrified of being incinerated and that knife of his wasn't so nerve-rackingly adjacent to some of my most favorite arteries, this Devon guy was starting to annoy me.

"Mind if I ask *you* a question?" I hazarded.

You worthless bag of fill-in-bad-words-here, I added silently. Ellie heard, anyway, and stiffened beside me. *Don't make him mad!*

But if we meant to get out of this, we'd have to distract him somehow. And have you ever noticed how these sludge-dwelling slime-toad types always like talking about themselves?

Well, I have, so I went on. "'Cause I'm really wondering how it all actually happened. I mean, did you come up with the idea first and Clifton was imitating you? Or . . ."

Devon kept driving, not answering. We hadn't reached the causeway roadblock yet, but in the gathering dusk, the smoke and flames loomed nearer, and dark shapes moved in the gloom.

But I could see from his eyes that he was listening. And he couldn't very well talk about this with anyone else, could he?

Still, he must've been dying to, and Ellie and I were his only possible audience.

Because once he got us over to the mainland, where he likely knew a dozen good places to hide our bodies, I knew darned well that Devon Sipp meant to kill us, too.

There was nobody coming toward us in the opposite lane, and this cheered me somewhat. It meant the causeway road-block was still set up, so at least we wouldn't be able to get across immediately.

Ahead, more red and blue lights strobed the murk, and guys in yellow rubber fire coats were hustling around determinedly. Trucks lined the road, both volunteers' vehicles and the big red or yellow tankers and hose rigs from nearby towns. They were all so urgently focused on the fires that nobody paid any attention to us as we eased past them. Then . . .

"Clifton was only supposed to use his notary stamp. I paid him, took care of him really good," Devon said suddenly as we approached the incline onto the causeway's two-lane deck. "But he had to horn in, try to steal my plan. Let me do the hard part, when Alvin got . . . you know."

Right, I did know: propelled headfirst into a hatchet. "I don't get the rest of it, though," I prodded. "The big picture."

To our left, under a fading sky, spread Carrying Place Cove, a wide, glistening mudflat now at low tide, and there were no fire hydrants here. That accounted for the tankers lined up along the roadside. Devon slowed the truck as more brake lights glowed ahead.

"How did it all work? Who did what?" I asked.

He must've known that with the truck slowed down, I'd be tempted to jump out instead of waiting for his answer. That's why he'd gripped the knife again, turning it so it stuck out the back of his fist, with the tip aimed at my liver.

Still, he *did* answer. "Look, it was simple. Alvin was well known to make lots of wills. This would be just one more, so no reason to think he *hadn't* made it. So Perry Wilson printed the blank form, Clifton notarized it, and I faked the beneficiary listing and the witness signatures."

Of course he had. "So all you had to do then was make sure Alvin wouldn't make another one before he died. So . . ."

"So you killed him, and that way he couldn't," hardly seemed a promising conversational gambit.

Devon's expression darkened. "Correct," he agreed, not seeming to like the memory he was having, either, even as he said it.

We edged forward again in the line to get onto the blocked causeway, behind a van with Massachusetts plates and two Yankee baseball bumper stickers.

Devon frowned. They were letting only one car onto the

span at a time in case the fires flared again on either side. As it was, enough smoke spiraled up to make the trip hazardous just on that account.

"Freakin' traitors," Devon muttered, scowling at the Yanks material. The Red Sox were the only ball team to follow around here, and the license plate just made the sticker seem worse. . . .

Funny how your mind can still drift trivially when your life's in peril, or maybe it was just my way of thinking outside the box, because I had an idea suddenly.

"Anyway, I promised Perry Wilson a big payday, too," Devon said, returning to his explanation.

And Perry had wanted the money to use in luring his sisters back home, I supposed . . . not that it would work, but he'd thought it would.

"And what about Clifton? I get that you paid him, too, but then why'd he show up at Alvin's house just now?"

At this Devon went silent, but he couldn't restrain a tiny glance in the rearview. So of course I looked also, and . . .

And just then a hot gust blew off the grass fires, lifting the sheet of canvas in the truck's bed to show Clifton lying there underneath it, tied up and mad as hell. Gagged, too, with his own red bandanna and tied securely into the truck bed for good measure, so he couldn't just jump out. The canvas flopped back down over Clifton again, hiding him.

"Big jerk was going to take my will out of the desk and put his own in its place. So *he'd* end up inheriting," said Devon.

The car ahead of us eased forward onto the causeway. Devon let the brake off and the clutch up, and we rolled forward, too, then stopped again.

I hadn't given up on my idea from earlier—jumping out, I mean—but the time still wasn't right. Now I glanced at the cat in the bag on the floor. It was asleep in there, I gathered, or at least it was lying quietly for the moment. Biding its time until it finally got loose and clawed all our lungs out, maybe. I felt like clawing some lungs out, too, only not quite yet.

"Clifton," said Devon grimly, "wasn't supposed to be part of this at all, and neither were either one of you, so—"

"And what about my car?" Ellie demanded, interrupting him. "I guess you must have something to do with that blowing up, too, right?"

At this, Devon looked puzzled, and when he was about to reply, Ellie cut in again.

"Here comes Bob Arnold."

The car just ahead of us was up on the causeway but hadn't moved forward any farther, so it was blocking us in. At the same time, in our vehicle's rearview mirror, I spied Bob moving up the line of cars waiting behind us.

He was stopping to speak briefly with each driver. Seeing this, Devon threw the truck in reverse and stomped on the gas. I'm not quite sure how he managed that with the big, sharp knife still in his hand, but he had its pointy tip back up against my side again so fast that it didn't matter, anyway.

In the next heartbeat, we were screeching to a halt, then flying forward again as he aimed the truck off the pavement to the right, toward the strip of stony beach running along the base of the causeway on the bay side.

The deepwater side, in other words. *Oh, great,* I thought as it hit me that he meant to drive onto that beach and cut around the road altogether to avoid the causeway roadblock.

Whether or not the tide was low enough for that remained to be seen, whether we wanted to or not. And if it wasn't, the next thing we'd see was the doorway to what Sam called Davy Jones's locker room.

Because it might *look* dry enough, but depending on the tide, that beach might just be a sort of sandy soup; and if you drove onto it and then a biggish wave rolled in, when it rolled out again, that biggish wave would carry your vehicle directly—

"Ahh!" cried Ellie, gripping my knee very firmly with her left hand, as the truck shot forward.

"Ouch," I whispered, barely believing what I was seeing.

"Fudge," said Devon as the truck barreled crazily through a slurry of loose sand, swerving and fishtailing.

Only that's not quite the word he used, and I didn't, either, as we jounced down a ridiculously steep granite-boulder pile, thudded onto a concrete slab, shot straight off into thin air— with our wheels, I supposed, still merrily spinning—and landed hard.

Which *stopped* the spinning, and so much for my worry that the beach might be soupy. The bones in my spine, on the other hand, felt as if they'd been liquified on impact, and so did my brains and whatever those stalky things are that hold a person's eyeballs in place.

Right now my eyes seemed to have rolled neatly up inside my head, and when they rolled back down again, I felt sure they'd have the word *tilt* lettered onto them, like cartoon eyeballs.

And meanwhile, Devon kept the truck bucking and roaring over wet stones, one hand gripping the steering wheel and one on the handle of the knife, which he still had jammed against my ribs.

Gasping, Ellie leaned forward and tried not to slam her head on the bouncing dashboard while she gathered up the cat bag. The cat moved a little when she settled the bag on her lap, then became still.

The cat hunkered inside the bag was still waiting for its chance, no doubt. Me, too, but at forty miles an hour and with low tide–exposed rock ledges flying by in the gloom, I still didn't like our odds of surviving if we leapt for our lives.

I mean, seriously, this was ridiculous. And then it got more so. Now when the truck jounced *up* instead of thudding *down—ouch*—I could see past the roadblock to the causeway's far end and the headlights of cars waiting to be let through.

Past them in Pleasant Point, people moved around in their yards, spraying the roofs of their small houses and sheds with garden hoses. Thin arcs of hose water glittered diamond-like in the yard lights, and they were spraying because . . .

"Oh, give me a break." The words burst angrily out of me, because I'd had it now, I really had, and the raging fire that had broken out ahead of us just put the cherry on top.

Sloping up from the beach ahead of us, and from there across the flat shoreland that the Native American settlement was built on, the massive new blaze was devouring rotten trees, discarded lumber, chunks of driftwood. . . .

Embers from the grass fires must've set this stuff alight, I realized, and there was no way to drive past it. Other than, I mean, going *through* it.

Devon tromped on the gas pedal.

"Listen," I said. The fire crackled, and below that an ominous hum droned, like that of angry bees. "Listen, why not go *under* the causeway and then back up to the road from the other side?" I suggested urgently.

In fact, there was no way to drive back up to the road from the other side; it was all boulders piled up against the roadbed to prevent erosion. I hoped he didn't remember that.

But the disgusted look he shot me said he did, and so did the fact that we still hurtled stubbornly and almost certainly suicidally toward a hot, hellishly terrifying, fiery wall of . . .

"Uh, you guys?" Ellie ventured uncertainly.

Somewhere along the line, he'd rolled the window down. Now he stuck his elbow out and drove one-handed, a maneuver that, considering our current situation, nearly gave me heart failure.

"What?" he said around a grin. After rooting in the vehicle's ashtray with his right hand, he found a longish cigar stub, jammed it into his mouth, and applied a lighter from his breast pocket.

Ellie shot him a look that should've vaporized him, and not just for the stinky cigar. "Uh, you might want to—" She stopped. Now she was frowning through the windshield, but not at the fire. I followed her gaze.

Then I spoke flatly. "Devon? Roll up your window." But he didn't.

A small black cloud, like a pulsating inkblot, hung against the deep blue evening sky. Halfway between us and the blaze, which was now spreading rapidly into the town's vulnerable backyards, the cloud looked suspended thirty feet or so in the air.

Vibrating. And . . . *humming*. And it wasn't suspended; it was holding itself up there with millions of beating . . .

Wings.

"Yeeks," I managed to say before the cloud veered around and arrowed straight toward us. "Roll up," I snarled, "the damned window."

Which this time he did, again taking his hand off the wheel while we were going very fast. But this time I didn't care, because in a few moments we'd be blasting through a wildfire while riding in a gas tank–equipped vehicle, and that was bad enough.

But gasoline or no gasoline, I did *not* want this truck's cab to be full of angry bees while we were doing it.

Because, as I may already have mentioned, I was plenty angry myself. I mean, who did this guy think he was, anyway?

"Devon!" I cried. "Stop. We're going to crash into—"

A wall of fire? A pile of rocks? A vehicle? I couldn't tell, and I definitely wasn't up for finding out the hard way, but his eyes were intent now, fixed on the conflagration ahead.

So there we were, racing at a rip-roaringly hot wildfire, gaining speed. I looked over at Ellie, still with the cat bag in her lap. She stared ahead, expressionless. But *determined* . . .

Devon wrenched the steering wheel suddenly to the left. The truck's front tires hit the base of the causeway's roadbed fast and at an angle; we didn't quite do a truckish backflip. But almost. Then, laboriously, the vehicle began to climb. A few yards, then a few more. If we made it to the top, we would come out just beyond where the roadblock sawhorses stood.

In other words, we'd be past the roadblock, and after that, Devon could just head for the hills, and I doubted anyone here was going to quit firefighting long enough to give chase.

In fact, we might not even be noticed, especially now that peoples' household propane tanks were starting to explode. By the time our front tires scrambled onto the roadbed again, the world around us really seemed to be coming to an end, full of smoke, flames, explosions, sirens. . . .

Devon flung the cigar stub out the window without looking and gripped the wheel, grimacing. The truck's rear tires spun as the vehicle struggled to push itself up the last steep few feet and onto the pavement.

Blue smoke and the stink of burning rubber filled the cab. Ellie's hand gripped mine as outside, flames loomed inches away and the heat coming into the truck made my scalp prickle.

"Go," I whispered to Ellie. "Out your door. Jump."

But she wouldn't—the flames were too terrible—and she wouldn't let go of my hand, either.

"Devon, listen to me," I said desperately, trying again. But he just kept gunning the engine until it shrieked, moving us up toward the road a little more each time. Toward . . .

Drat. Toward more fire. New blazes were springing up faster than the hose-wielding firefighters could extinguish them, and now a particularly nasty-looking patch of flame had flared up right in front of us.

And while I'd thought driving through a fire at high speed

would be bad enough, now it seemed that instead, we were about to inch through one, slowly enough to ensure that we got roasted.

Or, as I'd feared before, that we'd be blown to bits when the gas tank exploded.

"Devon, listen to me now, you—"

He *stomped* the gas pedal, whereupon the truck rocked back onto its rear tires and *lurched* up over the   edge of the bluff, then stalled there.

Flames filled the windshield, and fire tendrils licked around to the vehicle's side panels. Popping and sizzling sounds from beneath the floorboards scared a squeak out of me as I yanked my feet up onto the bench seat and Ellie did, too.

Devon turned the key. The engine turned over once and died. He turned it again.

Click-click-click. Then nothing.

Ellie touched the door handle and yanked her hand back with a gasp. "Hot," she breathed, shaking her fingers, and then she began yanking off her sweatshirt to use like a pot holder. But even when she got the door open—if it opened—she'd still have to jump out into those flames.

Devon turned the key again, the knife he'd been menacing me with forgotten, lying between us on the seat. "Come on, come *on* . . ."

The engine kicked over and va-roomed, and we rocketed away from the bluff's edge. And then somehow . . . we were up over the edge of the bluff and onto the pavement. In just a moment we'd be past the sawhorses and flares and highballing down Route 190 toward the mainland.

That meant we weren't going to burn to death, or at least not right this minute, so I couldn't help feeling relieved. But now that Devon had pretty well confessed to having committed Alvin Carter's murder, he really couldn't let us live, could he?

Or Clifton Ferrier, either. I hadn't checked lately, but he'd been tied in, so he was probably still in the truck's bed, likely bruised and battered or worse

But then, just past the end of the causeway, something was in the road ahead, and relief came over me. It was Bob Arnold, standing there in his blue uniform, straddling the yellow line with a big flashlight in one hand and his service weapon in the other, his round shape and shiny pink forehead instantly recognizable.

Behind us, the tide was coming in fast at the foot of the bluff that this truck had just somehow clawed its way to the top of.

Devon's look hardened.

"Oh, no," I whispered. "Don't!"

But he didn't put his foot on the gas as hard as I'd feared he would. Instead, he pulled slowly toward Bob until we were right up alongside the Eastport police chief, then rolled the driver's-side window all the way down with his left hand.

The knife, I noticed, had gotten back into his right hand somehow, and its point was turned around once more so that it aimed again at many of my most essential internal organs. In other words, Devon thought I'd better shut up now. So I did, but when Bob peered in, I let my eyes do the talking.

"Well, well," said Bob sternly, "you all came across that channel just now, did you?" His tone as he leaned farther in said, "What are you? Nuts?" And he gave no sign that he'd even seen the *Help us* looks I'd started shooting at him, much less interpreted them.

"Hi, Bob," I managed. "We were just . . ."

But we were just *what*? Wildly, I searched my mind for some plausible errand we might all be out on together on a night like this, when everything was on fire.

Then Ellie spoke up. "Bob, we've got an injured cat here, and the veterinarian said if we got there right away, she would—"

See, on the one hand, the last thing we wanted was to get past

Bob Arnold. Once he was in the rearview, we were on our way to our graves, I felt sure. I mean, what else could Devon do with us?

But the thing was, remember that handgun I'd seen Devon brandishing out at his mom's place?

Yeah, I didn't, either. But at the moment he had it aimed at Bob. It was in his left hand, whose wrist was cocked back so that the gun's barrel angled nearly straight up.

Bob hadn't seen it, I thought. But Ellie and I had, and we didn't want to get Bob killed, did we?

No, sir. We most certainly didn't. I let out a breath I hadn't known I'd been holding as Bob backed his head out of the driver's-side window and stepped away from the vehicle.

Raising his arm to wave us on, he seemed about to say that this injured-cat business was just the kind of nonsense he would expect us to be involved in at a time like this, but go ahead.

But then he didn't step any farther away. Instead, faster than I'd ever seen Bob move before, he snaked his arm in through the vehicle's window and thrust his hand down at Devon's hand.

The hand with the gun in it. The gun went off.

At the same moment, Ellie let the cat out of the bag.

With a yowl guaranteed to strike fear into the hearts of rodents everywhere, the cat sprang angrily from Ellie's lap to my right shoulder. There, digging in what felt like a set of velociraptor talons, it teetered briefly and painfully before pushing off strenuously with its rear claws.

So I yelled, adding to the general consternation in the truck's cab. Meanwhile, by now the unhappy animal had its front claws deep in Devon's scalp.

Startled, he let out a bellow and gripped the cat's body with both hands to try to pry it off. To do this, of course, he had to drop both the knife and the gun, which had just discharged. Bob seized the opportunity to (a) step right back up to the truck again and (b) grab Devon by the throat and begin shouting in his face.

"Out of the vehicle! Out of the vehicle now!" he commanded, along with delivering other remarks mostly having to do with Devon's personal hygiene, his intelligence, and his general level of bone-deep, "ought to be slapped sideways" annoyingness, which Bob seemed to rate as extremely high.

The truck's door swung open, and Devon tumbled out. I stared, openmouthed, as he fell slackly away from me, not understanding until I saw all the blood he'd left behind on the bench seat that the accidental shot from his own weapon had hit him.

Ellie stared. Me too. "Is he . . . ?" she asked.

"I don't know," I said, and in fact, I didn't know much. If you'd put me into a cement mixer and tumbled me around for a while, I couldn't have been more discombobulated. But it was over, we were safe, and . . .

Sensibly, the cat sprang out as the truck lurched beneath us. Ellie sat up from where she'd been bent over to dab at a cat scratch on her ankle and looked around suspiciously.

"What was that?" she wanted to know, and so did I.

As if in answer, the vehicle shuddered, then moved again—backward.

Oh, this wasn't good. The first lurch had swung the open driver's-side door; the second slammed it shut with a bang.

And, of course, it wouldn't open again, or the other one, either, no matter how we yanked and rattled the door handles. We were rolling slowly but steadily back toward the bluff's edge, and toward the heaped-up boulders and granite ledges waiting below.

Also, I believe I may have mentioned that the tide had been out and now it was coming in again?

So the sand-and-stones beach where we'd driven ten minutes ago was under enough water by now to turn it into a mucky trap. Assuming, I mean, that we didn't get killed just tumbling down the bluff . . .

"Jake?" Ellie said worriedly. "You'd better . . ."

Yeah, no kidding. I slid behind the wheel. The key was in the ignition. I turned it; grinding sounds were the only result.

"Freakin' thing won't start again," I said, although by now this was fairly obvious, and so was the fact that Ellie and I should start saying our prayers, if any.

Again, with the ignition. Again, nothing. But, boy, were we ever rolling now, and when I hauled on the steering wheel, it felt frozen. Putting my weight into it, I found I could barely move it half an inch in either direction.

"The brakes," Ellie reminded me kindly, meanwhile looking as if she was ready to shove me aside and jump behind the wheel herself.

"Oh. Yeah." I stomped the brake pedal, which let out an agonized squeal, followed by a great deal of metal-against-metal clattering, but did not do much stopping.

"Hmm," I said thoughtfully.

But not really. There was nothing more to think about. We were rolling toward the bluff, and we were going to go over it, and that was all there was to it.

"Fasten," I told Ellie, "your seat belt, and put your arms over your face."

She did, and I did the same. Then I struggled more with the steering wheel and brakes but got the same unhappy results.

Finally, I gave up and braced myself, although how you could really get ready for what was coming, I wasn't quite sure. On the road, a crouched-down Bob Arnold turned from his first-aid efforts for Devon Sipp and saw what was happening. After jumping up, he hustled toward us while shouting into his radio.

But there was nothing he could do. By then we had so much momentum going, stopping us would've taken a big grappling hook and the kind of monster tow truck usually used to haul eighteen-wheelers out of ravines.

But none of these were in evidence at the moment.

"Here goes," said Ellie quaveringly as the truck's rear wheels rolled over the bluff's edge.

But instead of following, the vehicle's body slammed down and the hood tilted upward. We were looking through the windshield straight up into the sky while the truck teetered, as if trying to decide whether to go the rest of the way or not.

And now I could hear waves below us.

"I hope we don't drown," I said.

"Don't be silly," Ellie replied. "The fall will kill us."

A laugh escaped me. "Oh, terrific," I said, taking Ellie's hand as the truck's front end soared and an awful crunching and grinding sound came from beneath us. And then . . .

Then without warning something big and shiny flew up over the vehicle's front end and hit the hood very hard with a heavy metallic *thunk*!

After I got done with my flinching and screaming, I saw that the thing hadn't just *hit* us; whatever it was had pierced the hood of the truck like some enormous curved claw and lodged itself there.

"Hey," Ellie whispered. "We're not moving anymore."

As in we weren't rolling over the bluff's edge, she meant. Instead, we'd stopped. I didn't understand why, and then from somewhere came a high whining sound, as if some very large piece of machinery was . . .

"Ellie." I couldn't help giggling when I saw it backing up toward us. "Ellie, it's a tow truck."

A really *big* tow truck. Also, that thing lodged in the truck's hood was a grappling hook and the cable attached to it . . .

Because now I saw that there was indeed an attached cable, and in circumference it was the size of my two forearms pressed together. *Oh, thank you*, I thought.

The machinery whined, the cable snapped tight, a shudder went through the pickup truck, and the noise coming up through the floorboards beneath us sounded like somebody was demolishing our vehicle by throwing rocks at it.

Big jagged rocks, hurled from below . . .

When the winch pulled us back up over the edge, a crowd of whirling red and blue lights greeted us: cop cars, volunteers' pickups, an ambulance, and that big tow truck, still stubbornly dragging us toward it, reeling us in like a fish.

"Cover your faces," yelled one of the volunteer guys.

Then he ran up and removed the truck's windshield by the simple method of taking a crowbar to it.

Greenish safety-glass pellets exploded inward at us, and an instant later we were being helped out of the cab through the ragged hole where the glass used to be, the volunteers urging us to move faster than even I thought was necessary, until I *was* out and saw the smoke rising from beneath the truck.

"Yikes." I really couldn't wait to start walking away from all this, but when my feet finally hit the ground, my legs turned unhelpfully to water.

"Yeah, there's hot embers everywhere," said the volunteer who caught me as I fell. "Including under your truck."

Leaning on her and not bothering to correct her idea of who owned that cursed green vehicle, I tottered across the grass to a first-aid tent that had been hastily set up.

Ellie and another helpful young firefighters' auxiliary member were right behind us, tottering similarly. Just then her husband, George Valentine—Ellie's husband, that is, not the volunteer's—pulled up fast in his own pickup truck, skidded to a swerving halt as he caught sight of us, and jumped out. Wearing a Red Sox ball cap, a denim jacket, and canvas work pants, he rushed toward me, then spotted Ellie and ran on by.

"I heard your name on the scanner," he told her, sounding scared trending toward relieved. "Are you all right?"

Not waiting for an answer, he seized her by her shoulders and flung his arms around her, and I left them there together in favor of entering the tent, where they gave me some water and sat me down to wait. For what, they didn't say, but I was in no mood to argue.

Or to go anywhere, either. All that I was in the mood for, suddenly, was to stare vacantly into space while all my systems turned back on and reloaded themselves into my brain circuitry.

"Hey." Bob Arnold stood over me. Sweaty, sooty, big messy-looking scratch across his forehead . . .

"You thought of the tow truck," I said. It was all I could do not to fall down and kiss his feet, I was so grateful to him.

Of course he'd thought of it. It had been his idea for the town to buy the big vehicle a couple of years earlier, and in all the time since, it had never been used.

Until now.

He squinted past the toothpick he was vigorously chewing. "Told you that hook would come in handy someday."

I managed a half smile. But the moment when Devon's truck tipped over backward with us in it kept replaying in my head. As it would, I imagined, for a while.

"He confessed," said Bob, and that got my attention. "In the ambulance, Devon told them he killed Alvin Carter," Bob went on. "They got it on audio, lucky for us."

That puzzled me. Why would he . . . ? "I don't get it. Can't he just plead guilty when he goes to . . . oh." "Trial," I'd have finished. But I said, "You mean . . . ?"

Bob nodded unhappily. "Yeah, he's gone. I guess he must've known he was on his way out."

Out of this life, that is. I looked up questioningly again.

"Getting the confession recorded," Bob explained, "was Devon's idea."

"Huh," I said, not quite sure how to process this. "So the murdering jerk had a nice little moment for himself at the end?"

And now someone was going to have to go and tell his mother that he was dead.

Bob shrugged exhaustedly. "I really couldn't say what kind of moment it was, Jake. I mean, who knows what people think when they're dying?"

Just then George and Ellie peered in through the tent flap, looking for me, and Bob took this as his cue to leave.

"All right, we'll sort this all out tomorrow. State cops'll no doubt be wanting to talk to you both," he said.

Yeah, no doubt. I tossed my emptied water bottle into the recycling bag by the tent's exit. Outside, the flames had mostly been beaten down at last, leaving a smoking swath of blackened grass with the skeletal shapes of burned trees sticking up from it.

Then the cars on the road began creeping forward; the shapes of men in the near darkness were hauling aside the sawhorses, too.

Nearer by, silhouetted against the last gleams of light in the west, Devon Sipp's pickup truck hung on the tow-truck hook: beaten and battered, its glass all smashed. It was about to be hauled up onto the tow truck's flatbed. But then . . .

"Hey," I said, remembering suddenly. "Someone's in the . . ."

Just then the tied-up bundle that was Clifton Ferrier sat up as well as he could and began bellowing through the bandanna that gagged him.

I figured that meant that Clifton was (a) alive and (b) somebody else's problem now. Relieved, I turned away to climb into George Valentine's vehicle.

After sliding behind the wheel next to me, George thrust his phone at me. "Call Bella. She's been blowing up my phone for half an hour."

"Oh, gosh," I breathed guiltily. In all the commotion I'd completely forgotten about her. She had not, however, forgotten me, and she answered on the first ring.

"Bella, I'm so sorry. Are you all right?"

"Of course I am," she replied briskly. "I'm still here at the hospital. The surgeons took the bullet out of Perry Wilson, and no one's tried putting any more of them into him."

Phew. I felt myself relaxing.

"How," she went on, "are *you?* What's going on, and why is George not answering his phone?

She'd already tried calling our house, but no one there knew where I was. So she'd kept calling people all over Eastport, at last fixing on George as likeliest to learn my whereabouts if he didn't already know them.

And now here I was, so that had worked out for her, and she sounded pleased. She wasn't always efficient, our Bella, but, by God, sooner or later she got the job done.

Yet another thing lifted my spirits, too: her tone. Crisp, confident . . . as if being given a serious, potentially dangerous job had rejuvenated her. This was the Bella we knew and loved.

A job, I mean, that depended more on smarts and courage than on actual, laboriously physical derring-do. . . .

George turned on the windshield wipers. They smeared across the glass, blurring oncoming headlights to spangled flares. But I didn't understand why this was happening until I realized it was *raining.* Not just drizzling or spitting, but really letting loose with a lot of cold, wet drops, big ones.

With the fires fading behind us and the lights of downtown Eastport glimmering ahead, I turned to whisper the good news to Ellie.

"Sounds like Bella's got her groove back," I said.

But Ellie was already sound asleep.

Fourteen

"It all started when that housekeeper, Mary Sipp, told her son, Devon, that Alvin Carter was on a will-making kick," said Bob Arnold.

As I'd suspected when I saw him rising from the bed of Devon Sipp's wrecked pickup truck, Clifton Ferrier knew a lot, and he'd been happy to discuss it in return for not getting charged with being an accomplice in Alvin's murder himself.

"And then what happened?" I asked Bob.

In the few days since Devon Sipp's death by accidental gunshot, Ellie and I had made progress on getting our households, our families, and our business back into working order, and had even made preparations for the cookie-baking contest.

Now Bob sat beside me at one of the long tables in the Unitarian church hall as the long-awaited judging for the annual competition was about to begin.

"Nice turnout," he remarked appreciatively. "Decorations are nice, too."

He was right on both counts: a hundred or so people, mostly

cookie contestants and their families, filled the hall, along with local and regional news reporters and even a Bangor TV camera.

And Prunia Devereaux's table arrangements looked lovely, especially the bunches of cherry-red rose hips and glossy green leaves that she must have come early to arrange in their glass jugs.

"Attention! Attention, everyone!" Prunia was at the front of the hall now, wearing a flowered dress, a green sweater, a string of pearls, and a green silk pillbox hat.

"Thank you, all of you, and the news media here, too, for coming out this morning to support . . ." Once the crowd had settled, Prunia began delivering the carefully-crafted speech she had written.

I pulled my own sweater tighter around my shoulders; the old Unitarian meeting house had only electric space heaters now that the ancient oil furnace had finally gone kaput.

Then . . . "Bob," I urged him. "I asked you . . ."

"What happened," he finished for me. This was the first time we'd been able to get together socially since the night of the fire.

"Well," he went on, "what happened then was that Devon thought up a plan for getting one of those wills of Alvin's—the last one, as in *last* will and testament—to designate Devon himself as the only heir."

So far, so fine. "Devon knew about Clifton because his mother also told him it's who notarized Alvin's documents," I said.

"And about Perry Wilson," Bob agreed. "Specifically, that Perry printed blank wills for Alvin, which he could fill in."

At the front of the hall, Prunia spoke easily and well about the cookie-contest entrants, identifying a good quality belonging to each contestant and making a big deal of it: for instance, how helpful the person was to the library, the arts committee, the schools, or whatever. Running the contest each year was a sizable undertaking, but she did it and she was good at it.

"But why were Prunia and Alvin Carter such friends?" I asked. "You wouldn't think . . ."

Bob took a small crustless white bread sandwich from a serving plate of them. Filled with a mixture of chopped Spam, pickles, grated raw carrot, and mayonnaise, they were an old Eastport delicacy called jitterbugs and were improbably delicious.

Bob ate his in a bite. He loved these ladies'-lunch finger foods, which was why I always invited him to events like this.

"She'd made," Bob said simply, "a project of him." He sipped tea, his little finger rising delicately. "Wife died, and Alvin retired and moved here. This was thirty years ago. He's been alone all that time, and I guess Prunia felt sorry for him. You know how she is."

Oh, did I ever. She'd never met a situation she couldn't fix . . . in her own opinion, anyway.

Bob continued. "Wasn't till recently his chain of clothing stores went bust, though, and he ran out of money."

I turned slowly to Bob. "I beg your pardon?"

Bob nodded, as if everyone knew this. "Oh, yeah. Too bad for anyone who really thought they were going to inherit from him, but the state cops have been looking into Alvin's finances, and when he died, poor old Alvin was as broke as a joke."

"So it was all for . . ."

"Yup." Bob ate another sandwich, while at the front of the hall, Prunia was winding down her thank-yous and acknowledgments.

"All that murder business, all for nothing. Devon got his will made by Perry, got it notarized by Clifton Ferrier, and had sneaked it into Alvin's desk drawer after he killed Alvin," Bob summed up.

"That's why he was on the property that morning when Ellie and I were first there, and right there in the house, too, to finish the last step in his plan," I said. "And with so many other wills that Alvin *did* make floating around, no one would suspect the one that named Devon was a fake."

All this time, Ellie had been listening from where she sat on my left; now she leaned forward. "So then, once he knew what Devon was up to . . ."

Bob nodded. "Right, then Clifton did exactly the same thing as Devon had done, only with himself as beneficiary. When you ran into him that last night, he was there to take Devon's will out of the desk drawer and put his own in."

Ellie nodded comprehendingly. "And presto, now *his* will is the last one, and *he's* Alvin's sole heir."

"Right," said Bob, "but first you interrupted him and then Devon caught him. He popped a tiny chocolate éclair into his mouth, smiled happily around it, swallowed.

Ellie laughed, not entirely pleasantly. "Poor guy. His day sure went south fast, didn't it?"

As she spoke, those truck headlights of Devon's probed the sky again in memory, as did the feeling of his knife's tip aimed at my left ventricle.

"It sure did," I agreed, not entirely pleasantly, either, because for one thing, picture me trying to explain it all to Wade, who hadn't been a bit pleased.

Up on the podium, Prunia was thanking all the contest's entrants again, plus the helpers for today's judging ceremony, the ladies who'd picked rose hips, the sandwich makers and, of course, Unitarians, who'd so kindly, et cetera.

Meanwhile, the finalists sat nervously at the head table. I caught Mika's eye and winked, *You go, girl*! She smiled shakily back.

"And now, without further ado!" Prunia exclaimed, and all the cookie contestants looked terrified.

"Here goes nothing," Ellie breathed as Prunia began to read off the list of cookie-contest winners for this year.

"Bar cookies, Miriah Johnson!" Prunia announced, and a fair, freckled forty-year-old with red curls stood up proudly.

"Refrigerator cookies, Sandra Oates!" Polite applause rippled through the audience as Sandra got up and approached the podium.

"Everything really does look lovely," whispered Ellie, and it did, too.

Up and down the tables gleamed the gold-scalloped edges of the white china cups and saucers, the antique silver teaspoons, and the hand-painted dessert plates brought over from France decades earlier by someone's great-aunt Somebody-or-Other.

"Yes," I agreed. "But, Bob," I added, turning back to him, "what about Perry? I still don't get who shot him and why."

"Drop cookies!" Prunia enthused from up front.

"You took Perry up to the health center, didn't you?" Bob said.

It was a statement, not a query. "Yes, but . . ."

"Clifton went there that same day to see the dentist," said Bob, "about his bad tooth. And *while* he was there . . ."

Right. As I'd now already realized, that's when Clifton decided that to be on the safe side, it was time to get rid of Perry.

So he shot him—once out in front of Perry's house and once at the hospital. Good thing Clifton was no champion marksman, no more than Perry was himself. . . .

But now Perry was home, and Billy Breyer was about to be let out of custody. It had taken a while to get hearings held and the paperwork completed, even with Mick Flaherty's help.

And I'd had *almost* all my questions answered.

"And now for the most hotly contested cookie group, the one we're all waiting for, the 'invented or developed by contestant' category!" announced Prunia.

"How do you suppose Mika's going to do?" I asked Ellie nervously.

I had no idea what to expect. In the few days leading up to the event, Mika had gotten secretive about her cookie-contest entry, not even telling us what kind of cookie she was entering.

Ellie sighed. "I *think* she's still going with a variety of snicker-doodle, but . . ."

But there was nothing we could do but wait and see; in the end, for all our big talk about rigging the contest, there had been no way to do it. Too many jurors would've had to be bribed, and word would've gotten out in about twelve seconds, anyway, if we had tried.

And besides, it wouldn't have been sporting. So Mika was on her own, just as she'd have insisted on being. Hoping that it all turned out reasonably all right and oddly confident that it would, I looked happily around the hall, where the murmur of women's voices filled the air, along with the mingled perfumes of brewing coffee and fresh baked goods.

"When are the girls getting home?" asked Ellie, choosing a miniature scone from a plate of them labeled OLIVES AND BRIE. "I'd have thought I'd be seeing them by now."

Anna and Helen Breyer, she meant. With Billy on his way home, like Ellie, I'd thought his sisters would arrive soon, too. But I hadn't seen them. Also, I wasn't sure how an olive-and-cheese scone would taste, but I had my suspicions.

"Poor Perry," I said. "Have his own two sisters been in touch at all since he was shot, do you know?"

Ellie shook her head. "I asked Prunia. She said she called them and left messages, but neither one called back."

A heavy sigh rolled up out of me. "So I guess he must've burnt those bridges permanently," I said.

Too bad, but sometimes you really can't go home again. Or sometimes, as in the case of Perry's sisters . . . The hundreds of photographs of them that he'd wallpapered a whole room with

rose up in my mind's eye again, a chilling sight. Yeah, sometimes you just shouldn't.

"And now . . ." Prunia was still at the podium. Mika went on
waiting patiently but looked ready to dissolve with anxiety.

I took one of the olive-Brie scones to calm my own nerves.
Something called honey butter had been provided to anoint the
scones with, so I did that, and then hesitantly, I bit in.

Chewed. Swallowed. Took another smallish bite, just to
make sure. And then . . .

"Oh, holy criminy, Ellie, these things are—"

Prunia said, "Of all the many wonderful varieties of cookies
our excellent Eastport bakers entered, one batch stood out."

"Fabulous!" I whispered. The mild yet smoky, creamy Brie,
the toothsome bits of green olive, and the scone itself, its crumb
rich and moist but not in the least gummy . . .

Meanwhile, the suspense was killing me.

"The winner is . . ."

Mika sat up straight, looking spiffy in white khaki pants, a
sailor-striped T-shirt, and a navy cardigan draped over her
shoulders, with the sleeves tied loosely around her neck.

When I try doing that, I always look like I'm about to be
strangled by a renegade clothing item. But never mind . . .

"Ellie, what if she doesn't win?"

Ellie shrugged in reply. In the past week, no appropriate
child care had been found, and the job at the college had let
Mika know they couldn't wait for her decision much longer. So
Mika badly needed some kind of good news, and ideally, she'd
get it delivered by an experienced mother's helper who worked
for reasonable wages.

But we still didn't even know if Mika's cookie was any good,
contest-winning good, I mean, until . . .

"Mika Tiptree! With her delightfully different drop cookie,
the Snickerdoodle au Chocolat!"

Ellie and I looked at each other. *Huh?*

Neither of us had ever heard of it. But plates of them were being passed, so we each took one—well, I took two—and did our usual cookie test: break, sniff, bite, and finally taste it.

"Oh, my goodness," Ellie breathed blissfully.

"Yeah," I managed faintly, "this isn't half bad."

It was all the way good, was what it was, no question about it. The cookie was beige, round, flat, and crinkly on top, just like as regular snickerdoodle.

But across that crinkled top, Mika had drizzled the very thinnest swirls of chocolate glaze—not buttercream icing, mind you, but only melted chocolate, powdered sugar, and a little hot milk.

The stuff was barely there; she'd designed it that way. And yet . . .

"Wow," I said, taking another.

"So," Ellie sighed happily as around us, enthusiasm for Mika's creation built. At the head table she was beamingly taking congratulations from the other contestants, and to judge by the way she was scribbling in a notebook, she was also taking cookie orders and appointments for media interviews.

"You know," I said thoughtfully, "if I'm not mistaken, we may have created some competition for ourselves. Looks like a lot of people want chocolate snickerdoodles to take home."

"Yes. Fine," Ellie said impatiently, too good-hearted to care about that in the midst of Mika's triumph.

Sam and the kids were up there with her now, along with my father. Bella was at the Chocolate Moose, because, as she'd said, she really couldn't stand the suspense. I got up, caught Mika's eye, and waved a happy *See you back at the house* at her. She nodded joyfully at Ellie and me and went back to her winner's duties.

"Not that this solves all her problems," I said as we moved toward the exit, past long tables loaded with trays full of every possible kind of cookie.

And sandwich and tart and petit four and . . .

"Oh, of course not." We reached the hall's big old arched double doors and went out through them. "But a little boost to the old self-confidence never hurt anyone."

We paused on the flat granite slab that served as the hall's doorstep. The noonday sun was warm, but now in the first week of October, the breeze had an unmistakable chilly edge on it, even in daytime.

We began walking. Just then Bob, who'd somehow gotten out ahead of us, came down the street in his squad car.

"You two take care," he said as he slowed alongside us. "Stay," he added meaningfully, "out of trouble."

He pulled away as Ellie and I kept walking toward down-town and the Chocolate Moose, and when he was gone, she let a breath out in relief.

"I wish he'd just lower the boom and get it over with," she said.

About all the snooping-related deeds we'd done, she meant. Illegal, dangerous, or both.

"He's not going to," I said.

We reached Water Street and turned downhill, went past the redbrick Peavey Memorial Library, with the cannon on the lawn out in front of it, two restaurants (one Mexican, one pizza), a pair of two-centuries-old bank buildings turned into galleries (one painting, one sculpture and jewelry), and the low shingled shape of the WaCo Diner, its blue awnings snapping in a breeze.

"Because the thing is, Ellie, that in the end it all turned out all right."

In the past week, all kinds of cops had interviewed us, sepa-rately and together. But we had had nothing new to offer and, after all, they already had a confession from Devon. So after their first couple of visits either to my kitchen or to Ellie's, they'd lost interest, and we'd heard nothing more from any of them.

"Oh, sometime we'll get a lecture from him, I'm sure. Once the dust clears," I said.

Out past the fish pier, seagulls sailed above white-topped waves. Ahead, the googly-eyed Chocolate Moose sign hung over the sidewalk; two bikes leaned against the cast-iron café table and the pair of chairs we'd set up out front.

"Helen! Anna!" we cried in unison.

Inside, Billy Breyer's teenaged sisters were happily ensconced in their usual booth, with their bags and jackets flung everywhere around them and a shiny new red spiral notebook open on the table before them. They were making, it looked like, some sort of a schedule, but now they shoved it aside.

"Have you heard?" Anna asked joyfully. "Billy's coming home!"

And of course we had, but we let them tell us all about it again while Bella, who'd been the only one available to open the shop this morning, beamed from behind the counter.

"He's getting here tonight!" Helen enthused.

"And now that *he's* out, *we're* home!" Anna exclaimed. "Oh, it's so good to be here!" she added, pressing the back of her hand to her forehead theatrically and giggling at herself.

Helen, though, wasn't in quite such high spirits. "Although we're not staying," she put in quietly.

Ellie stared. "But . . . why?" she asked after a moment during which she and I glanced worriedly at each other. Had their aunt Prunia's terrible influence actually rubbed off on them— and so fast?

Anna sat up, touching the tips of her fingers together calculatingly. "It wasn't easy, but we got it all hashed out with her. Fishing in summer, boarding school in winter," she said. "It was an offer we couldn't refuse."

My mouth pretty much just fell open. "You talked her into that? Prunia, she agreed to . . . ?"

The girls nodded together.

"We'll finish this semester here in Eastport first," Helen said. "Then . . ."

"Because, see, Prunia could tell that we'd beat it the first chance we got," Anna explained. "Like, run away and just not come back."

The very thought sent a chill through me, and to her credit, I gathered it had through good old Prunia, too.

"And honestly, the school she picked for us, it's not so bad." While saying this, Helen got up and twirled to show the pleated plaid wool skirt and green knee socks that, along with a vest and crisp shirt, were part of her school uniform.

"There are," Anna agreed, "some cool girls there. And some good courses, too, for when we do have our own boat, like how to apply for a bank loan and how to file business taxes."

Helen grinned. "Don't tell Aunt Prunia, though. She doesn't realize how much the school has improved since she went there!"

Then Mika arrived, and Bella headed home to check on my father, whose late-night strolls had been curtailed lately by the arrival of baseball's World Series season. Good old sports.

"Good heavens," Mika exhaled, sinking happily into a chair. She'd been up before dawn, baking for the contest, and it seemed that winning had taken some energy out of her, too.

But she spied the girls' notebook, whose first few pages had been neatly ruled into columns, and her interest in that was lively enough.

"It was Bella's idea," said Helen. "I told her we weren't going to be fishing over this winter, so we needed other money-making ideas."

"That's why we're making a schedule of when we don't

have classes and would be available to work for you," Anna added.

"Oh," I said regretfully, "I wish Bella had talked to me about it first." It was indeed a fine idea, except . . . "You see," I told the girls, "business is slow over the winter, so we don't need any help in the shop then."

"Oh! No, not you," Helen corrected me.

"We meant her," Anna said, pointing at Mika, who looked as mystified as I felt.

"She needs babysitting. We need jobs. Bingo, it's a perfect fit!" said Helen.

"It could work," said Mika, sounding cautiously interested. She eyed the girls speculatively.

"We will be so careful," said Helen, "with your kids."

"We'll be on time," Anna added earnestly. "We'll play games. We'll—"

"All right, all right," Mika gave in, laughing. "Why don't you both come up to the house right now and meet them, then? And if that works out, we'll talk about hours and money."

So Helen and Anna gathered their jackets, bags, and notebook and hurried out to their bikes. As they pedaled away, with their smiles radiant and their tangled curls flying, they looked like storybook heroines dashing off to their next happy adventure.

Ellie watched them go. "Funny how families that might look similar on the outside are so . . ."

"Different on the inside," I finished.

I knew she meant Billy and Perry, each with a pair of younger sisters and each from a family with a tragic past. And yet so utterly unalike in every other way.

"I guess things really aren't always what they seem," said Ellie.

Yeah. Not even very often, I thought. Anyway . . .

"That's really something about Bella, though," I said, changing the subject as we cleared up napkins and cups and finished setting the kitchen to rights.

"That she suggested the girls for Mika's babysitting?"

"Yup."

I wiped the front of the glass-fronted display case, now humming along contentedly since Sam had repaired it, then replaced all the paper doilies on which the last few cookies—just oatmeal-raisin and fig roll-up, mostly—still rested. Business had been brisk this morning, it seemed.

"I think maybe Bella knew all along," I said.

"That Mika had doubts?" Ellie swept crumbs into a dustpan and emptied it.

"No, I mean that Bella did. That she knew it was going to be too much for her, a toddler and an infant for hours on end."

"But she wanted to decide for herself," Ellie said, "not have the decision forced on her?"

"Correct. She's not stupid, but she's as independent as a hog on ice."

My cell phone burbled; I put down my wiping cloth.

"Jake?" It was the lawyer Mick Flaherty. "Hey, listen, your young man's coming home."

I told him I'd heard, and that I hoped I was let out of our bargain on account of this.

Talking to Mick about my past wasn't on my to-do list at the best of times, but after my recent reminder about what life was like when you were mixed up with murderous criminals, I'd have preferred being shot out of a cannon.

"Oh, hey, one more thing," Mick said after he'd let me off the hook. He was indeed a tough old lawyer, but he was a gentleman at heart. "When you were snooping around," he said, "did you by any chance happen to run into . . . ?"

Outside, a tour bus rumbled slowly into town. It eased down

Washington Street and around the corner, then angled into the parking lot across the street from the Chocolate Moose.

"Uh, Jake?" said Ellie as a lot of late-season tourists with cameras and field glasses slung around their necks got out of the bus, stretching and blinking.

"A department-store dummy?" Mick finished.

"Oh, you're kidding," I said, suddenly seeing the solution to a puzzle that had been flummoxing me for days.

Ellie spoke nervously. "Jake, a lot of those tourists are heading . . ."

Correct. They were heading our way, weren't they? And us with our display case nearly empty and the coffeepot dry.

"See, when his stores went belly up, there were a lot of old-fashioned display mannequins in the windows, but they were leased, not Alvin's property at all," said Mick.

A couple of the tourists spied our sign hanging out over the street and began telling the others. Excitement rippled through the group; there were fifty or so of them.

"Anyway, those mannequins are pretty valuable nowadays, and one's still missing," said Mick as from the other end of Water Street the Unitarians' old Chevy station wagon approached.

It pulled up out front, and Prunia Devereaux began unloading cookie trays from the back of the station wagon just as *another* vehicle, this one a repurposed black Chevrolet hearse belonging to the Elks Lodge, pulled in next to it.

Oh. My. Heavens. We'd completely forgotten the Elks Lodge special order. . . .

Prunia hurried in, the little silver bell over the door jangling brightly as she passed beneath it, and shoved two trays loaded with positively delicious-looking cookies from the baking contest onto our counter, then went back out for more.

"A department-store dummy," I repeated into the telephone,

remembering yet again the corpse-like figure I'd rolled right into when I was under Alvin Carter's porch.

All at once I couldn't seem to decide if I was sobbing with hilarity or just plain sobbing. It didn't matter, though, because I really didn't have time to do either.

Rushing past me, Ellie shot me a look. The wave of tourists rolling out of the bus was about to crash into our store, *and* the Elks were here to pick up the load of cookies they'd ordered.

"Mick, thanks for everything. Talk to you later. Gotta go," I said before hanging up just as the first of the out-of-town visitors came in.

And then the frenzy began: in the next half hour we sold every single one of the forty dozen cookies that Prunia had just delivered.

She'd brought the coffee urn, too, from the Unitarian church hall, where it had apparently just been filled again before everybody dispersed, so there was plenty for everyone, and our cold-drinks cooler got a workout, as well.

At last, when the rush was over, the coffee urn dry, and the cooler similarly exhausted, Ellie and I sat alone at one of the little cast-iron café tables.

"Cheers," she said, lifting a chocolate-dipped macaroon with half a brandied cherry pressed into it.

"Cheers," I echoed, hoisting an almond toffee wafer.

We each took a bite and washed it down with water, which was all we had left to drink in the place.

"You know, I don't know what in the world we're going to do with ourselves now that things are back to normal," I mused.

"Ha," Ellie said knowingly. "We'll just see how long that situation lasts."

And she was right, of course.

* * *

That night, Wade and I sat out on the porch in the autumn dusk. I leaned into his shoulder; he slipped his arm around me.

"Did you know the penalties for falsifying a notary stamp are the same as for perjury?" I asked.

Inside the house, Sam and Bella chattered happily, doing the dishes together. Mika was in the dining room, working up a syllabus for her new teaching gig; the Breyer girls' babysitting audition had gone smashingly.

Out in the driveway, Sam's old pickup truck hunkered on the new tires I'd bought for it, my way of rewarding the trusty old vehicle for not killing us out on Route 190 the other night.

"Because that's what the notarization of a document is," I said. "A sworn statement, on paper instead of in a courtroom."

"And a guy who would sell that kind of a promise . . ."

"Right. Clifton Ferrier was already a lowlife, so I'm not all that surprised he decided to make bank on Alvin Carter's death, especially since he didn't have to kill Alvin to do it."

"Because Clifton knew that Devon would take care of that part," Wade said.

Right again. "All Clifton had to do was wait until Devon had done it, then replace Devon's fake will with one of his own. But that's the part I don't get."

Wade nodded contemplatively. "'Cause Devon was such a straight arrow, you mean? Worked lots of jobs, helped his mother, even got her a handyman type for the heavy chores . . ."

Butch, he meant, who, as far as I knew, was still bunking in the Sipps' shed, fortunately for Devon's mother, Mary. Actually, I had a funny feeling that good old Butch might be moving up to the big house soon, but that was another story, to be continued.

In the distance a foghorn hooted plaintively.

"Yes, that's just it," I answered Wade. "Devon wasn't the type to—"

"To stay on that land, working himself sick until he's crippled with that belly pain and by then arthritis, too, never getting steady employment with, say, any benefits or a pension, getting older and not seeing any other future ever . . ."

And his mother always struggling to pay the bills, as well as to save face about it . . .

"Yeah," I said finally. "I do get it now."

Guys got old, or they got injured. Having no money and no way to get any was a hard way to live. It was why I wasn't sorry that Helen and Anna Breyer would have an education to fall back on if need be: wanting to fish was one thing, but having to was another.

Meanwhile, Devon wasn't going to invent anything or start a business or get discovered for anything. Getting Alvin's money was the only way he'd ever have a different life.

And he knew it. So he'd grabbed for something.

And missed.

"That's why Mary Sipp was crying, I'll bet, the day of Alvin's death," I said. "She didn't know for a fact what Devon had done. But she *felt* it. He was her kid, after all."

"And she knew his heart," Wade agreed. "So yeah, I get that part, too." He looked out at the silent street. "But what was Prunia Devereaux's reasoning? Why'd she set so much store by an ornery old grump like Alvin? Did she just want his money, too?"

It was getting colder out now; I let Wade drape his denim jacket around my shoulders.

"No, I think that of everyone, she was the one who probably knew all along he was broke," I said.

Geese flew low overhead, their wings softly whush-whushing in the dark as they headed south.

"For all I know, he even told her," I said. "But Prunia does what she believes is her duty, you know. That's what all the attention she paid to Perry was all about, too, and all those trips to get Alvin Carter's wills notarized."

I'd asked her about this, finally, at the Moose, when she'd finished unloading all those cookies.

"She didn't take any of that seriously at all, or even give it much thought. She was just trying to keep him cheered up and occupied," I said.

I'd asked her about not wanting to witness them, too, and she'd looked thoughtful before replying. Finally:

"Just because I was trying to help him, that didn't mean I wanted to get mixed up in his affairs," she said.

Which made sense, and that was Prunia, all right: all over everything, but in the end she kept herself to herself.

When I repeated this to Wade he nodded, and we were silent a while. Then . . .

"Sam's work is straightened out?" Wade inquired, and I said it was. Now that Billy was back and could work again, all was well.

"And Mika's, too," I added. The Breyer girls weren't a permanent child-care solution, but they gave Mika some breathing room to get a longer-term plan together.

And they helped Bella to save face, since they needed the work almost as much as Bella needed to ease back from it.

My dad stepped out onto the porch, wearing a fleece jacket and a woolen cap with the earflaps pulled down. The porch's yellowish overhead light carved deep lines into the nut-brown leather of his face.

"See you later," he said. His deep-set eyes crinkled at us, and then he was gone, down the front steps and away under the nearly bare maples lining the street.

I made as if to get up, but . . .

"Let him go," said Wade quietly, his arm tightening around me. "He's a grown man."

I leaned back. Wade was right, of course; people should be able to do what they wanted.

Mostly.

Upstairs, a music box played in the children's room, the soft, sprightly melody floating sweetly out onto the woodsmoke-perfumed night air. Woodsmoke from people's chimneys, I mean. The long drought was over, we'd had rain every day this week, and there hadn't been a grass fire since . . . well, since that night.

Wade sighed deeply, getting up. "This whole business about neither you nor Ellie having a working phone with you, though," he said.

Of course, that would be the thing he objected to. It was what I objected to, also, because in the end that was what had nearly killed us: me having lent mine to Bella, that is, and Ellie's, as I found out afterward, having been lent to her daughter, Lee, until Lee's broken one could be replaced.

"Yeah, I'll watch out about that," I promised, having already ordered spares for each of our cars. Speaking of which . . . "But listen, Wade, just one last thing. About Ellie's car explosion . . ."

Which, actually, it wasn't, or at least not the way we'd thought.

"You're kidding," Wade said when I relayed what the state cops' mechanic had said about it.

Bottom line, the battery had exploded. "Some kind of an electrical system malfunction," I said. It was why she had been having trouble starting the car. "Meanwhile, that reminds me, I gave the remote starter back to my dad," I added.

Not that I'd used it. It's amazing how easy it is to forget that your car might blow up, if it doesn't do it right away.

Streetlamps went on. "I guess some things are about to change around here," said Wade.

Teenaged babysitters, Mika out working, Bella doing what she'd always done, but less of it . . .

And the kids growing up. Upstairs, the music box slowed and stopped.

"But," Wade added, crouching beside me to lay his cheek warmly against mine, "some things won't."

Recipe

Old-Fashioned Chocolate Sauce

This is the chocolate sauce that Jake and Ellie put into small jars with Chocolate Moose labels on them to give as gifts. So delicious, no one ever guesses how easy it is to make! Here you go:

Melt together two tablespoons of butter and two ounces of unsweetened chocolate in the top of a double boiler or in a saucepan over very low heat. Stir in a cup of sugar and half a cup of water. Add half a teaspoon of vanilla extract and continue stirring over low heat until the sauce thickens.

And that's it. You can spoon some of this chocolate sauce over a scoop of vanilla ice cream as soon as it's done, just to make sure it turned out okay.